The Air Loom

George Beckman

Copyright

Dedication

This book is dedicated to everyone who believes in the freedom to choose their own leaders.

Acknowledgments

Writing is not a solitary business in my world. Ruth is a plot-flaw expert and always knows where every character is in every scene. Donna is a proofreader with skill and patience. Mark sees books in acts, and helps me know when the curtain is going down on an act. Matthew helps clean up book blurbs. I cannot express enough thanks to my colleagues on //LineByLineTime. (Twitter-X)

Table of Contents

Copyright...ii
Dedication...iii
Acknowledgments...iv
Chapter 1..1
Chapter 2..8
Chapter 3...12
Chapter 4...18
Chapter 5...23
Chapter 6...28
Chapter 7...33
Chapter 8...39
Chapter 9...43
Chapter 10...47
Chapter 11...53
Chapter 12...64
Chapter 13...70
Chapter 14...75
Chapter 15...79
Chapter 16...85
Chapter 17...89
Chapter 18...95
Chapter 19...100
Chapter 20...105
Chapter 21...111
Chapter 22...118
Chapter 23...123
Chapter 24...132
Chapter 25...139
Chapter 26...148
Chapter 27...153
Chapter 28...161

Chapter 29...166
Chapter 30...173
Chapter 31...181
Chapter 32...187
Chapter 33...192
Chapter 34...196
Chapter 35...201
Chapter 36...207
Chapter 37...215
Chapter 38...220
Chapter 39...227
Chapter 40...234
Epilogue...239
Books By George Beckman...240

Content Advisory

I write wholesome books. While the main characters are wholesome people, Freebooters aren't. *The Air Loom* is the third book of the trilogy, and the characters are now New Adults. The war against the enemy becomes more violent.

Lurking in the Caves
Cunning Paranoid Evil
A Complete Madman

Chapter 1

The scale of the stronghold below was staggering. The *Silver Seed* hung in the mist of a cloud. Small bands of Freebooters, crazed men, ravaging towns were nothing to this new threat.

We took turns at the telescope, studying storage tanks, pipes, buildings, and a partially completed airship.

I stepped to the wheel and trued us in the air. "Dolph, get lots of pictures. We have time."

Dolph turned the black knob to bring the image into focus. He switched the ground glass for the film holder. "Steady." He pulled the film cover, and the shutter clicked. When the cover was back in place, he removed the carrier. "OK."

"The afternoon sun is lower," José said. "Our shadow is far to the east. We can go lower."

I eased the levitation lever, thinking out loud. "They must be storing the hypnotizing liquid in those tanks."

Laura focused the telescope. "Or something worse. We know how many minds one Blue Vial can alter. Those tanks are immense."

The camera lens clicked.

I examined the airship under construction with a hand scope. Cradles were being constructed as if for lifeboats—but this was Colorado, and the airship was not designed for water.

Dolph took a long look through the telescope and locked the mount. "What are those egg like objects."

I counted twenty-eight.

1

Laura adjusted the telescope. "I believe they inflate. Look now. There are stacks of them lying flat."

"They are going to haul them in the slings of the airship." José's voice showed wonder. "When they hit the ground, gallons of hypnotizing gas will be released."

"Ooo, that gives me the shivers," Addy breathed.

Dolph peered into the glass. "A bit to the starboard—"

José slipped into the rifle pod under the pilothouse. I held the wheel steady, and the shutter flicked.

"We have been seen!" José climbed quickly onto the deck. He handed Laura the spyglass.

I pulled the lift lever, and the deck pressed beneath me. Through the observation glass at our feet, I watched men spilling into the yard from the side of the mountain.

"That should be enough," Laura said. "We're too high for rifles."

The men mounted large guns on tripods. "Those are big guns. I'm taking us into the clouds!" I said.

The altimeter spun, and wispy fog floated past. Droplets formed on the forward windows.

Laura glanced up from the eyepiece. "Those are not guns—they're telescopes."

I didn't want the enemy getting a good look at our ship, and took us further into the clouds. I set the propulsion lever for Slow.

Dolph gathered the camera and film plates. "Let me make sure these pictures are good."

After all these years, José still refused to use contractions. "This ship is hard to spot when you know where to look. If we head south and then come out of the clouds, it is doubtful they will find us."

How did they spot us? "They must have lookouts."

I came to a decision. "Let's move so we can watch again." I pushed the propulsion lever forward, and the air tubes began to hum.

We emerged from the clouds south of the compound, turning toward the yard. The telescopes on the ground were still aimed toward the northern sky. I focused on a puzzling single structure standing near the bluff. It reminded me of pictures of the

2

Eiffel Tower. We took turns at the telescope but came to no conclusion.

Always the planner, José said, "Let them think they have destroyed us."

We stood in a circle, deep in thought.

"Get low enough for them to shoot at us?"

"Yes, draw rifle fire, but watch for larger guns."

Memories of the cannonball ripping through the breezeway of the *Cloud Queen* tightened my throat. She was fashioned after a Mississippi riverboat. Gleaming white with red trim and two fluted stacks, she was beautiful. I didn't rest after that battle until she was restored to her former glory.

"What if we dynamited the place? Destroy the tanks—the airship?" Even as I said it, I knew my words were spoken in frustration rather than logic.

Laura studied the scene at the telescope for a long moment. "I'm afraid we are only looking at part of this bee hive. Who knows what's under that mountain."

Dolph came forward. "Captain Will, the exposure is perfect. Are we starting home?" He was anxious to see Finn's progress with the aircycles.

I shook my head. "We must think. That airship down there is huge, but the bow is still just a frame. The boiler, motor, and airscrews are not in place. We have several weeks." *I hope.*

Laura let José have a turn at the telescope. "I am afraid that airship is not the last they are building. That ship cannot carry all the eggs they is preparing. They are gearing up for more than one ship."

"We need to get back to Eagle's Crest. For now, we let them think they have destroyed us," I said with finality. "With this ship off their minds, perhaps they won't feel pressured to hurry their plans. Dolph, how much smoke can you create?"

It was the kind of challenge Dolph loved. "I can make smoke. How much time do I have?"

José grinned. "You have time, but the sooner the better." He winked.

"If everyone has seen enough, I'm taking us back into the clouds." With no disagreement, I pulled the levitation lever.

3

"I'll see about lunch." Laura tightened her pinafore apron tie. We had been married for almost two years, and I never tired of her tiny waist and jet-black curls.

Dolph didn't stop for lunch, so I took a plate to the engine room.

"My plan is two-fold," he said. "I will cut back the air supply to the boiler causing the fuel oil to smoke. Second is this brazing torch. I have filled it with a concoction that will smoke like crazy— someone holds it at one of the rifle slits."

"Good work, my young friend." I handed him the plate. "Take at least a few bites. You keep telling me you're a growing boy, and I don't want your mother thinking we starved you on this trip."

"Growing boy with an important job," Dolph said between huge mouthfuls that would have brought a scolding from his mother. "Finn is depending on me to fill his big shoes."

We swooped low over the compound, and not a single person on the ground noticed. On the second pass, José went to the rifle pod and fired at the filled eggs. Three small streams began to squirt out of a bag. That got their attention.

Men swarmed out of the side of the mountain with rifles. Using the range finder, José helped me keep a safe distance from the ground, and bullets began to rattle harmlessly on the underside of the ship. At one hundred-twenty feet stem to stern, thirty-five at the rear beam, we were hard to miss.

I spun the wheel, and she came around. I eased the propulsion lever, and we hovered. José slid back down into the rifle pod.

"They are rolling out a big gun," he called.

"Tweak the levelers, Dolph," I said in the speaking tube.

The ship tilted to the starboard, and bullets continued to pepper the hull.

"They are unlimbering the big gun! I do not have a clear shot at this angle!"

"Smoke, Dolph!" I backed the ship away to the west, and the roll of black drifting over the nose was impressive.

4

The men below swung the clumsy cannon barrel toward us.

The deck gave way beneath my feet, and I pulled the levitation lever back. Nothing happened. A glance at the revolution meter showed the engine had slowed to one hundred turns. Pressure in the flash boiler read eighty pounds.

The thud of the cannon firing rang against the hull.

"They shot too high," José called.

"Dolph! Report!" I yelled into the speaking tube. The ship slipped lower. Gripping the lift lever and adjusting the propulsion levers with my right hand, I tried to balance our fall and our retreat. "Dolph!"

"Working on it!" Dolph was not at the speaking tube, and something rattled in the engine room.

"I have to see where we are going down!" I spun the wheel, and the ship pivoted sluggishly in the air. The stern was sinking lower. Laura stood on her tiptoes, peering out the front windows.

"Maybe a quarter mile to a small meadow!"

We'll never make it. "Take the wheel. When we are far enough away, stop propulsion. We must stay in the air."

I dashed down the hall and swung into the engine room. Finn's batteries were a quarter spent, and the pressure was at forty. Finn's words played in my head: *With no engine, the batteries may prevent crashing if we're not too high.*

"Sorry, Will. I choked the fire too much, and it went out." Dolph worked the striker. "I panicked and forgot to turn off the oil jet." He snapped the igniter again. "I think the striker is under oil."

I went to the door. "Addy, bring the torch! Keep it lit!" I cracked open the sight slot and peered inside. The injector was still above the oil.

Addy was at my side, the torch belching black smoke. I shoved the nozzle in and cranked open the flame.

"Can we fly with the torch heat?" she asked.

"Trying to light the fire. Hold it. Point it down as much as you can—toward the middle. Dolph, inject a little oil." The needle on the battery gauge rested on the peg, steam pressure falling to thirty-eight.

5

Dolph turned the valve, and the flame caught but flickered feebly. *The blower's running but not pumping air.* I slid open the intake tube inspection cover. The tin pipe was filled with fuel oil.

"Addy, keep the torch going. Every little bit will help."

The firebox door oozed smoke, my eyes burned, and it was hard to make out the gauges. Something scraped the hull beneath us.

"Brace yourselves!" Laura called down the hallway. Another crunch, louder this time, screeched its way along beneath us.

I grabbed a hammer from the toolbox and swung the claw at the underside of the tin air intake. "Dolph—bucket!" I swung again and again. I dropped to my knees, using both hands.

Outside, something cracked, and the ship shuddered. The claw penetrated the tin, and oil spilled onto the deck before Dolph could get the bucket under the gash. I worked the claw into the hole and pulled sideways to widen it.

More limbs cracked. The blower gasped in gulps as air and oil were sucked into the impeller in spasms. Then, the welcome roar of the boiler flame could be heard.

I wiped my eyes with my sleeve. Smoke hung in the air, and Dolph coughed.

The pressure rose to forty pounds. The pipes to the engine rattled.

Dolph rushed to open the water drain valves on the line. Steam and water snorted out.

I watched the revolution gage, praying we wouldn't lock the engine. She knocked twice, and Dolph closed the valves when the flywheel became a blur.

Addy was choking. "Go into the hall," I said.

"Will, I am so sorry!" Dolph moaned. His earnest eyes searched mine. This young man who helped design the aircycle and prepare the smoke was suddenly reduced to the boy he had been just a few years before.

The pressure climbed to one hundred. I held my kerchief over my mouth. "All is well."

"I could have ruined Finn's beautiful ship. Got us all killed."

"Dolph. When you got up this morning, did you say, 'I think I'm going to wreck the *Silver Seed* today?'"

6

Thick smoke hung in a layer. "No, Captain Will," he croaked.

"I didn't think so. Step into the hall and get some air. Then get busy and check everything. When the smoke clears, wrap the hole I made and cinch it with wire. Set the batteries to charge."

"Yes, Sir. I'll clean the floor!"

José had come to the door. "We are running the fans at high speed, and I have the upper hatch open. In the meantime, come look."

"Dolph, trim the ship." I followed José and Addy to the rear salon, the deck flattening under our feet.

A cloud of black hung over the hill behind us, and a smoke trail followed us. "Think they saw that?"

"Oh, they saw it," José said. "They would not be able to see the ship from the compound, but that cloud is rising in an updraft. Perhaps they heard trees breaking."

"Well, when we try to make the enemy think we are going down, we do a good job of it."

"I was convinced," Addy said.

Chapter 2

Smoke continued to follow us. Dolph found it difficult to control the boiler flame with the extra oil pool in the boiler pan.

"Captain Will, I'm afraid we are building too much heat. I have the injector almost off. We need to land and clear out the extra oil in the firebox."

Laura used the hand scope, scanning the terrain. At last, we hovered inches from the ground in a wide meadow miles from civilization.

"Addy and José, take rifles out just in case." It always made me nervous to have an oddity like one of our airships stranded on the ground. "I'll have Dolph and Laura take the ship up a few feet to inspect the hull."

José and Addy went to the side door. Laura turned the periscope. "All clear."

"Laura," I said, "remember our rule. If something happens, you must launch."

I followed José and Addy out, wearing my holster and pistol.

The ship lifted, and I walked underneath. Flying had become second nature, but the massive ship only feet above my head had my full attention.

The sheeting was ripped open in two places, revealing the wood structure. There was a large crack in the port side of the rifle pod glass. I pushed on it, and it held.

The huge knife at the rear remained intact and tucked tight against the hull. We had shredded the balloons of more than one enemy ship with it. A long narrow limb lay wedged between the blade and the hull. When I pulled, it hung on the long, vicious teeth, and I worried it back and forth. When the pine branch was clear, another breach in the sheeting was revealed. *Could be worse.* Finn would have to check the knife mechanism.

I rapped on the rifle pod and indicated for Laura to bring the ship down.

In the engine room, I spoke gently to Dolph. "The ship is OK. A few tears in the sheeting, but we can land. Let's get the burner cleaned out."

8

Laura brought the ship to the ground, and Dolph shut down the boiler. Fuel in the burner pan continued to flicker lazily, and we finally resorted to cutting off most of the air. When the flame finally went out, smoke seeped into the engine room again.

"I made a real mess of things, Captain Will."

"Any of us could have done the same." I opened the firebox and we stood in the hall. "We need Finn to design a set of fans to exhaust the area at times like these."

When the fire box cooled, Dolph began to dip fuel oil from the pan. I formed a piece of tin to make a more permanent repair to the blower intake.

Laura joined us. "José is convinced that no one is around." She smiled. "Except for a small deer. He is butchering it now."

I hadn't heard the shot. Fresh meat would be welcome.

Dolph discovered the striker was still not working. "My mess keeps getting worse," he lamented.

"Dump your smoke concoction from the torch, and we will use it to start the boiler."

It took three tries to get the brazing torch lit. Dolph resorted to cleaning the jet. It was almost evening before the ship lifted into the darkening sky.

I couldn't wait to be home, in the big lodge with friends I thought of as family.

"We need to contact Eagle's Crest. No need to tell Finn about our problem. It will be easier in person. Just tell them there is damage and what supplies will be needed to fix the ship."

Dolph began to key. SILVER SEED STOP
MARIA HERE STOP WILL GET FINN STOP

José's sister was growing up. I was impressed with the speed she sent the message. But no one was faster than Dolph.

FINN HERE STOP

RAN INTO A BIT OF TROUBLE STOP ALL IS WELL AND ON THE WAY HOME STOP HULL NEEDS PATCHING IN THREE PLACES STOP

My mind blurred with the rapid staccato of the key.

9

SLOW DOWN FRIEND STOP LET ME CHECK THE CODE TAPE STOP

Dolph grinned. "He's in the workshop. I'm too fast for him."

"No time to show off. We need Finn to make an accurate list."

GOT IT STOP WHAT HAPPENED STOP

I moved to the key.

LOST POWER MOMENTARILY TRYING TO MAKE THE ENEMY THINK THEY HAD SHOT US DOWN STOP GOT CLOSER TO THE TREES THAN WE WANTED STOP

"Thanks," Dolph said gratefully. "I will tell him everything when we are home. Finn may want to make some design changes."

The fun chatter with Eagle's Crest that followed calmed my unease, and I slept well that night.

As we often did, we read and played darts and chess during the days. The *Silver Seed* could be flown with two at the controls, and she made good speed with a tailwind. But Colorado was a long way from California. I found my mind wandering while Addy and Laura played the final game of a chess match.

We sat at the long table that stretched across the beam of the salon. The turn of Addy's lip signaled she was about to make a clever move. She slid her bishop into place. "Check—and mate in three."

Laura studied the board. She would lose her queen and then a rook. She tipped the king over. "Wow, Addy. Seventeen moves! I'll go start your pie."

"I'll share!" Addy teased.

José gave Addy a sideways grin.

When at last we approached Eagle's Crest, we all gathered in the helm room, eager for our first glimpse of home. Smoke curled from the lodge fireplace, and folks gathered in the yard. Minnie and Mrs. Rodriquez would have a feast for us. I reached for Laura's hand.

The row crops glistened in the afternoon sun after the first rain of October, and the glass windows of the greenhouse winked at us.

10

When we settled, José opened the door to a cacophony of greetings. In the face of unknown evil, these faces were my hope.

Chapter 3

The race kept our minds off the Freebooter threat.

Laura and Mary churned the pedals of their aircycles. All of Eagle's Crest was cheering. Laura was flying nearly twenty feet lower than Mary to take advantage of the wind being blocked by the lodge. Mary rounded the pine and appeared to be in the lead. Both women leaned into the handlebars.

It was not our first race. Finn continually improved the propeller design on the aircycles and both women spent hours pulverizing the Levitrite into finer grains to get more lift from less electricity.

Laura's bloomers were billowing in the breeze. Minnie said they were quite risque, but Laura insisted she was a woman of the nineties.

Mary edged out Laura for the best of three. Her face was pink with excitement, and Nathan grabbed her cycle before she landed and carried her on the bike to the crowd. Mary squealed with delight.

I helped Laura park her aircycle, and we walked hand in hand to the lodge. Minnie, Dolph's mother, had a lusty fire in the fireplace. I brushed the wisp of hair in front of Laura's ear.

"Finn, the bikes are better than ever," Laura said. "We raced for twenty minutes, and I feel great."

Mary turned a teasing eye toward Nathan. "I could have gone for another two rounds if someone hadn't snatched me out of the sky!"

"I thought you would give me a ride!"

"I can give you a ride, but you might get scared at one hundred feet."

"You get me up a hundred feet, and I will admit I am scared!"

Mary picked up her top hat and goggles, and we followed her outside. She climbed on her aircycle and began to pedal. The bike went up about six feet. Mary twisted the altitude grip. "Grab on, Mister."

Nathan reached up, grabbed the landing stand, and looked up. "Go."

"I think you are in trouble, Nathan," Minnie called. Even Maria had closed her book.

Mary began to pedal with a vengeance. Nathan was a barrel-chested, powerfully built man, and I wasn't sure Mary could lift him. Mary was gorgeous, but behind her beauty was a woman of conviction and steel. Her determination showed, and the pedals spun the dynamo faster and faster.

Nathan's feet lifted off the ground, and they began to rise.

"How high?" Mary teased.

"Put me on top of the lodge. I need to check the flashing around the fireplace."

We watched as Mary edged toward the lodge. She struggled to gain altitude as they crossed the yard.

"This is kind of fun," Nathan called.

Mary was standing in the pedals, pulling up on the handlebars. The aircycle inched higher.

We cheered when the bike rose over the edge of the building, and Nathan pulled his feet up to clear the roof. He made his way to the ridge, and Mary flew the aircycle back to us.

An exhausted Mary walked in circles, catching her breath. José brought a long ladder.

After supper in the lodge, the telegraph radio started clicking. Everyone knew Morse Code, and a hush fell on the large room. I recognized the methodical coding of Professor Gruber.

WESTERN UNION NEWS FROM COLORADO STOP ENTIRE VILLAGE NORTH OF DENVER UNDER INFLUENCE OF MIND GAS STOP SUPREME NAVARCH BRAGGING AN ARMY BATTALION UNDER HIS CONTROL IS STOPPING TRAVEL NORTH STOP P GRUBER

"What is a Navarch?" José wondered.

13

We looked to Laura, and she went to the keypad.

Professor Gruber's answer came quickly. GREEK STOP LEADER OF THE SHIPS STOP

Finn stirred. "There will be no help from the army."

Dolph ran to the shop to get the message recording tape.

"They must have a small airship somewhere or another way to deliver so much gas," I mused.

Finn studied the pictures. "If the wind were right, one of the eggs in a wagon could be released."

The thought of gas seeping into the houses of an entire town made me shudder.

A sober silence fell on us.

José stood and then sat again. "You were right about him building more ships. The question is—how *many* ships?"

Addy backed up to the fire. "One is too many."

"We must be back in the air in a week, ten days at the most," I said. "They must be stopped before they can use the gas on more people."

Mary was always the practical one. "Laura, how much money do we have?"

"We made over seven thousand during the last Flying Riverboat Excursions run," Laura said. "After expenses, we have more than one hundred ninety thousand."

Addy blew air between her lips. "We are rich."

"That we are," I said. "Next time we advertise an excursion run on the *Cloud Queen*, we want no complaints from you!" I teased.

"But will I always have to be the stewardess?" Addy asked. "I hate that starched getup. I feel like I'm dressed in cardboard."

"Addy, you are the best stewardess we have." Laura didn't mention Benny. When doing Steamboat Excursions, Benny's absence was palpable.

"I'm the only stewardess!"

"And that makes you the best."

Dolph was puffing when he hurried in. Finn read the message, and we passed it around the table.

As we had so many evenings, our conversation turned to what seemed to be the never-ending struggle with Freebooters.

14

"So let's review what we know about this Supreme Navarch," Laura said. "Finn, what do you make of the tanks at his stronghold?"

Finn tapped one of the pictures. "I have made some measurements using this wheelbarrow as a scale. The tanks are at least three thousand gallons each. He's going to use the gas on more than the army."

"Six tanks of that awful stuff," Laura whispered.

"Four tanks are for gas, two for liquid. This is good. He first makes the gas and then converts it to liquid. The extra step will take time."

Laura wasn't relieved. "Six gallons would be too much."

Mary huffed, "All we need is the world running around blindly following the orders of a crazed lunatic!"

"Freebooters are like a bee hive," José said. "This Supreme Navarch is the queen. I believe all orders originate with him. Until we can stop him, we only drive them back." He paused for effect. "We have done that twice and are back at the beginning."

Not the beginning—this is bigger than we ever dreamed.

Laura and I leaned close and watched the fire.

The next part was tricky. "We are going to have to go into the compound and see for ourselves." I felt Laura tense. "José and I." I gave her a sideways glance. "We have done it before."

She looked down at her hands in her lap and nodded.

"We must be very careful," Nathan said. "Roads to that compound are being guarded by the army—what used to be the army."

José grew restless, pacing along the long table. "Aircycles. We come in by night. They will never suspect us."

"I have preliminary plans for a new aircycle design with four riders in tandem," Finn said. "If we made them with bullet-shaped lightweight faring, we would have more power and less wind resistance."

José eyes showed his excitement. "Could one or two fly one? Could we drop two off to spy, and the others fly the machine back?"

"That is my hope. It will take some time to design."

15

"We may not have time, Finn," I said. "We must be back in Colorado before the Supreme Navarch has time to launch a ship."

"We'll study the pictures again," Finn replied. "I am convinced this Supreme Navarch is not ready for a large-scale attack. The ship under construction is huge, and we all remember how long it took to build the *Silver Seed.*"

I was well aware of my tendency to run into action before thinking. "The sooner we can infiltrate the compound, the sooner we will know what we are dealing with.'

"Don't worry, Captain Will. Finn and I have all the parts on hand. We will have the quadcycle ready in a few days."

Finn looked skeptically at Dolph. "Don't promise what we may not be able to deliver—but, yes—we will start work on the frame immediately."

When the two were gone, Addy asked, "Besides Will and José, who would be the other riders? I'm a good racer."

Maria looked up from her book. "It's not only speed. The riders need endurance."

The room went silent.

"You can't know how far you will have to ride." Maria returned to her book.

Laura fixed her gaze on me. "Maria is right, and women have endurance. You didn't think I was going to let you have all the fun, did you?"

I'm not going to win this one.

Addy batted at José's arm. "And don't think you're leaving me behind, Señor."

"Hey, I said nothing. I am innocent."

Addy laughed. "Sure."

"Let's plan to race Thursday, at ten o'clock in the morning," I decided. "In the meantime, José and I will remount the steam cannon on the *Cloud Queen.*"

Finn had retooled the cannon, creating a rifled bore to shoot pointed shells. José made quick work of bolting the mount. I took extra care attaching the steam hoses.

I lamented at the sight of the bow—deck chairs replaced by machines of war.

16

Our next project was to build a massive set of piers for the *Silver Seed*.

Chapter 4

Addy hovered twenty feet above the area between the cabins and lodge.

"How long?" I asked.

"Forty minutes." Her face and arms glistened.

A bulging leather knapsack hung under the aircycle. "How much weight?"

"Seventy pounds—rocks—one gear left over from the *Silver Seed*. It's—heavy."

"Who helped you lift off?"

"I helped—myself, Will," she puffed. "I'm not helpless."

Laura slid her arm around my waist. "Good job, Addy. I'll go up when you're done. We'll show these men we women have stamina."

Addy looked down and smiled. "I can do twenty—more minutes."

"I will tell Minnie to have extra breakfast ready for you," I said.

As we walked toward the lodge, Laura said, "She will need it." She was quiet for a moment. "You know she has her mind made up."

"I know. I keep thinking Nathan may be the better choice."

"Because he's a man!? Addy is thin. Tiny. She'll more than pull her weight."

I nodded. *But will she have enough power to lift a quadcycle back to the Silver Seed?*

At breakfast, José and I decided we would race mid-morning, best out of three. It was pointless, as José was the fastest aircycle rider at Eagle's Crest, but we enjoyed the competition.

I wandered out to the workshop and puttered around the *Cloud Queen*. She had helped us win many battles against the Freebooters. I loved the old ship's regal pilothouse and idly turned the big wheel, testing the rudders. I recognized Laura's footsteps when she gave a little skip outside the pilothouse door.

"Thought you might be up here. Are you thinking about this coming storm?"

18

"We seem to spend much of our life fighting off Freebooters—too much. Sometimes I get tired."

"And sometimes you get bored."

I smiled. I often wondered what I would do if the world were free from the hypnotizing gas. Would I run excursions with the *Cloud Queen* for the rest of my life? I knew I couldn't settle on a profession and give up the skies. José had mentioned creating a freight line—"Air Trains," he called them. We would tow cargo over the mountains.

Laura put her arm around me. "Lots of decisions to be made. Lots of dangerous decisions, I am afraid."

"Yes."

"Will? Laura? Can you come to the Workshop?" Finn called. "I have some things to show you."

The shop, attached to the hangars for the airships, was a marvel of devices and inventions. Huge chalkboards hung on two walls, with drawings and math equations covering every inch. The two code radios, drill presses, a forge, and a large telescope were impressive. Long work benches were scattered with tools, gears, springs, and levers. Finn and Dolph created marvelous inventions in the vast room.

Dolph measured the height of a small lacquered wooden box suspended by copper wires from a container of Levitrite. It floated above one of the work benches. There was no sound. He pointed to a knob on the box for adjusting the electricity and looked at Finn. "Almost a perfect balance."

We had been flying for almost six years, and yet I resisted the temptation to wave my hand above it—to be sure it was not hanging from the ceiling by invisible wires.

"It still seems magical," Laura remarked.

"It is not magic." Dolph's enthusiasm was contagious. "Electricity from batteries in the box flows through the Levitrite, creating lift, in direct proportion to the current. Just like the dynamos of *Cloud Queen* and *Silver Seed*." He looked to Finn.

"Absolutely correct, my young friend." Finn studied the knob. "How long has it been at this voltage?"

Dolph looked at the railroad clock on the wall. "Twenty-seven minutes and thirty-seven seconds."

19

So like Dolph, not thirty-six seconds, not thirty-eight.

"We have added sodium chloride to the water around the Levitrite, making the current more effective," Finn said. "It was Dolph's idea. For the life of me, I don't know why I didn't think of it earlier."

"Simple chemistry," Dolph said. "Laura, it was in the books you got for me. The lift increase is twelve percent. We can lift more with less energy." Dolph pushed a paper with his calculations across the table.

Laura took the paper and studied the figures. "No mistakes. You are using your math skills well!"

Laura had always wanted to teach and ran the small school for the children of Eagle's Crest when we were home. Maria organized the lessons when Laura was gone.

The floating box inched closer to the table, and Dolph made an adjustment. "We won't make an hour. The batteries will be spent in forty minutes."

"Great work, Dolph," I said.

Finn took us to his drawing board. A four-person aircycle was sketched from three perspectives.

The long frame was like a double bicycle built for two. "I see four dynamos, Finn."

"Each set of pedals runs a separate dynamo. I have designed circuitry so they will couple. This way, everyone does not have to pedal at the same cadence. In fact, one person pedaling could conceivably keep the cycle in the air."

"With four aboard?" Laura asked.

Finn, ever the scientist, furrowed is brow. "Yes and no. Of course, it would take considerable voltage to provide lift."

Addy slipped into the room and stood by José. "I will have to start training with more weight!"

"How soon until we have a prototype?" I asked.

Dolph pointed to pieces of tubing. "We are already preparing the frame."

"I have ordered more seats," Finn said. "They should arrive at the Lab soon. We can go down with the *Cloud Queen.*"

I worried about the progress at Henderson Lab. After defeating the Adjunct Commander and his plan to take over

California, we turned the subjugated army post into a lab. The main goal was to find an antidote for the hypnotizing gas.

"What does Professor Gruber say about progress?"

"No change."

"Peter has not come out of the fog?" Laura asked.

"I am afraid not. Professor Gruber said the lab is very clean." Finn smiled.

I chuckled inside. When the laboratory used a small amount of hypnotizing gas on our volunteer, Peter, the instructions given to him were not intended to cause any harm. He was simply told he liked to keep the lab clean.

"You are going to owe him some broom time, Finn," I teased.

"I suppose so, but I will gladly do it without gas to help me." Finn sighed. "I still remember when I was in the fog—doing things and yet helplessly wondering why I was acting the way I did."

Finn was ashamed of the way he had treated Mary. Given general Freebooter commands, Finn had been told women were to be servants of men. Attracted to Mary's beauty, he had been like a love-sick puppy. Coming out of the fog, he remembered enough to know he had treated her in lecherous ways.

José stuck his head in the door, his smile crinkling his eyes. "Ready to race, Will?"

"Always."

When we were outside, I asked, "Do you think Addy can keep up in a four-person aircycle?"

"Yes. She is tough. She is only beaten by Mary and Laura."

"You are not saying this because you—"

"I love her, Will, but that is not why I am saying this. Addy can pedal."

"Have you told her?"

"I think she knows."

I stopped and turned to José. "Have you told her?"

"It is hard. These are important words."

"Yes, but if you love her, you need to tell her."

José brushed his chin. "Then I guess I better be brave."

"José, you are the bravest person I know."

"Yes, but I am not brave when it is Addy."

21

I moved the conversation back to choosing riders. "Nathan might be the better choice for the quadcycle. He's an ox of a man."

"Nathan is a powerful man, but does he make two times the power? I think he weighs two times what Addy weighs."

José was right. Finn called it weight to power ratio. Addy was slight but wiry. "OK," I said. "Let's race. But I think you should tell her you love her—soon. It is only fair."

"You win the race, and I will tell her tonight."

Chapter 5

José and I launched and hovered above the porch of the lodge. When we had the aircycles evenly matched, Laura called, "Go!"

I increased my pedal cadence and twisted the propulsion grip. The aircycle moved ahead. I stood and pedaled hard and inched ahead of José. If I could get to the light pole before him, I could cut it close and pick up needed time.

I opened the propulsion grip all the way and felt the dynamo resisting. I continued to stand, pulling up on the handlebars, and pedaled harder. I didn't look back to see how large a lead I had. "Never look back" was Mary's motto.

I steered for the light pole, depending on the wind to move me to the side enough to clear the handlebars.

I felt good and kept the aircycle low but did allow it to gain a foot or so of altitude. After the turn, I headed into the wind and crouched low, trying to reduce the drag.

I could hear José behind me, spinning the pedals evenly and fast. After I turned at the pine, I had twenty feet on José. I had never been able to do any better than follow him around the course.

With the wind now with me, I stood again, spinning the pedals with all my might. The bike was buffeted by the wind, but the same breeze moved me along at a fair clip. I eased the elevation grip ever so slightly to allow more electricity for the propulsion tubes, and doubled my effort. My legs burning, the aircycle moved briskly along. When I crossed the finish line, I looked back to see José still twenty feet behind.

My legs felt like rubber as I eased down to land.

"You are fast today!" José called.

When he came close, I said, "You didn't let me win just so you could talk to Addy, did you?"

"You only won one. We are racing for best out of three."

I got off the aircycle and walked in a circle. I glanced at my pocket watch and said, "One more minute?"

"No resting," Laura said. "Back up you go!"

Several had come out to watch, and more arrived when the news of my win spread. Even Mary stopped hoeing weeds in the corn and pushed back her floppy hat.

I lost the second race but managed to edge José out on the third. I thought my legs would fall off, but it felt good. Laura gave me a hug. José glanced over, and I pointed my finger at him and mouthed, "Tell her." He nodded, the right corner of his mouth lifting.

Addy challenged Nathan to a race, and Mary drew near. Nathan was the faster of the two, but Addy held up one finger. "Wait," she said. "I think it is only fair to weigh the aircycles."

Nathan lifted each machine. "They feel the same, but you can choose the one you want."

"Oh, I don't care which aircycle I use. I want each bike to be the same percentage of our weights."

Nathan looked puzzled. "You are going to weigh your bike down so the total weights are equal?"

"No, Nathan!" Addy used an exaggerated tone, as if speaking to a small child. "You and I get weighed in the lab. Then we weigh the bikes. *Then*—we make the human-to-bike ratio the same!" She put her hands on her hips, grinning up at him.

"I weigh a lot more than you."

"Yes, and I can see you are all muscle," Addy said with exaggerated enthusiasm.

Mary plopped her hat back on, tilted her head slightly, and winked at Nathan from under the brim.

In the lab, Addy weighed one hundred three pounds, and the bike weighed thirty-five. Addy went to where Dolph was ready with paper and pencil.

"Rounds to thirty-four percent," she said. "I am lifting a bike that is one-third of my weight!"

Mary covered a smile.

"Your turn, Nathan." Addy watched closely as Nathan slid the weights across the bar.

"Two-forty-two," Dolph reported.

Addy did some quick math. "To make the bike be thirty-four percent of Nathan's weight, the bike needs to weigh eighty-two pounds, right, Dolph?"

24

"Eighty-two."

"I rounded down for you, Nathan." Addy was enjoying this. "Keep going, Dolph. I think we will add forty-seven pounds to Nathan's bike."

Dolph had his tongue in the corner of his mouth. "Forty-seven."

Addy patted Nathan's shoulder. "Don't worry, Friend. All that muscle will be able to make the bike work better!"

José nodded in admiration. "I think she has you, Nathan."

Addy handed Nathan her leather knapsack. "I have been training with this. The gear in the bag weighs twenty-two. You will have to take some rocks out—I've been training with seventy."

Nathan raised his eyebrows.

The group, eager for the game, watched as Nathan tried different combinations. "Listen, Kid, don't be surprised if I still win this race!"

Addy slid the bar weight to forty-seven. "No lift-off yet," she said happily.

Nathan arranged two gears on top of each other, and looked at the scale.

Addy put the toe of her boot on the scale and tested it. "So, close, Nathan, so close."

I handed Nathan a small rock, and the bar lifted.

"Close enough," Addy said.

Nathan hefted the bag easily. "Maybe the winner should serve pie to the loser for a week."

"Addy, I will give you an extra piece of pie tonight when you win, now that you will have a server," Laura laughed. "Nathan, maybe you should keep that ballast handy. Addy may want to race again tomorrow to improve her lead."

"Only one way to find out," Addy laughed. "Are you ready? Best out of three?"

Everyone at Eagle's Crest came out. We used benches from the lodge and sat happily watching. Maria continued reading her book, giving an occasional glance at the scene.

"I find it balances best if you tie it here." Addy pointed to a bar on the landing stand of Nathan's aircycle. She handed Nathan a length of light line. "You can even use my lucky twine."

When all was ready, Addy lifted her aircycle. "This feels nice and light without the seventy pounds." She half-closed one eye. "I think that is sixty-seven percent of my weight. Add in the bike, and I've been lifting my weight! Your eighty-two pounds should be easy."

Nathan lifted off and mock-groused about the bike being sluggish. They went up even with the eve of the lodge, and Laura started them.

Nathan easily won the first round but was breathing hard when he returned. In the second round, he held the lead for the first half, and then Addy began to pull alongside. When they turned at the tree, Addy steered to the outside but kept pace. When no longer in the turn, she began to pull ahead. She stood in the pedals and leaned into her work. She crossed the line a full length ahead.

Laura started them on the third round. Addy was like a cat, all quickness and speed. She pulled ahead almost immediately. Nathan plowed along, keeping his head down. I think he realized he had been beaten when Addy rounded the pole.

Cheers came up as they rounded the tree and started for the finish line. Nathan closed the gap, but when he pulled near, Addy put on a burst of speed, feet flying. She crossed the finish line half a length in the lead.

Nathan made a quick landing. "That kid is determined!"

Addy continued to fly in a circle over us. "This is a puzzling moment! How could a one hundred three pound girl stand a chance against all those muscles?" she teased. She turned the cycle toward the pole, calling, "Time me!"

We watched in admiration as she made two more rounds, the last only seven seconds slower than the first. When I was sure she would land, she hovered over Nathan. "Now's the real test. Grab on, Nathan."

Nathan's smile was huge as he reached up, getting a grip. "You already won, you know."

Addy began to pedal furiously. The dynamo whined at a higher pitch, but the bike did not rise. Nathan did a little toe raise, pushing off, and they hovered in the air, the breeze inching them to the side. When his feet brushed the ground, Addy eased the lift grip and let him down.

Nathan stepped aside, and she landed with a thump. The aircycle started to tip, and Nathan steadied her. She caught her leg on the seat as she swung it over, and he caught her arm until she could drag her right foot off the aircycle.

"Oh, my," she exclaimed, face red, taking deep breaths. "Wow!"

Laura slipped off her apron and handed it to Addy.

Addy wiped her face and arms. "I'm going to need to clean up," she mumbled into the cloth.

"I don't think there is any doubt, Addy," I said. "You won the contest."

José stood with a glowing smile on his face. Addy handed back the apron.

Nathan peered down at her. "You OK, there?"

"Yes, thank you." She stuck her hand out, and they shook. "Thanks for being a good sport."

She walked over to José and leaned her head against his chest. He lowered his head and whispered something in her ear. She grinned and hugged him around the neck, whispering to him. We watched José help a wobbly Addy toward her cabin.

Laura came close. "About time," she whispered to me. "And I love you, too."

27

Chapter 6

Minnie and Mrs. Rodriquez prepared the perfect lunch. It was a cool fall day, and there was a lusty blaze in the fireplace. Addy helped Mrs. Rodriquez carry in the food, and they chatted in Spanish. I felt ashamed to think she had picked up Spanish so quickly working with Mrs. Rodriquez while I, José's best friend, still only knew a few words and phrases and spoke those with an accent that made him smile.

At Eagle's Crest, we didn't have many rules, but we made it a practice to only speak of pleasant things while eating together. The long table had become a place of refuge, and the meal was punctuated with pleasant chatter about the greenhouse, fields, and the race. Paul had hiked into the hills and carried in a buck over his shoulders. Letty, Laura's mother, complimented the venison.

After lunch, I stood. "There is nothing like a good meal to help one think," I said. "So, how is the quadcycle project going?"

"We're making good progress with the frame and mechanicals," Finn reported.

A large coal popped onto the hearth, and Maria scooped it up, tossing it into the fire. She settled back in an overstuffed chair with her book.

"Al, how goes the repair to the *Silver Seed* hull?"

"Nathan and I have the new sheeting in place. We also tested the knife. There was no damage."

"Finn, as soon as the quadcycle is complete, we will begin testing." I looked to Minnie and Letty. "Could you please make faring for one of the aircycles we already use? Addy and Mary will be able to give us an idea of the advantage of less wind resistance."

"We must go to Henderson Labs," Finn said. "I want to see the progress on the antidote."

I don't remember when I didn't love Laura, but we fell deeply in love in the pilothouse of the *Cloud Queen*. Now, at the wheel over the San Gabriel mountains, my feelings had not changed. Laura stood, as she often did, in the doorway. The breeze gently tickled the hair in front of her ears. But there was a sadness about her.

We wanted children, and she had lost another baby the week before. It was early, but this was not the first time. I was saddened, but I knew the repetition distressed Laura. She loved teaching the little ones at Eagle's Crest and had always imagined herself as a mother. As the possibility became more remote, she felt these disappointments deeply.

Addy came up the stairs, two at a time. "Henderson Laboratory sent an all-clear."

"Thanks. We will begin our descent." I rang for Half speed and called down for us to come to two hundred feet.

Laura stepped in front of the pilothouse and surveyed the clear area near the main bunkhouses. "Looks good."

"Drop the landing marker," I called into the speaking tube. "Land at will."

Once the marker touched the ground, landing became the simple matter of the engine room watching the dial as the clockwork mechanism wound the cable. We touched down gently, and I lashed the wheel and rang for Stop.

Professor Gruber met us outside the shop with a box. "These are filter masks. You must not breathe in the gas. The entire laboratory is filled with the gas today."

I pulled on the mask, and Laura helped tighten the straps. I got her hair caught in a strap, and she went to a mirror in the *Cloud Queen* to get untangled.

"What about you, Professor? You don't wear a mask?"

"I'm afraid it is too late for us working here. The gas is everywhere. We just ask that you do not tell us to do a specific task or that we should like something." He brushed his mustache. "Peter tells me daily that I will develop the antidote." He chuckled. "As if I needed prompting."

We stepped inside the old barracks building. A small steam engine in a nearby shed provided electricity. Gruber's shop was filled with books and chemicals. Several volumes were open on various benches. Bubbling liquid moved from beaker to beaker through glass tubes.

29

"Are we any closer to understanding the gas?" Finn asked, his voice muffled.

Professor Gruber gestured to liquid bubbling near us. "We are closer to knowing how the gas hypnotizes, but the antidote has been a complete failure. He gestured toward Peter, polishing one of the lab tables. "It has been three weeks and still he cleans. He says he is happy to try antidote after antidote, and we can continue the experiment."

"Peter," I said. "How are you?"

Peter wiped his hand on the rag he had been using and shook my hand. "Good to see you, Will."

"Peter, is your desire to clean becoming any less?"

"I am not sure it is because of the command I received after I was given the gas. I enjoy cleaning. It is good to keep things clean." He turned back to his polishing.

I looked at Finn. Peter had recited the exact words we used when he sniffed the gas.

Finn showed Professor Gruber the pictures of the Supreme Navarch's stronghold. "We are especially concerned by these eggs, as we call them. We believe they are bladder-like." He pointed to the layered stacks near a building. "They are stored flat until filled. Luckily, that ax leaning on the building gives us a reference point."

The professor held a magnifying glass to the photo. He grabbed a ruler and made some measurements.

After several minutes, he put the lens on the lab table and began making calculations. Peter picked up the lens and polished the glass.

"Three battalions were given the gas. In your opinion, did they use the eggs?" Finn asked.

"Yes. It is possible to create a mixture that remains liquid until exposed to air. This is the way the Blue Vials work. Open the stopper, and the liquid begins to bubble. The Freebooters take a sniff and pass it on. When the stopper is replaced the bubbling stops."

"How much liquid do you think one of the eggs will hold?" I asked.

"According to my calculations, each egg could hold at least twenty-five gallons. They can't make them much bigger because of

30

the difficulty in handling them. Some of the chemicals would vaporize, but most would remain in a liquid state—heavy enough to break the bladder when dropped from a sufficient height." The Professor turned the photo toward us. "As you have guessed, and I agree—these cradles on the sides of this airship are to hold the bladders."

I watched blue liquid dripping into a beaker.

The professor scribbled some calculations. "I believe the entire Denver population could be under their control in a single night."

"Will it work while people sleep?" José asked the professor.

"We cannot be sure. But if a speaking trumpet was loud enough, people might wake up. Perhaps a steam whistle?"

"Why would the people not just shoot the airship down?" José was disgusted.

"Good question. We are not sure how high they will be when the first eggs are dropped, or what effect they will have. Perhaps people will be stupefied and not fight back. The main thing for us is to keep them from starting."

"One thing for certain," Laura said. "We don't know what they are planning. But this goes beyond pretty women walking around with parasols gassing people one at a time."

"We have to get into that compound," I said, "and soon."

Professor Gruber pointed to tall poles. "These are the lights?"

"Yes," Finn said. "Apparently the Supreme Navarch keeps some lights on all night. It will make it easier to land."

"Easier for them to see you as well. You must be very careful."

"We will land away from the compound and walk in," I said.

"Good," Professor Gruber said. "There is one more problem I can see. Look carefully. This building seems to be connected to the mountain. An extension of the mountain."

"We believe he has caves under the mountain," Laura said.

"I am afraid you are correct."

We spent the next hour with Professor Gruber. He showed us the step-by-step analysis of trying to find an antidote for the gas.

31

"We know how to make the agent, in the form of the blue liquid. We know what is in it—chemically. What we don't know is how it works. I am afraid this is the product of a mastermind. Perhaps a sick person, but brilliant." He smiled. "With genius there can be insanity. Not me, you understand, but sometimes." He winked.

Chapter 7

Finn liked ceremony, so we gathered in the shop and watched as he and Dolph whipped a tarp from the new quadcycle. We cheered and clapped.

It was beautiful. The cloth faring skin fit tightly and had been painted grey. The machine stood on two stands, front and back, with an opening for each rider.

Finn walked around the aircycle rapidly, talking fast. "The pedals are independent of each other, each with its own dynamo. Each person can pedal at their own speed. I have a mixing box, here." Finn tapped a wooden box with a screwdriver. "It will combine the electricity of each dynamo to give power to the Levitrite and the two propulsion tubes. These tubes contain fans that will create tremendous thrust. Dolph and I have worked on the mechanism and find the fans are quite efficient."

Finn put his hand on the front handlebars. "This rider is the driver. The lift boxes are in this lightweight frame above the riders' heads. The frame is only heavy enough to support the lifters when not riding. These high tensile wires actually hold the cycle in the air."

Finn paused. "This aircycle only weighs seventy-seven pounds but will have the power of four persons pedaling. It is almost twice the power for the weight."

"Is it ready for testing?" Addy bounced on her toes.

Maria slipped in, holding her page with her finger.

"This is as good a time as any," Finn said. "But there are differences between this and the other aircycles. First, this unit can back up."

"I made the motors reversible, so the twist grip has a neutral position. Rotate it forward, and the thrust goes toward the front. Get in, Dolph."

Dolph climbed onto the front seat and began to pedal. "There is a click mechanism, so the driver can feel it move into the reverse position." The fast-moving air sent papers fluttering off a workbench.

"Not too fast, Dolph. We don't need you flying up to the ceiling!" Finn teased.

33

"I have the lift turned off." He twisted the grip, the fan slowing and reversing.

"Brakes!" Addy said.

Dolph was out and opened the second seat flap. "We thought we should have a second set of controls. It may be that a cycle this long would be out of balance with one rider flying the machine from the front saddle."

I'm in a world of wonders.

Finn gripped a knurled knob on the steering post. "Twist this lock on the handlebars so it will turn the rudder."

"So, one person can ride this?" José asked.

"We hope so, if need be. We never know what might happen." Finn gave an apologetic smile. "Not trying to look for trouble, but on this mission, it is possible some might be captured, or—"

The workshop was quiet until someone coughed.

"We will be extra careful," I said.

"I geared the dynamos to match the pedaling cadence most of you use. Of course, calling for levitation *and* propulsion increases the resistance."

"This is well done, fellows." I admired the beautiful black quadcycle frame with red trim. "I think you may have outdone yourselves."

"Maria painted the accents." Dolph blushed. "And we should thank Mom and Letty for sewing the faring," he added quickly.

"Yes, thanks to Maria, Minnie, and Letty." I clapped, and applause echoed in the workshop. Minnie hugged the smiling Maria and Letty.

We carried the quadcycle out, and Addy brought the aircycle with faring.

"Now, don't rush up to three hundred feet," Finn cautioned. "This is a maiden voyage. Test each feature slowly."

"What order should we sit?" Laura asked.

"Well, we want it balanced. I have miniature levelers installed, but balancing the machine as much as possible makes sense. I would like to start with a lighter crew, so it makes the most sense to have Will, Addy, Laura, and José do the first test. If Will and Laura want to be the first two riders, José would ride in the stern."

Laura winked at Addy. "I want to ride behind Will."

Addy eagerly rubbed her hands together. "Fine with me."

We climbed onto our seats.

"Can you hear me?" The canopy created a muffled echo, but the response from the others was clear.

I began to pedal. "Let me try to lift us by myself." I pedaled faster and turned the levitation grip. The bike trembled but did not lift off. I stood, and with great effort, the bike shifted its weight on the ground.

"Will, you have the propulsion grip in reverse. Put it in the middle, neutral position," Finn said.

I turned the grip, feeling the click, and we lifted sluggishly off the ground. "Laura, join me."

Immediately, the quadcycle lifted, and I eased the levitation grip. We hovered five feet over the ground. Clapping and cheering came from below.

"How are you doing, Laura?"

"Fine. Try forward a bit."

I turned the propulsion grip, and the propeller tubes began to whisper. The quadcycle eased forward.

"OK, everyone, let's pedal at medium speed." I set a cadence, and I could hear the swish-swish of the pedals. It was a new sensation. Balancing the quadcycle lift and forward motion was the same as the other cycles, but I didn't feel the immediate drag in the pedals when I added lift or propulsion.

We settled to the ground, and I opened two clips on my faring door. "Finn, Dolph, this is as natural as can be. Can we try a race?"

Finn touched his palm to the electrical box. "Running nice and cool—I don't see why not."

I set a cadence and the others followed. I brought the quadcycle to fifteen feet. Mary pulled alongside on the aircycle, spinning the pedals easily.

Finn's voice was faint. "Ready, set, go."

I set a medium pace. When we pedaled in tandem, the quadcycle gained speed, and we began to move faster than I had imagined. I increased the elevation and headed for the light pole. When we rounded the pole, the quadcycle leaned into the turn, our feet swinging out. Laura squealed.

"Alright, let's go!"

I stood in the pedals, and the others joined suit. I opened the propulsion to Full and trimmed the lift. The propeller tubes increased in pitch, and air rushed out behind the bike.

We made the turn at the pine and moved toward the finish line. Over my shoulder, I saw Mary approaching the pine.

When we crossed the finish line, I brought us near the ground and reversed the propulsion. The quadcycle slowed, but braking was not instantaneous. "Addy. On three, you are going to let us down. Everyone, be ready to jump in if she can't do it."

I counted to three, and we began to sink slowly. At five feet, Addy was spinning hard. We hovered. I eased the grip, and we settled to earth.

Cool air brushed my cheeks as I climbed out of the quadcycle. Laura's hair was damp.

"Finn, it is too hot in there. There's not a breath of air!" Laura pushed wet curls off her forehead.

I put my hand out to Finn. "But it's great. Addy was able to let us down!"

Mary landed. "That thing is fast. You beat me by fifty or sixty yards."

"But what about the faring on the aircycle? Does it help?" Finn wondered.

"It makes it easier. I want to race José on the second aircycle before we add faring. I think I can win."

José smiled. "We will see, Mary, we will see."

We stood under the big tree and drank water. Exercise helped calm the growing unease in my belly.

While they set up for the race, Laura tried taking the quadcycle up from the second seat. Each time she tried, the rear came up, but the front stayed on the ground.

"This is like riding a bucking horse," she laughed.

"I need to adjust the auto-levelers." Finn stuck his head in and removed the box's side. He pulled a screwdriver from his pocket and made adjustments. "Try it now."

36

The rear came up the moment Laura twisted the grip, and she let it clatter to earth.

"Oops. Wrong way." Finn made a correction.

Cheers and whoops reminded me of the race taking place. I looked up in time to see Mary crossing the finish line almost one hundred feet ahead of José. The faring made a great improvement.

Nathan moved toward the quadcycle. "This whole unit does not weigh as much as the bike I raced Addy with. Let me try."

Nathan took it up ten feet and circled the watchers below. "Not bad, Finn, not bad," came his muffled compliment.

Mary was in the air again, pedaling toward the light pole. "Catch me, Mister!" she called.

Nathan leaned into the pedals, and the quadcycle followed. Nathan's powerful legs worked hard, but Mary easily outstripped his efforts. She waited for him at the finish line, and they were laughing when they landed.

"I tell you, if Nathan and I were part of the crew of the quadcycle, there would be no catching us."

It was true. After timing several races, the fastest team always included Nathan and Mary.

When we put the aircycles in the shop, Minnie was ringing the dinner bell.

Finn began to design the quadcycle launching mechanism for the *Silver Seed*. This required one of the cabins to be reworked for the purpose.

"The idea is for the four riders to be able to fly out of the cabin through double doors in the floor here." Finn indicated an area marked in the middle of the cabin. "We will rig a trapeze so the cycle can be suspended while the doors open. Then, when its supporting its own weight, we let it go."

My stomach tingled with excitement.

Al and Nathan made the cuts, and Finn began installing motors and gears to open and close the doors.

37

When the mechanism was complete, Finn and Dolph took the *Silver Seed* above the compound. The blue-gray lower hull floated majestically as the bay doors opened and closed.

"She is beautiful," Laura said quietly. "I love to see her hanging in the air."

The huge ship settled to the earth in front of the airship bay, and Dolph was first out the door. "Step one, success!" He could hardly contain his enthusiasm. "Finn let me fly her from the helm room while he tested the doors."

"And you did a good job." Finn grabbed Dolph's shoulder, rocking him back and forth. "Nathan will finish framing the interior of the launch room, but we are on schedule."

Every day, two teams rode the aircycles. Laura, Addy, José, and I worked with the quadcycle, building our endurance. Dolph produced a system for air to be pulled into the faring to keep us cool.

I wasn't sleeping well at night. I couldn't decide if it was excitement or frustration. Each day we were delayed was another day the Supreme Navarch could launch his next attack.

Chapter 8

The *Silver Seed* hovered thirty-five feet above the landing area at Eagle's Crest, the quadcycle swaying from its tethers as José and Addy climbed into their seats. After Laura was in place, I slipped onto the front seat.

Finn pulled a brass lever, and the doors swung away to each side. The floor giving away under my feet was unsettling. The queasiness reminded me of the first time I looked down the drop ports on the *Cloud Queen*.

I checked the twist grips and called back to the others. "Match my cadence." I pedaled slowly, at about thirty revolutions a minute. When the others matched my pace, I twisted the elevation grip, watching the two chains that held us go slack. Nathan unhooked the quadcycle and nodded.

I eased the elevation grip, and we slipped through the opening. Immediately, wind from the side caught the bottom of the quadcycle. We tilted sideways, swinging like a pendulum from the Levitrite cubes supporting the cycle.

I tried to go back up, but we had blown backward. The rear of the quadcycle bumped against the hull of the *Silver Seed*. We tipped, and sparks cracked. The quadcycle nosed up dangerously, and we began to fall. Addy squealed.

"Pedal!" José yelled. "The rear lifter is shorting!"

The nose tipped so high it was difficult to pedal. I leaned forward with my legs banging against the handlebars. "Pedal for your life!" Our descent had slowed, but the *Silver Seed* receded from view.

"Lean back on José's handlebars," Laura panted.

"Got it," Addy said.

For a moment, we seemed to hang in the air.

"Oh!" Laura exclaimed. "I can't keep my feet on the pedals."

We began to fall again.

Moments later, my foot slipped. I felt like a monkey, hanging on to my handlebars, sitting against Laura's handlebars, fighting to get my feet back on the pedals. The sounds of feet slipping punctuated our descent.

39

For a short moment we hovered, and then someone lost their footing again.

I checked the elevation grip, and it was wide open. "How far to the ground?"

"Soon!"

I tried to stand again, but we hit with a sudden jar. Both feet slipped and I lost my grip on the handlebars. My back slammed against Laura's handlebars. The cycle landed on the rear wheel and toppled to our left. When we hit, my wrist bent back, pain shooting up my arm.

Al and Paul lifted the quadcycle off us, and I looked at the others. José and Addy were a tangle of arms, legs, and faring, with Laura beside them. I realized I was on Laura's foot.

I wiggled out of the tangle and stood, holding my wrist. "Everyone all right?"

Laura rubbed her ankle. "I think so." I helped her up, and she stepped gingerly on her foot. "I'm OK. I'm OK." I wasn't convinced.

Addy scrambled to her feet, and José rolled onto his side. His head was bleeding, and Addy knelt and pressed her shirt tail on the wound. "Oh, José. Oh, oh."

Laura bent down to look at José's head. He sat up. "OK—just banged up." He struggled to his feet, Addy with two hands on his arm.

Laura hobbled around the cycle. "Our beautiful quadcycle. What a mess."

The *Silver Seed* touched down, and Finn flew out the door. "Too high! Everyone alright!? Oh, no—terrible. Everyone alright?"

Dolph was on his knees, inspecting the wiring to the rear Levitrite box. "Burnt to a crisp," he said. "A direct short. The resistance made it harder to turn the dynamos—robbing the system of power!"

Finn put his hand on his shoulder. "Not now, Dolph."

Mary came from the greenhouse and put a cloth on José's head. "Anyone else bleeding?"

"Banged up," I said. "I think we will be fine. Let's get the cycle into the shop."

Addy steadied José. "I am taking José to the bunkhouse. Mary, please come." As they moved away, José was wobbly in the leg.

"I learned something," Finn kept saying. "I learned something. I designed three equal lifters, and when the rear lifter was damaged, the cycle went out of balance."

Dolph looked at the damage to the rear levitator. "Finn, we can protect the cables better going to the levitators."

Finn nodded. "Right, Dolph. We were over confident. We have been flying for six years and have become complacent. We have to build in more safety features."

"Should I take notes?"

"Yes. I think the auto-levelers were part of the problem," Finn said. "They never shut off, but when the quadcycle tipped, the leveler shifted the current to the shorted rear. That made pedaling much more difficult." Finn hissed, "We were fools to let them launch from that height."

"We have to check for side wind," I said. Dolph wrote fast.

My wrist throbbed, and Laura and I made our way to our cabin. We wet cloths and wrapped her ankle and my wrist. We lay on our bed and fell asleep. It was getting dark when Addy tapped on our door.

My wrist was black and blue and throbbing. Laura said her ankle felt better.

"Do you think your wrist is broken?" she asked.

"No. It must be sprained. I can move it—it's just stiff from the swelling."

Outside, Addy waited on our little porch. "José's head hurts. Mary said we should watch his eyes. Mary said it can be serious if one pupil gets bigger than the other. So far he seems OK. He slept. He insists on coming to the lodge. Al is helping him."

I couldn't remember José complaining about pain in the past.

In the lodge, wonderful smells filled the air, and the little ones were setting the table. Finn and Dolph came in from the shop.

"Dolph and I have made some notes, and we are fixing the frame of the quadcycle," Finn said. "I'm really sorry about this mess."

41

"Not all your fault. When we started to descend out of the *Silver Seed*, the wind caught the faring and caused us to swing. The levitators acted like a hinge, and our feet swung sideways. I panicked and opened the levitators, and we struck the ship, causing the damage. It was my fault."

"There is no fault here," Paul said. "We are learning how to fight a different kind of war with new tools. Mistakes are part of developing this equipment."

"All four of you could have been killed today," Finn said. "I would not be able to forgive myself."

I saw the incident had shaken Finn's confidence. "Finn, we all know there are dangers. We are at war. Not the kind of war where army meets army. This is a war of mind control. The important thing is that we learn from this. And Finn—we don't have much time. How long until repairs can be made?"

Finn seemed to regain strength. "By morning, Dolph and I will have the quadcyele lifters redesigned. I would like to have Al and Dad there early to repair the frame and make modifications."

"Take as many as you need." I flexed my wrist. "I don't think I can do much with this arm. José, how are you feeling?"

"I am fine. Head hurts, but I can work."

I didn't sleep well that night, and neither did Laura. After breakfast, José, Laura, and I puttered around the *Silver Seed*, checking and rechecking equipment and supplies. We discussed at length what we would wear and carry. We decided on knives and small twenty-two revolvers. We would carry the minimum amount of food and water. We hoped we would not be in the compound long. "In and out" was our mantra.

I chafed at the delay.

Chapter 9

Finn showed me a new quadcycle. He redesigned the position of the lifter boxes. "If we lose a levitator, the cycle won't go nose up or down to such a degree. The main lifter is directly in the center. Safer."

"Well done. This time, we practice and practice. Make sure we have all learned to ride the quadcycle," I said.

"The wrecked unit is also almost ready. Dolph has reworked the levitators, moving them closer to center. Paul was able to straighten the frame."

"Then we will practice with two teams."

Later, in our cabin, I asked Laura if her ankle was ready for pedaling.

"I think so. It is still stiff this morning, but after I move around it is fine." Laura pulled her hair back with two combs. "Will, we need to take this carefully, anyway. We can afford no more mistakes."

I sat on the edge of the bed. "I know. But with the army north of Denver hypnotized, it is up to us to stop this nightmare. We cannot allow gas to be dropped on civilians. Who knows what commands might be given?"

"What do you think the Supreme Navarch's goal is?"

"Power. Power and control?"

"Yes, but how much? Is he trying to take over the country?" She sighed. "Do people like that ever get enough?"

"Enough is never enough." It was a sad truth.

At daylight, Laura and I, Addy, and José made up the first team.

"I put a temporary switch to disconnect the front or rear Levitrite lifters as a test," Finn announced. "Hover at low altitude and turn them off one at a time. Be ready to turn the lifter on again."

Two blade switches were mounted on the handlebars. I slipped into place and worked the lever. "Seems simple enough."

We launched, and I took us up ten feet. "Ready, everyone. I'm going to disconnect the rear."

There were murmurs of approval, and I lifted the handle.

The bike dipped in the rear, causing my stomach to roll. I was tempted to reconnect the switch, but the angle didn't keep us from pedaling. "Everyone OK?"

"Yes," José called.

I studied the ground, and we were not sinking. I brought the lever down, and the bike righted itself. "Let's try the front."

I was more alarmed when the bike nosed down. I eased us forward. "At least I can see the ground better," I joked.

I connected the lifter, and we rode for forty-five minutes, making the race loop over and over. The new bike provided better ventilation for us and was more stable.

Dolph stood with a chalkboard. "Every lap has been a full two minutes faster than a single aircycle."

Mary, Nathan, and Finn rode with Addy as well. Finn would rather have worked in the shop, but I convinced him he needed to be in shape. They did two rounds in just under four minutes and landed.

Finn was first out of the faring. "You were right. I need to ride every day."

We also mixed the teams in case of illness or injury. With eight pilots, we felt confident any team could land and spy on the Supreme Navarch.

I was impressed with the Mary, Laura, Addy, and José team. They were fast, and Mary was an excellent pilot.

Finn had fabricated a winch device to be hooked to the top of the quadcycle so the bike could be lowered but remain attached until we were sure the riders were in complete control. We used several combinations of riders to practice drop-off and pickup.

Dolph timed each exercise, and our confidence increased. We were ready.

44

We had a special meal in the lodge three weeks after our return from Colorado. I felt excited and anxious at the same time. It was our last evening at Eagle's Crest for a while. I wasn't looking forward to four or five days of flying. The *Silver Seed* had beautiful cabins and comforts, but the trip meant flying twenty-four hours a day. On other long trips, we played chess, darts, and read. This trip, we planned to log time peddling the quadcycle.

Minnie had outdone herself, with roast chicken, mashed potatoes and squash. As we ate I began to relax.

After we had eaten, I stood. "Friends, we are embarking on a dangerous but grand adventure. For me, the danger is overshadowed by the knowledge that we are engaged in the fight of our lives. Our fight is for freedom. We know the United States is based on freedom. Our constitution guarantees us freedom, but the Supreme Navarch is determined to rob us of that freedom. Autocrats cannot be allowed to control the world."

I paused, taking a drink of tea. "The real danger is that if we lose this endeavor, our ability to know what is best could be taken away. One whiff of the gas and we would end up in the fog, not knowing why we are doing some things—not even realizing we are doing them. We do not know what devious commands may be given as this war continues. Being numb from the fog, we wouldn't even care."

This is the big threat. Those in the fog seemed content to muddle around as if it were normal. Any command could be given when the gas was administered. True chaos would occur if the right commands were given to enough people.

Finn opened a box Dolph had brought him. "These are the new handheld coders." He held up a small box with a wire sticking out of the top. "I have devised a way to send code for short distances. Dolph and I have tested these. The range is such that you can communicate with the *Silver Seed* as it hovers high above the Freebooters' stronghold."

I turned one of the devices over in my hand, and I marveled at the intricate parts that must be inside. There was no crank. I gave Finn a questioning look.

45

"It has a dry cell battery. Push the button on the side with your thumb, and then the big button on the front is the code key."

I pushed the side button and tapped FINN IS A GREAT INVENTOR. "Seems easy enough."

Even though we were not transmitting, Finn understood the clicks and smiled. "Thank you. Dolph was a big help. Conserve the battery by only pushing when you are sending or receiving."

Finn took the box and tapped THANKS WILL. There were smiles. Addy rapped CLEVER with her knuckles on the table. Code had become a second language for us.

BUENO Mrs. Rodriquez slap tapped, and there was a ripple of applause. The level of commitment at Eagle's Crest was astounding.

"These boxes use a different wavelength than our other code units," Finn continued. "If these were to be captured, we don't want Freebooters listening in our conversations. I have modified the radios in the *Silver Seed* and the *Cloud Queen*. A switch will change the frequency instantly. Dolph has them labeled."

"One last precaution. Always begin a code conversation with BB for the battery box. This way, the receiver will know that the sender hasn't fallen into enemy hands."

Finn thought of everything.

We stared into the fire, happy to be together. José and Addy were sitting in two chairs, holding hands. Laura and I left when the coals were dying and slept restlessly. I knew I was keeping her awake and went to our small sitting room. I eventually dozed in the armchair.

46

Chapter 10

The steady whine of the propeller tubes comforted me. We flew high, as Finn told us there was less air resistance. I thought perhaps there would not be as much air for the propeller tubes, but Finn assured me flying high was best. Several of us got headaches flying at nine thousand feet. Extra cans of fuel lined the hallways and every empty space.

Because we flew twenty-four hours a day, we broke the shifts into four hours, keeping a minimum crew at any one time. One person watched the engine room, and two were in the helm room—one at the wheel and one at the elevation rudders.

Laura and I often worked together in the helm room, and from time to time, restless crew members came to talk. It was difficult to sleep during the day. Our cabins could be made completely dark, but my mind knew it was a bright day outside.

By the third day, we were exhausted, and I found I could sleep well at any time.

We played chess, checkers, darts, read and held math races on the chalkboard. Even Finn was able to peddle the quadcycle vigorously for thirty-five minutes. By the middle of the fourth day, I was ready to arrive.

"I think we should take one extra dry cell down for the code sender," I said. "We can hide it somewhere when we get on the ground."

José and I were in the rear lounge looking over our supplies. We each had a small canvas pack Minnie had made for us. We would wear our knives and pistols. José packed a length of rope.

"Are you ready for this, my friend?" I asked.

"I am ready."

High clouds darkened the sky, and low fog clouds whispered in the canyons and valleys. The *Silver Seed* would not be seen.

We scanned the rough terrain below as the ship descended slowly through a veil of cloud, unsure where a mountaintop might be. Laura pointed. "There's the slender lake. We are close."

47

I turned north, and we slipped higher, so the clouds almost blocked our view. A mist fell on the windows.

"Probably raining harder on the ground," I said.

"Yes, take your slickers. You can always leave them."

The compound came into view. It was larger than I had remembered.

Laura began sketching a map of the compound. "The hill above the compound should give you the best access."

"And a good place to spy on the yard below." I turned the wheel. "It's midday. Let's move north until later."

We climbed into the clouds and ran the propeller tubes for fifteen minutes. The *Silver Seed* rocked in the rough air over the canyons below.

We ate in the lounge while Addy and Nathan manned the ship. We descended from the clouds in the late afternoon, moving south again. The sun slanted in under the clouds, casting long rays over the mountains. Addy was in the shooting pod, and we all surveyed the area.

"What about over there?" Laura pointed to a copse of trees on the northern side of the compound. "We could let you off just in the clouds. They will never see the quadcycle."

"On the trip back, how are you going to find the *Silver Seed*?" I wondered.

"I will blink the light in the gun pod," Finn said. The light winked twice, glowing against the fog.

I was anxious, and when nervous, the smallest detail multiplied into problems. "Good."

"It is cold, that is good. We won't get hot in the quadcycle," Addy said.

The *Silver Seed* hung low in the clouds, motionless until twilight came. "It's now or never," I said.

We walked, single file, into the launch room. Laura, José, Addy, and I climbed into our seats and turned the snaps on the faring.

Finn leaned toward us. "Ready?"

"Ready."

48

Finn reached up, checked the cable hook, and lifted us above the deck. He pulled the lever, and the bay door gears whirred and clicked. Wind ruffled the faring.

Finn went to a speaking tube. "Bring the ship to port thirty degrees. Ahead Dead Slow." The faring became still.

"Let's spin at about one per second," I said. The pedals began to spin. I tested the lift, and the cycle became light. I gave it a bit more lift. "Steady."

Nathan unhooked the safety chain. I eased the lift grip, and we floated down, the cable following. The trick was quickly getting below the *Silver Seed* so wind would not batter us against the doors.

The new design was much easier to manage, and we were twenty feet below the ship in moments. The cloud thinned quickly, and visibility increased.

"Everything feel good?" I asked.

There were murmurs of yes.

I reached for the code box. BB HOLD US HERE. I increased the lift, and the cable went slack. "Unhook us, Addy."

The mechanism clicked. "We are free."

"Steady pace. Here we go." I steered down, circling over the small flat. The air was chill, and we weren't peddling hard. When we were about twenty feet above the ground I eased off the propulsion and we hovered.

"You ready, José?"

"Ready."

We landed gently on damp soil, and the quadcycle started to tilt. I twisted the grip and moved a few feet forward. This time, the cycle sat solidly.

I slipped out of my door flap and met Laura coming out of hers. She wrapped her arms around me, and I lifted her off the ground.

"Be careful, my love. I need you. Come back to me."

"You are *my* love. I only want to get this done and return to our lives." I kissed her and marveled at how I never got tired of how her hair smelled.

Laura unlatched the second seat steering lock and readied herself.

49

José and Addy kissed, holding hands until she was on her seat behind Laura. We closed their flaps and stood back as the pedals began to spin.

The quadcycle lifted off and quickly disappeared into the mist. José tapped out BB CYCLE RETURNING. We waited until the key clicked ARRIVED SAFELY. I followed José into the trees, feeling very much on our own.

The copse was not as dense as it appeared from above. We picked our way along a deer trail and crept up to the manmade bluff over the buildings. Light poles lit a large area, with sheds and outbuildings lurking in the shadows.

José uncoiled the rope and tied it around his waist. "Put a couple of loops around that sapling and let me down."

I played out no more than fifteen feet of rope when the line went slack, I tied it off. Long moments passed. I resisted calling to him. The line tightened, and when José's head appeared, I helped him up.

"Just as we thought. The building comes right out of the mountain. They are right below us."

The spidery structure was puzzling, almost on stilts, separated and strengthened by arches. It had platforms, rooms, and stairs. "That building is mostly iron," I said.

A square tube connected it to the large building. "I think that is a tunnel to pass from one building to the other."

The smell of cooking filled the air, and we wandered toward the aroma. A vent, eighteen inches in diameter with a cone-shaped cover to keep out the rain came out of the ground. Standing in the warm air, talk of cooking and the clatter of pots and pans drifted up the vent. Even though we had just eaten, the scents made me hungry.

"Hey, boy, hustle these rolls out there before they are cold," echoed up the tube.

José motioned me to follow, and we moved back into the trees. "There will be more of these vents."

We wandered west and found a trail winding down the hillside toward the compound. A canyon dropped off beyond.

50

It was almost dark, and José lit the small coal oil lantern. "We must keep an eye on this side. Men may come here to work on the vents."

Walking a rough grid, a pattern became apparent. Every hundred paces or so, we found smaller vents. Near one vent, we could hear shouting.

"I will not have delays! I am the Supreme Navarch!"

"Yes, Supreme Navarch," echoed several voices.

"Why are we lagging in gas synthesis? And why is the Air Loom not producing gas faster? I have provided you with the latest equipment—and this is my reward. Delays!" Something slammed down.

An Air Loom?

"Sir, the speed of gas production was based on a smaller model. For some reason—the larger model is not as efficient."

The Supreme Navarch's voice became low and menacing. "Are you saying that my design is flawed?"

"No, Sir. The design is a scientific marvel." There were murmurs of agreement. "Perhaps we are not operating the inputs efficiently."

"Make it efficient! I will not have delays. I am the Supreme Navarch."

"Yes, Supreme Navarch."

"How long since the workers have passed the Blue Vial?"

"Yesterday, Supreme Navarch."

"And what commands were given?"

Silverware clinked, and I ducked under the cover to hear better.

"Standard, Sir. Edict forty-three."

"Change the edict. I want the vial passed again tomorrow morning. Tell those fools they want to work harder and longer. They do not feel tired."

"But—the last time we passed the Blue Vial so soon we—"

"I will not tolerate insubordination!" the Supreme Navarch screamed. "You hear me?! No arguments!" His voice got low again. "Am I understood?"

"Yes, Supreme Navarch."

We stepped back from the vent. "This must be his office or meeting room," I said.

"Yes." José gestured with his chin. "He is loco—like a spoiled child who is not allowed to have a piece of candy."

"Loco is a good word for it. We can't allow a man like him to give commands to the world."

Chapter 11

We searched the sloping hillside, mapping vents in our minds. A light drizzle caught on my eyelashes, and I swiped them away with the back of my hand. The undergrowth was thick in places, and we had to avoid clumps of small trees.

"I think these tunnels have been here for years." José shook a shrub with a two-inch trunk that grew close to a vent.

We worked our way north, the moon making a shrouded appearance. José held out his hand. A swish of branches made my breath catch in my throat. We ducked, waiting.

When a form moved against the shadows, I drew my gun. As the dark shape moved to our left, I made out wide antlers. "Is that an elk?"

"I think so. I have only seen pictures in books."

I slipped my gun back into the holster. "He kind of spooked me."

The elk moved up the hill.

Just when we thought the tunnels could not go any farther into the mountain, we came upon several huge vents hidden among an outcropping of shale. Below, we heard the wheezing groan of machinery. One of the vents was sucking in great quantities of air. The echoes coming up the tubes gave the impression the devices were far below us.

A chugging sound led us to a large chimney pipe. We got to the downwind side and smelled fuel oil. "That's one big steam engine," I said. "I suppose to generate electricity." Air whistled into two more intake pipes. We stood in the warmth of the smoke stack.

"So, how do we do this?" I asked. "We could just go back to the ship, get dynamite, and drop charges down the vents."

"There are too many vents. I think we need to understand what is happening inside." José gazed up toward the sliver of moon disappearing behind the clouds. "We must kill or capture this Supreme Navarch. Twice we thought we had defeated the Freebooters, and now they are back. The scope of this is beyond anything we could have imagined."

53

"It has occurred to me—we thought the Adjunct Commander in Sacramento was the leader. Foolish of us. The word adjunct doesn't mean the top person."

"Supreme should be the top, yes?"

"One would think. But what if there are Adjunct Commanders in other places?" I shuddered at the thought. "Even in other countries."

"We can not hurry—there is no room for mistakes. We need to learn more about the patterns of their activities."

Either no one was tending the engine below, or the machinery masked their voices. We decided to hike back down to the kitchen vent.

We communicated with the *Silver Seed*, reporting that we had found vents and were settling near one for the night. We kept the conversation short as we didn't want to spend the battery. I wished we had a crank sender with us. I longed to chat with Laura.

I slept fitfully with my back against the warmish pipe. We huddled together under both our blankets, with my slicker over us, and José's over our legs. It rained twice in the night, water dripping off the vent cone. My stomach growled.

At four-thirty in the morning, we heard clattering in the kitchen, and the air from the vent began to be warmer. Wood smoke came up from a stovepipe we had not noticed. The smell of bacon being cooked made my mouth water.

When the sun peeked over the mountains, I was glad for its warmth. A convoy of supply wagons was being unloaded in the yard below. We crawled under a low bush and watched men in the yard. Several were filling the egg bladders with a long hose. Once, we smelled a sickly sweet smell and scrambled to our feet. We ran back, holding our breaths.

I held my finger to my lips, indicating we shouldn't speak.

We sat in silence against our vent. My ankles and feet were soaked.

I couldn't tell any difference in the way my mind felt. At last I said, "We need to stop the Freebooters. We should only speak in positive terms until we are sure we didn't breathe enough gas." José nodded.

After thirty minutes, I said, "We're OK."

54

"Yes. But Professor Gruber can find an antidote any time."

We edged out to the bluff, happy the wind was over our shoulders. José pointed to some clothes hanging on a line. "The uniform is easy. A hat, shirt, and pants in ugly green."

"Perhaps we should help ourselves to those a little later."

"Some of the men look Mexican." José nodded to a group of men carrying demijohns into the main building. "I will look like I belong."

Several women came out, carrying baskets of clothes. Two men guarded them with rifles as they took down the dry laundry and hung out the new.

That night, we sent a message to the *Silver Seed*. BB BIG COMPOUND MANY MEN STOP WOMEN DOING LAUNDRY STOP

THE PATTERN CONTINUES STOP SEETHING STOP

I recognized Laura's word. "Laura is boiling mad."

"Everyone is mad," José said, "or should be."

"We cannot blow up the compound with dynamite. Too many innocents." I said.

"If one stays, we have a chance of rescue. We can flip a coin."

"No, I'm going."

We watched for two more days, carefully noting all movement and marking times. The aircycle came down with food and water each night. Using the code boxes, we synchronized our watches with the *Silver Seed* each evening.

The greatest activity was at eleven in the morning. Women brought out laundry, and wagons were unloaded. All afternoon, building materials were carried under the arches of the building on stilts and pulled up inside with cables. On the second day, construction began on another level.

José slipped down that evening to get a uniform off the line. When he returned, he held a woman at gunpoint. She only wore a plain white dress. "She was trying to get away. Maybe I should have let her go, but I think she may be useful. She knows the inside."

55

She was a tiny person, only coming to my shoulder.

"We are not from here," I said. "We're not going to hurt you."

The woman stepped back. There was a yellowing bruise above her wrist.

"We won't send you back." I looked at José, and he lowered the gun and handed me the clothes. They were wool and well-made.

"We're sorry to have frightened you, but we hope to rescue more people than you."

The woman gave an almost imperceptible nod. Her eyes followed the rise of the hill behind me. "I must get away from here. Far away!"

"Please don't run. We need to talk. Then, we'll help you get away."

"Yes. Look, I have put the pistol away."

The woman twisted a small handkerchief into a knot.

"I'm going inside the compound. I need to know how we might do that without being caught." The woman crossed her arms. "But first, I am Will. This is my friend José. What is your name?"

"Susan." Her arms remained crossed, glancing over her shoulder.

"Glad to meet you, Susan. Let's move to that clump of pines."

Susan picked her way among the rocks. Her bare feet looked cold.

I dug in my pack and handed her a pair of socks. "What can you tell me about this place?"

She sat on a boulder, pulling up the socks. "Why would you go in there? They will give you the gas."

"Why didn't they give you the gas?" I asked.

"Many women are gassed. I taught myself to hold my breath —in the stream at home. My brothers and I had contests."

"How could you hold your breath so long? Isn't the gas filling the room when they pass the Blue Vial?"

"The vial only bubbles when the stopper is out. After a whiff, the stopper is replaced. It's ceremonial, very solemn. Everyone waits, head down, with both hands outstretched. The

56

ceremony leader takes the vial from person to person." She held up one finger. "The secret is to hold your breath and act right."

"What do you mean, 'act right?'"

The corner of Susan's mouth twitched. "Blow out a tiny bit through your nose instead of drawing in." She held her hands together, raised them to her face, lifting her chest. "It is important to put a silly look on your face."

José was smiling. "Well done. Have others done this?"

"One woman did and escaped when hanging the laundry. Now they guard us."

I was impressed. "How long until they will miss you?"

"Probably not until morning. It was time to bring in the laundry—I went first. I told the guard I would take some clothes down, and then meet him behind the sheds." Susan's eyes went steely. "He's a dumb sot and easily convinced."

"And he did not raise the alarm?"

"I hoped he wouldn't. He broke the rules—letting me go ahead. He may not want to be questioned."

José cocked his head. "Wait. The other guards will not miss you?"

Susan shrugged. "By this time of day, they have stopped by the saloon. It's against the rules, but they are not exactly dedicated."

"But they are under the influence of the gas?"

"Yes," Susan whispered.

She planned this well.

"We work two periods each day. At night, the lights go out at nine-thirty, and everyone is to sleep." Susan shivered. "It's pitch black in there. The Supreme Navarch wants everyone asleep—early."

"Have you met or seen the Supreme Navarch?"

"Only at General Assemblies." Susan dusted her hands together. "He's a weaselly little man with a weak chin. He always stays on stage with The Twelve—The Chosen. They are the only ones he trusts. More like bodyguards, if you ask me."

"What happens at General Assemblies?"

"The Supreme Navarch yells at us. If we're lucky, he gets hoarse and stops early."

"Do just the women go to General Assemblies?"

"Oh, no. Everyone must go." Susan mimicked a tiny voice. "We are all family here! Family!" Susan waved her arms in a grand gesture. "And I am your protector!"

José chuckled.

I continued my questions. "How many women are inside?"

"I am in group one. There are twenty of us. There are two groups. I don't know how many are in the other group."

"What do you do besides laundry?"

"We clean, make beds, and do laundry."

"Cooking?"

"No, the Supreme Navarch insists men are better suited."

"Where does he stay?"

"He has a room where he meets with The Twelve."

"Inside the caves or in one of the buildings?"

"The meeting room is in the caves in the mountain. It is huge." She paused. "Not really caves. At least it doesn't look like a cave. It is finished inside—big square hallways. There's a maze of them in there. It's easy to get lost. Pay close attention to all the turns and side tunnels."

I turned to José. "Perhaps I could pretend to be a cook?"

Susan brightened. "The kitchen staff is changed often. You might be able to join unnoticed."

The sun had gone down, and I offered my coat to Susan. She stepped back, shaking her head.

Her chin was quivering, and I took off the coat. "Here— you're cold."

This time, she accepted. The coat almost touched the ground, and she pulled it tight around her.

"Susan, you don't have warm clothes. No shoes. It's close to freezing each night. We have a way to take you away. I think it would be best."

Susan glanced at the hill again.

José turned. "I will start a fire."

After José left, Susan drew back. I stepped back as well, leaving plenty of distance between us.

"Have you heard of a flying steamboat and another airship that defeated part of the Freebooter army? In California?"

"We heard the story, but steamboats don't fly."

58

"I am Captain Will Henderson." I gestured in the direction José had gone. "He's my shipmate and best friend." I took a tentative step forward and put out my hand.

She started to reach out but pulled her hand back to her cheek. "Then, it's true?"

"Yes, it's real. We can take you to one of the ships, tonight."

Susan crossed her arms again. "I don't think I want to fly. Couldn't you give me shoes and let me go?"

"Do you know where this place is—how to get home?"

A tear rolled down her cheek. "They blindfolded us when we were brought by wagon."

"This is rough country. Without food, I don't think you will be able to get far. You won't know who to trust."

Susan drew herself up, squaring her shoulders, the coat hanging on her thin shoulders. "Why should I trust you? For all I know, you work for him." She pulled a stub of a butter knife from her pocket, gripping it hard. She had scraped it on something to give it a crude edge.

I put both palms toward her. "If you will wait with us, you will see more than a flying riverboat."

Her hands went to her sides, tears rolling down both cheeks. "I'm just so tired." Her shoulders slumped, all her bravado gone.

I wished I had a picture of the *Cloud Queen*. I put my hands on my knees so my eyes were level with hers. "Please trust us. Trust me." Her big eyes glistened. "You can help in the fight against all that is happening down there. Draw us a map of the tunnels you are familiar with." She was crying hard now, almost hysterical. "You are cold and hungry. Please come with me—at least to the fire."

Susan gave me a grim nod and followed me, the butter knife still in her hand.

José stood by the small fire, and Susan warmed her hands. She had stopped crying.

The message box clicked BB WE HAVE A WOMAN FROM INSIDE STOP SHE IS SCARED STOP

Susan looked nervously toward José, but he kept the box under his slicker.

BB SEND MARY LAURA ADDY DOWN STOP BRING COAT STOP

59

"Don't worry. He's talking to our ship."

"You two scare me."

"We're all scared," I said. "But what scares us the most is the Supreme Navarch succeeding. We can't let that happen."

José cooked three eggs. Susan didn't take more than a bite or two.

"Do not be nervous," José said. "You will like the women who are coming."

She let out a long, shaky breath.

LAUNCHING QUADCYCLE STOP

José lit the lantern and we made our way to the small field, Susan walking between us. She stumbled once, and I realized she was weak from mistreatment. José held the lantern high.

Air in the propulsion tubes whispered above, and when I looked carefully, I could see an area where the stars were obscured. The *Silver Seed* was right above us, and I hadn't noticed. The quadcycle landed beside us.

Susan stumbled back from the machine. "Oh, I don't think I could go in that! That's—flimsy."

Laura, Mary, and Addy stepped out, and we made introductions. Laura wore her black top hat and a short cape.

I hugged her. "So far, so good. Susan says there is a big turnover in the kitchen staff." I puffed out my chest. "I am going to be a cook!"

Laura laughed. "Good. When you come home, you can start helping more!"

Mary exchanged backpacks with me. "Not fancy. Rations are low. We are going north during the day tomorrow. We hope to have venison for you soon."

"Thanks." I looked forward to something besides potatoes, cheese, tortillas, and beans.

Addy gave Susan a short coat and handed me mine.

I stepped back while Laura and Mary talked quietly to Susan, and at last, she climbed into the quadcycle. José and Addy stood to the side, whispering quietly. Addy was the last to take her seat.

Laura lifted off three times, the bike only rising an inch or two. "How are you feeling?"

"Do I need to turn the foot things?" Susan wondered.

"Only if you want to. If you don't want to try, that's fine."

Susan turned the pedals several turns. "I've seen a bike. One with the big wheel in front. This is kind of fun."

Laura picked up the cadence, and Mary and Addy matched her speed. Susan continued to turn the pedals slowly.

"Here we go!" Laura turned the lift grip.

When they lifted straight up, Susan gave a squeal, "Oh! I don't like this!"

Mary's cooing, "Don't look down. Hang on tight. Look straight ahead. Look at my shoulders. Don't look down," faded into the night.

The pod light blinked occasionally. Then flashed, ALL ABOARD STOP GOOD NIGHT STOP

José and I waved into the quiet air.

The next day an exercise program began, led by a tall, muscular man. He shouted orders and a cadence. Men flopped their arms and legs around in a half-hearted manner.

That night, the quadcycle brought a detailed map of the forward part of the cave. Several passageways led further from the opening but only had a question mark where they ended.

"Susan did the best she could," Laura explained. "That poor woman—girl—was half starved."

Addy pointed to the assembly hall and the kitchen to the east. "From the main entrance, go past this auditorium, turn right, and you will come to the kitchen. It has double doors, but Susan has never been inside the kitchen."

Laura touched my arm. "Susan was taken from a town not far from here. We took her home."

"It's only right."

After the quadcycle rose, I paced from the kitchen vent. *The auditorium must be right below.* Two vents came out of the ground that were far apart. The auditorium was large.

61

The garbage was taken to the gully at ten-thirty each morning. Three men handled the duty, but sometimes more. *It must come from the kitchen.* I walked the hillside, imagining the network of tunnels below me.

José studied the map. "Sixty, maybe a hundred feet to the assembly hall."

"I think I could slip in with the garbage detail."

"Lots of coming and going."

That evening, Laura and Addy came down with food. The venison had just been cooked, and they brought plates. I almost felt civilized, eating with a plate on my lap.

Laura was trembling when we said goodbye. We watched as the quadcycle lifted. At the vent, I slept fitfully. Images of being captured and locked in a cell crowded my thoughts, pushing any pleasant dreams aside.

At four I took a walk, wandering from vent to vent with the map, trying to imagine what was below me. José had fried potatoes and venison when I returned. I changed into the green shirt and pants. The morning was not cold, so I left my coat.

When the exercises began, we walked to the trail.

I put my pistol in my pack. "Hide it in that junk pile near the dump. I will find it."

"Good luck." We shook hands.

Chapter 12

Two men dumped garbage from gunny sacks, letting it roll into the ravine. When the last man left, I hurried down to the garbage pile. I found a ragged gunny sack and filled it with trash.

Waiting was the hard part. A third man came, and I made a big deal out of shaking the garbage out of my bag. The man stood for a few minutes, gazing across the canyon. He glanced at me and grunted. "Guess we better get back."

I shrugged and walked behind him across the compound. Three women carried clothes baskets filled with wet green uniforms.

José and I hadn't been able to see the facade against the mountain. A building with a shed roof faced the yard. Huge double doors in the shadows stood open, and I tucked my folded sack under my left arm as my companion had done.

The interior showed a wide, brightly lit hallway stretching out before me. It was warm, but the air felt damp and slightly stale.

To our right was the huge auditorium with seats like a theater. We passed three sets of open double doors. A raised stage with a purple velvet curtain completed the effect. I wondered if they had plays to entertain the men.

Four hallways intersected with the main corridor across from the auditorium. We turned right after the last set of double doors, and the smell of food filled the air.

A tall, handsome man burst through swinging doors and pointed at me. "Hey, you."

Caught? So quickly? I stood straight. "Yes, Sir?"

"Get in here. Make it quick!" Inside the swinging doors was a massive kitchen. He handed me a bulging bag. "Get this out of here. It is stinking up the whole place. There are more. Hustle back."

"Yes, Sir."

I took the bag and retraced my steps to the dump. Two others followed me with bags. Once outside, one said, "So Ted had the ace the whole time. We fleeced that fool for ten dollars." The other man chuckled.

63

I dumped the bag over the edge, tossing my tattered bag onto the pile. Flies swarmed, a constant buzz filling the air.

The two other trash men seemed to have disappeared, so I made more trips, happy to be busy.

When I went in to get the third bag, the tall fellow said, "Where did those other men go?"

"I don't know." I tried to look unconcerned.

"Well, I need help in here. Two of my cooks are malingering." He pointed to two pots of steaming potatoes. He handed me a masher and a pair of gloves. "Make it snappy. The Twelve are going to the meeting room. The Supreme Navarch is having a strategy meeting, and they don't like cold food."

I bore down on the huge pot with all my weight. The head cook came with butter, milk, salt, and pepper. My stomach growled.

"You are a good worker," the cook said. "I may ask for you full-time."

I nodded, and started on the second pot.

A man dressed like a steward poked his head in from the other side of the kitchen. "Come on, Sid, let's get moving."

Sid glared. "A watched pot doesn't boil."

"Late cooks might end up in the pot," the fellow snorted.

Sid brought a rolling table. "Put the first batch of potatoes on the dolly. Go with Jenkins."

I lifted the big pot on the cart and followed the steward down several long hallways. I tried to memorize each turn in case he sent me back alone. *Two lefts, skip one, and a right.* I repeated the mantra in my mind.

We stopped in a long hallway outside a set of double doors. Jenkins went through the closest door, and I started to follow. He glanced back. "Stop," he hissed. "What is wrong with you. First day?"

I mumbled, "Yes, Sir. Sorry."

"Never go in there with work greens on. Only waiters and stewards."

"Yes, sir."

Two waiters came and dished potatoes into bowls. Another man arrived with a cart with vegetables and meat. Waiters made

64

hurried trips into the room. Each time the door opened, I tried to glance in. The room held a long table with a white tablecloth.

When the potatoes were gone, Jenkins hissed, "Don't stand there like a dolt! Get the wine."

I panicked. I had no idea where to get wine. "Sir, sorry, Sir. First day in the kitchen. Where should I fetch the wine?"

Jenkins looked annoyed. "Across from the kitchen!" he growled. "Bring twelve bottles of red and two of white. Hustle, man. Hustle. Double time."

I took the cart, steadying the empty potato pot, and went down the hallways. *Two lefts, skip one, and a rights is one left, skip one and two rights.* I hurried around the first corner and almost collided with two men. The cart's wheel hit a surly man's boot and he glared. "The Supreme Navarch wants more wine," I said.

At the kitchen, Sid looked up. "Going OK out there??

"Fine, Sir. I am to get wine."

"Leave the pot. Use the high cart." He patted a high two-wheeler with a fancy railing. "Don't break any. And don't help yourself. The Supreme Navarch has his bottles counted."

Back in the hall, there were doors every twenty feet. The first contained cleaning supplies. The second was a storeroom with canned goods. The third was wine. There were bottles in racks and bottles in cases. Many looked red. I picked up a bottle of clear wine and was reading the label when Sid came in.

He went to several cases sitting on the floor. "Take this. It is a fine French red. It will please."

"Thank you, Sir. I wasn't sure which is the best."

Sid laughed loudly. "I didn't say it was the best. I said it would please. Don't let them fool you, Boy. They just want wine."

"I am to take two bottles of white."

"The one you have in your hand will do—get another. The Supreme Navarch doesn't know much about wine but tries to impress."

"Thank you, Sir."

I set the box of red on the cart. I took the two of white, unsure what to do with them.

"Lay them across the bottles in the box, silly lad. And get a move on."

65

"Yes, Sir!"

"You are a proper boy, I will say that. What's your name?"

"Will, Sir."

"Keep calling me Sir, and I will keep you on full-time here." He went back through the kitchen doors, making them swing twice. I was starting down the hall when Sid came back out and called, "Hurry back. We have to mash potatoes for all the men."

"Hurry! Yes, Sir. I'll step smartly."

"Smartly, Ha!" He pushed air toward me with one hand.

I practically ran with the cart, making my turns from memory. The steward glared at me.

"Well, you took your sweet time."

"Sorry, but I believe I have a good choice for this evening."

Jenkins looked sour and pulled a bottle out of the box. "Hmm. French. Oh, he will like this."

"Yes, Sir. I hope so, Sir. Always good to please the Supreme Navarch."

Jenkins looked up, staring blankly at the wall. "Yes, it is always good to please the Supreme Navarch."

I hurried back to the kitchen and put my back into mashing potatoes. Sid added milk and butter as I made the wire click on the bottom of the pot. I mopped sweat on the sleeve of my shirt.

"You know how to work, I'll say that."

"Yes, Sir."

Steaming pots of potatoes kept coming, and Sid added his seasonings. Men in greens took them away by the cart full. I didn't look up until there were no more pots.

"Well, Will, I think that was the last of it. Time for the kitchen staff to eat. I'll bet you have worked up an appetite."

"Yes, Sir."

"Well, come on then. We eat in style."

I followed him to a room at the back of the kitchen. About twenty ate at a table, served by men who apparently had drawn the duty.

"So, Will, what was your assignment, before you were rewarded with garbage duty?"

I pretended to be swallowing. "Well, Sir, it is a bit embarrassing. I have been working with the Air Loom." I glugged

66

several swallows of milk. "Production has not been pleasing to the Supreme Navarch." Men began leaving. "I tried my best, Sir, but perhaps I am better suited for simple tasks than trying to coax the Air Loom to work faster. The Supreme Navarch wanted changes. I suppose I am one of the changes."

Sid seemed to accept my explanation. "Air Loom team. Well, we all have our talents, don't we? You and I may be better suited to the culinary arts."

I suppose I looked puzzled because Sid said, "Cooking, Boy, cooking. My Pappy cooked for Grant's officers. Runs in the family."

"My father is a grocer," I offered.

"It's all food. One getting it to the kitchen and one getting it out. I guess you will learn the other end." Sid sat back and sighed. "Sure like cooking. Hmm. We need to find you a bunk with the kitchen staff. You are on the culinary team, now."

I hesitated. "I was assigned to garbage detail. I don't want any trouble."

Sid, stood. "Listen, that's the low rung of the ladder here. Some are just there for disciplinary reasons."

"I suppose that's why I was assigned."

"You are a kitchen boy, now. No one will miss you. If someone asks, tell them you are a cook's assistant."

I stood straight.

"You don't want to bunk with your old buddies. They probably think you are a wash out."

"Yes, Sir." I hung my head.

"Do you have anything to bring from your former spot?"

"Not much, sir. One of The Twelve rousted me out in a hurry." I was not used to lying.

"We'll get you a duffel and more duds." Sid looked me up and down. "You'll do just fine."

67

Chapter 13

The general bunk quarters were rooms with twelve beds each. The cooks and kitchen staff were in a small side dormitory. I was given a bed, toilet gear, and clothes. Sid didn't seem to question my motives. Perhaps because I was assumed to be acting under the same orders as everyone.

I looked at my watch and realized it was past seven. Men were going and coming freely, so I wandered past the auditorium. The men I passed had already been drinking. There was no one outside, and I walked across the compound with my hands in my trouser pockets. After a last check, I ducked behind the shed and found my pack and radio. I slipped into some small bushes.

BB AM INSIDE AS KITCHEN STAFF STOP SEEMS SAFE STOP

I left the radio on for about thirty seconds, hoping for an immediate reply.

BB WILL TURN ON POWER FOR FIVE SECONDS EVERY ONE MINUTE STOP

I was in my second listening cycle when a twig cracked behind me. I fumbled in the pack for my pistol when José appeared.

"You scared me!"

"Sorry. I got your message, but could not see you in the moon light."

"I shouldn't stay out long, so I'm gonna to talk fast." I told José about my first meal on the job. "I was right outside the room where the Supreme Navarch was having a meeting."

"I was listening to the meeting at the vent. He is loco but crazy like a fox. He has other ships. I cannot tell where, but close—near. They will carry the gas pods. The ships will spread out. Even to Washington—where the President is. And other places."

"Did he say when?"

"He is still complaining about the gas machine, the Air Loom. It is not producing fast enough. He was yelling and throwing things. He is like a baby having a tantrum."

"I better get back. Are you doing OK?"

68

"Yes. I am camping by the kitchen vent but have a place up the hill with a view of several vents. When lights go on, I listen."

"And the *Silver Seed*?"

"Above. Laura sends her love."

"Tell her I am safe—love her." I paused, hating the distance. "You're doing a good job! Well done." I turned to go.

"You too. You make a good spy."

Inside, men were still wandering about. I found a saloon. Men were drinking, and women were dancing on a small stage. I got a drink and swished it in my mouth so I would smell of liquor. My nose burned, and my eyes watered. I stood by a wall and poured the drink in a spittoon. I put a silly smile on my face and returned to the bunk room.

Sid had a separate room but his door stood open. He looked up from a book. "You have a drink at the saloon?"

"Yes, Sir! Just getting to bed early, Sir."

At my bunk, it felt good to lie on something soft. I thought of José on the ground.

"Hey you! Got no respect, you!"

A large man stood over me. I recognized him as the fellow whose foot I almost ran over with the cart. I looked up, hands behind my head.

"I'm talking to you."

"Hey, I had to hurry. Everyone should hurry when bringing food and drink to the Supreme Navarch. It is good to please the Supreme Navarch."

"Yes, it is good to please the Supreme Navarch—but that don't mean you don't need a little respect. Don't you recognize the emblem?" He pointed to two circles on his shirt sleeve.

I hadn't noticed the rings.

The man reached down and grabbed me by the shirt collar. "What say we take this outside and see if I can't teach your mouth to say you are sorry."

I could tell he had been drinking, and I would not come out well if we fought. "I'm trying to get some rest. I have to hurry in the morning, too."

69

The man leaned close, blowing bad breath in my face. "Get up, you little rat! I ain't asking again." He pulled me up, and a button popped off my shirt. He shoved me toward the door.

Sid appeared in the doorway of his room. "What's the trouble?"

"I don't like the way this skinny rat talks to me."

Sid laid his book down. "Well, I don't like it when my men fight. What do you have to say for yourself, Will?"

"In the hall, earlier, I was in a hurry, Sir—running to get the wine. It is always good to please the Supreme Navarch, Sir."

The big lout let my shirt go and said, "Always good to please the Supreme Navarch."

"Supreme Navarch," Sid echoed.

The angry man snapped out of his reverie and said, "Oh, ain't you fancy with your talk. *Sir* to the boss. Trying for special treatment. Maybe I will teach you to call *me* Sir."

"It wouldn't hurt you to say 'Sir' now and again, Zeke."

Zeke blinked, and I could tell the alcohol was having its effect. For the first time, I noticed three small circles on Sid's sleeve.

I stuck out my hand. "Zeke. I didn't mean to offend. Won't happen again."

Zeke seemed puzzled for a moment. Sid gestured with his shoulder, and Zeke gave me a limp handshake.

When he was gone Sid said, "Follow me." He led me to the door of his room. He went inside and turned squarely, his shoulders almost touching both sides of the door. "Watch yourself, Will. You are a good worker. We don't want trouble from lazy sots like Zeke. Understood?"

"Yes, Sir."

"Good. Now, get to bed—and no more drinking tonight. No sense pouring good whiskey in the spittoons."

I started to ask but put my head down instead.

"Not much gets by me, Will. I have my ways of knowing what is going on around here."

I met his eyes. "Yes, Sir."

I went back to my bed and pulled the blanket over me. It smelled old, but it was cold this far back in the cavern.

70

Sid was a hard one to figure. He seemed more alert than the other men. Had he been given different orders? Did he hold his breath as Susan had? If so, why did he stay?

He certainly had his spies watching his men. I was sure he had not been in the saloon when I had poured my drink away. If he wasn't in the fog, were there others? Was there a counterattack afoot?

I slept well.

At four, the bunk house lights came on, and Sid walked up and down the rows of beds. "Up and at 'em, lads, up and at 'em. Rome wasn't built in a day, but we're not in Rome. Up, up—the folks that built Rome probably were fed on time." Sid carried a long broom handle and popped it against the iron bed frames of the men still sleeping. "Up and at 'em. Get a move on."

I buttoned my shirt as best I could with the missing button. I stopped at a huge lavatory off the bunk room. Men were coughing and cursing. I didn't see Zeke.

Sid had fires blazing in the kitchen in all the big stoves, and I welcomed the warmth. "First one in. Good, Will. Can you scramble eggs?"

"I'm no cook, but I can scramble eggs, Sir."

Sid pointed to a stove with two large skillets. "Keep both going, twenty each." He pointed to egg flats stacked nearby. "And Will?"

"Yes, Sir?"

"No shells. The Supreme Navarch came down here the last time he had a shell in his eggs." Sid pointed at nothing in particular with a large spoon. "Don't want the Supreme Navarch unhappy, do we?"

"It is good to make the Supreme Navarch happy." I put a dazed look on my face.

"Yes. It is good to please the Supreme Navarch," Sid intoned.

Was he correcting me, or didn't he notice the word change? I didn't dare look at Sid and began to crack eggs. I wasn't sure I could keep shell out of the eggs, so I watched carefully.

The constant motion in the kitchen was amazing. It seemed like a dance, with people passing and moving among each other.

71

One pan had burned egg on the bottom. I was unsure what to do, but a man frying bacon looked over and said, "Don't worry. Stir them in."

Sid came by once and said, "More pepper, before you scramble."

I kept my head down and worked as fast as I could.

Chapter 14

Two days later, I slipped out and talked to José. He was shivering.

"If you are too cold, go to the ship. I am doing fine."

"I am good. I have a tent around the kitchen vent. I sleep warm. I have another coat I will get. They are bringing more food, and I have been visiting the dairy late at night." José showed me a small bucket. "The Supreme Navarch keeps some quality cattle. Chickens, too."

I told José about Sid and the near fight I had gotten myself into.

"If you have to fight, move fast. Do not let them hit you."

"Easy for you to say," I laughed. "The guy was twice as big as me."

"Then, it is best to run." José made a fake swing in the air.

I told José about testing Sid, using the word happy rather than please. "Sid didn't correct me or act strange. I wonder if he is like Susan. Maybe he is not in the fog?"

"Be careful, because they may be testing you, too. And you don't want to end up in the fog."

The thought caused pin prickles in my stomach. "I must be patient, and I cannot come out as often as I thought. We start at four in the morning. We have an hour after breakfast clean up before we start for the mid-day meal and then a short break before we start dinner. They eat a lot down there!" I tried again to convince José to move to the warmth of ship. "I want you to go up to the *Silver Seed*." I casually changed the subject. "How is the fuel holding?"

I worried the airship had been in the air for over ten days. There was extra fuel aboard, but getting more at some point would be necessary.

"Finn says we will have to get fuel in eight days, or we will not have enough to get home."

"Tell Finn I am fine. If they go for fuel, you should go. If something happens below, you can do nothing for me."

"I know, but it makes Laura feel better if I stay close."

73

In the hallway, a group of men were moving down another corridor. I hurried to the corner after they passed. I recognized the whiny voice of the Supreme Navarch. I could only see the backs of heads, but he was shorter than any of the men, and none were tall. If I had been in the group, I would have been the tallest by two inches.

A man came out of a doorway, saw the Supreme Navarch, put his back to the wall, and saluted. He didn't move until the group was well past. Then he ducked back inside another room.

I slipped down the hall and stood behind some boxes, stacked in front of large doors that said Warehouse.

The Supreme Navarch stopped and folded his arms. "If it happens again, I am going to have Jenkins whipped. Do you understand me?"

"Yes, Supreme Navarch."

"What is the point of having tea if the tea is not hot!?" His voice squeaked when he said "hot".

"No point, Supreme Navarch."

"Then why was my tea not hot? It was tepid. Do you know the meaning of tepid?"

"Not warm, Supreme Navarch?"

"Tepid is lukewarm. Jesus said he would spew out that which is neither hot nor cold!" The little man began swaggering along the hall, lifting on his toes. "When I come in my airship, conquering all, they will think I am Jesus returned in a cloud! And I will *spew* out lukewarm tea!"

"Yes, Supreme Navarch."

The men were nearing the end of the hallway, and one man, walking slightly behind the Supreme Navarch, shook his head slightly.

At least some of them know this guy is crazy. Loco, as José says.

That evening, Jenkins came into the kitchen. He looked nervously around. Apparently, the fog did not make one immune to fear. "The Supreme Navarch is unhappy. That makes me unhappy. His tea was not hot."

74

Sid looked unconcerned. "The tea is hot when it leaves here. Who took the last tea down?"

The kitchen was silent. Jenkins pointed to a big man stirring the gravy.

Sid flicked his eyebrows. "Why did it take so long to get the tea there?"

"I—I may have stopped by the saloon."

"Saloon. That's not even on the way."

"*Repareringspils*," the man said. "A beer for repair."

Sid moved quickly toward the man and held out his hand. The man took off his apron and folded it into Sid's hand.

"Report to fuel supply."

The man moved quickly out the doors. "Will." Sid handed me the apron. You can make it snappy, can't you, Boy?"

"Yes, Sir."

"And cover the tea with a towel so it stays warm." Sid pointed toward a cupboard. "In there."

I got a towel and put it over my arm. Sid put in a large spoonful of tea and poured boiling water into the silver pot. "Never strain the tea. The Supreme Navarch wants to see tea leaves."

I closed the lid and wrapped it with the towel.

"Well, go with Jenkins. Get a move on!"

Jenkins walked briskly, and I pushed the pot and cups on a tea cart. When we got to the meeting room, I folded the towel over my arm. I arranged the cups and stood aside. I studied a schedule fastened to the wall.

"Have you served before, Will?"

I almost smiled, thinking of all the tea I had served on the *Cloud Queen*. The crew had tea down to a polished art. "Yes, sir. I have served as ship's steward." On the wall I could see the week's master schedule. I noted Fridays were Level 1 meetings.

"Hmm. Very good. Well, back you go. If you bring trays always shake a leg."

"Yes, Sir." I moved quickly back to the kitchen. A large calendar had been attached to the wall near the double doors. The third Saturdays were marked for general assemblies in the auditorium. Ten AM.

75

During my next talk to José, I told him about the man assigned to fuel duty. "He is a big fellow with a red beard and red hair. Lots of hair. He is on fuel detail, so they must be bringing fuel up to the compound. That may be our chance to replenish our fuel supply."

"Yes. Finn said they have been watching wagons going down, with tanks that are not guarded. When they return, the *Silver Seed* will help herself."

"If the redheaded man is with them—it will be a fuel run."

"I will tell Finn." José had grown a beard, and his hair was long. He looked cold.

"Go up to the ship. Get cleaned up. Get warm."

"I keep the code transmitter and two batteries tied in the tree by the big vent for the kitchen—on a limb that looks like a man's arm."

José is always thinking ahead. "OK. I will try to come out in a week. Be safe."

José shook my hand. "And you."

76

Chapter 15

The next evening, after we had served everyone, Sid called me to his office off the kitchen.

"Will, as you know, I keep track of my people."

"Yes, Sir."

"You know, we keep records here. Meticulous records."

"If you say so, Sir."

"So, I was looking at last month's records of those working on the Air Loom."

I felt my face getting warm.

"I don't find a Will on that list."

"Yes, Sir." I looked to the side and then met Sid's gaze. "I didn't use Will there." I hesitated. "I use Will here."

Sid gave me an unblinking stare.

"The Supreme Navarch was very unhappy with us. So I changed my name. I didn't want him to find me—in case he wanted to punish." I looked down at Sid's feet. "I know it was wrong, Sir, but I was weak." I looked up.

Sid shook his head slowly. "I don't think you are weak, Will. But you know I must watch my men."

"Yes, Sir."

"So, you know what I am about to ask." Sid reached for papers on his small table. "Which crew were you on?"

"Nights, Sir."

Sid ruffled the papers until he found the Air Loom night workers and scanned the list.

I took a chance. "Right there, number three, Sir." I pointed over the top of the papers.

"You don't look like an Albert Montoya."

I should've looked closer. "No, Sir. My parents died. I was Albert Smith, but the Montoya's raised me. Neighbors, Sir."

"Hmm. Say something in Spanish."

"En boca cerrada no entran moscas." I knew my pronunciation was terrible, but it was something José had said when I first told him about the *Cloud Queen,* and I liked the sound.

"And what did you just say?"

77

"More or less, I said if you keep your mouth shut, you won't get flies in it."

Sid fixed his eyes on me for a long while. "I think we will call you Will Smith. Be careful, Will."

"Yes, Sir." I could feel sweat running down my back.

I went to my bed and lay for a long time. I felt uneasy about José having gone to the ship.

When the scrambled eggs were done, Jenkins came. Sid sent me and another fellow with the carts for the Supreme Navarch's morning briefing. I had begun to learn that these meetings were not so much a briefing as a tongue lashing directed toward each department. His high voice carried into the hallway, occasionally squawking like a young rooster learning to crow.

"I am the Supreme Navarch! *No one* must fail to serve for the greater good! *No one.*" His voice went up each time he said "No one."

"No one," mumbled those in the meeting.

"Do you understand me? *No* one!"

"No one. Yes! Sir!" came the echo.

"Then why is the third storage tank empty?!"

No one spoke.

I started to take the towels off the dish covers, but Jenkins held out his hand.

"I don't think everyone understands me. We have a discipline failure. Failure! And I will not tolerate failure!"

"No, Sir."

The Supreme Navarch's voice got suddenly quiet. "No, Sir? That is all you have to say? Tompkins, you have been charged with the Air Loom operation."

After a long moment, someone coughed.

"I give you an important charge and you fail me. One week, and I am patient. Two weeks—and my patience is tested. And now we are at the *fourth* week, and still production is slow!"

Someone mumbled something.

78

"You fool! 'Yes, Sir' does not make gas. And Peters, I hope you are listening. The gas must be liquified according to my *exact* formula."

"Yes, Sir!"

"Take Tompkins! Follow me. Call for a General Assembly! Everyone except the Air Loom crew. *Everyone!*" he squeaked.

Chairs scraped the floor, and Jenkins motioned for me to get against the wall.

Two men threw open double doors down the hall and brought a man out, half dragging him toward us.

I flattened myself and stared at the opposite wall, unblinking, hand held in salute.

The men with Tompkins passed, and then the Supreme Navarch stopped in front of me.

"What is your name, boy?" The words hissed, and I didn't dare to meet the Supreme Navarch's eyes.

"Will, Sir. Will Smith." Fear rolled in my stomach.

"Do you pledge allegiance to me, Will Smith?"

"Yes, Sir!" I tightened my salute.

The Supreme Navarch stared at me, not blinking. I wondered why I was the object of the Supreme Navarch's interest.

"You pledge complete allegiance. Hmmm. We will see if you will, Will." He laughed. "Will will, Ha! That is the question. Will Will have the will? Ha. Three Wills in a row."

The Supreme Navarch looked at the two men with Tompkins and shouted, "Why have you stopped!? Get him to the General Assembly. And why is the GA klaxon not sounding? Am I going to have to go look in a mirror to see if my mouth is moving? Get the GA klaxon going. Get Thompkins on the stage."

The Supreme Navarch spun back to me. "You, Will Smith, will prove your allegiance."

I wasn't sure what I was to do.

"Don't just stand there. Move. Fall in. Fall in! Did you not hear me!?"

I moved quickly behind the Supreme Navarch.

"No, Will," he purred. "You will walk *with* me. I want to keep an eye on you in case your will is not my will." The little man laughed again at his bad joke. "It is a will morning. I will it so!" he said gleefully. He pointed to his right, and I walked beside him.

Horns began blaring, three long blasts followed by several seconds of silence. My ears rang as we passed one of the shrieking devices.

We turned down the long corridor, and Sid gave me a disapproving look as we marched past the kitchen.

We went in a doorway and up a ramp to a darkened room.

"Lights. Lights! Fools, lights!"

The lights high above showed us to be behind the purple curtain.

The Supreme Navarch paced back and forth. A man with a polished wooden case appeared, hesitating at the edge of the circle of men. "Come, man, come. We don't have all day."

Two others carried a table to the center of the stage.

"Put it down! Open it! Open it!"

The lid hinged back, revealing a matched brace of old flintlock pistols used in dueling.

The Supreme Navarch turned to me. His small, piercing eyes continued to stare without blinking. He handed me one of the weapons. "These guns were used in a famous duel among gentlemen, Will."

I hesitated.

"Are you so new to us? Come—Boy. Someone must have told you. You are today's executioner."

I did my best not to show the fear and shock I felt.

"Come, take the gun, Will. You should be eager to show your willingness to prove your allegiance." The small eyes still had not blinked. "Oh, look. He is a tender young fellow. Did you think I would let you wear a hood and pull a gallows lever?"

I accepted the pistol. My hand shook. A pistol with powder and a single ball, and I was in the room with the Supreme Navarch. My mouth had gone dry. If I shot the evil little man, it would be a sacrifice I would not live to tell about. Would killing him stop this Freebooter movement? I suspected not and hoped my reasoning was not the result of a lack of bravery.

The Supreme Navarch selected the other pistol. He smiled a sinister smile. "Oh, you didn't think I would let you do this alone, did you? Ha-ha! Ha-ha-ha! Why let you have all the fun? Open the curtain!"

The curtain whisked back in swift jerks, velvet swaying. The auditorium was only three-quarters full, with men scrambling for seats. A podium rolled forward on silent little wheels, and the Supreme Navarch climbed up the steps and held his hands for quiet. Someone handed him a speaking trumpet.

There was a hush as men hurried to fill vacant seats.

"Hurry, hurry. Fools. Get in your seats, or you will be up here as a sacrifice. Sound the klaxon!"

The horns echoed in the halls, and more men hurried through the doors. The women sat to the left, in a separate section. The horns stopped, and a silence fell on the room.

The Supreme Navarch launched into a rambling tirade about duty and the mission, and the failure of the Air Loom team. He repeated again and again that there was no room for failure. One sentence brought me to full awareness. "Soon, everyone will be under the influence of Autogen!"

Who's Autogen? I was struck with the fear that I was not at the central hub of the Freebooters.

As the Supreme Navarch droned on, I came to understand that his goal was "Perfect Autocracy" and that Autogen was the hypnotizing gas. I was snapped out of my reverie when I heard, "—Will Smith, this morning's executioner."

I stared straight ahead.

"Oh, don't be shy, Will Smith. Give the crowd a wave."

I put my hand up as high as my shoulder and gave tentative a wave.

"Oh, no, Will. You are this morning's leading man!" He grabbed my arm, and waved my hand back and forth. "Applause! Applause!"

The crowd clapped, and someone whistled.

The Supreme Navarch dropped my arm and turned to the audience. "Let's not go to extremes." He waved his hand dismissively and went back to the podium.

The men wrestled Tompkins forward, making him set his feet on a line. His ankles were bound, and his hands tied behind his back. Two of the Chosen Few had ropes attached to his arms,

81

holding him from each side. A blond man pointed to my line on the floor.

"Tompkins, meet your executioner, Will Smith. Will, this is Tompkins, a ne'er-do-well. A failure."

Tompkins looked at me with disinterest.

The Supreme Navarch turned his attention back to me. "Have you fired a flintlock before?"

"No, Sir. Never fired a pistol before," I lied.

"Pull the hammer back like this. Make sure it catches and doesn't slip and fire." He clicked his flint back.

I started to pull my hammer back when the Supreme Navarch stayed my hand. "Oh, no, Young Will, you will do it with the muzzle pointed toward your chest." His smile showed small gray teeth. "It will give you the proper impetus to ensure the hammer has clicked firmly into position."

I turned the muzzle toward my chest while the Supreme Navarch casually swung his pistol to my temple.

"Pull it back—carefully, Young Will, carefully."

When the hammer clicked into place, the Supreme Navarch said, "Aim your gun at Tompkins." He took aim as well. "Shall we? Together on three?"

Chapter 16

I sighted down the barrel, putting the bead on Tompkins' right shoulder. I wondered how much the ball might drift in such a short distance.

"One, two, THREE!"

I squeezed the trigger, and my gun roared, kicking my hand up. The smell of powder filled the air, a white cloud floating lazily away. The recoil surprised me, and yet Tompkins remained standing. Had I missed completely?

"Ha, ha, ha-ha-ha. You are a bad shot, Young Will." The Supreme Navarch put his pistol against my temple. "What should we do with such a bad shot?"

Time froze. Laura. I failed. I still had the revolver. If I ducked and swung, could I hit him hard enough to do damage? My fist tightened on the butt.

The little man twirled and shot Tompkins squarely in the chest. Tompkins' eyes stared at nothing as he fell to the floor, lifeless.

The Supreme Navarch put his hand on my shoulder. "Will, Will—did you think I was going to give you a loaded weapon? You fool! Double powder but no ball. Ha-ha. I am the Supreme Navarch. I know all. I am all!" he screamed.

He handed off the pistol and dashed up the steps of the podium. The blond man tried to hand him the speaking trumpet, but he batted it away.

One of the men took my pistol. I flexed my shaking hands. "Back to work, Boy," he said, turning away.

Uncertain which way to go, I stepped back.

The Supreme Navarch pulled a six-shooter from a shoulder holster under his coat and brandished it. "Back to work, you *fools*, or we will have more executions. More, you hear me!" He waved his finger, pointing here and there in the crowd of men. "And it might be you! It might be you!" The gun came down, and the Supreme Navarch steadied himself on the podium.

83

The curtain sailed closed, and the blond man helped the Supreme Navarch down. White flecks appeared at the corners of his mouth, and sweat appeared on his forehead. "You—it might be you," he whispered.

Two men brought a rolling chair, and the Supreme Navarch fell heavily into the seat. His head snapped up, and he waved the gun around the room. "Just a momentary spell. But don't let it fool you," he whispered. "I am the Supreme Navarch, and I grow stronger and stronger each time. Remember to keep me safe. Bring me my medicine or—" He slumped in the chair, his chin on his chest.

Two men rolled him off the stage. Tompkins was thrown onto a stretcher and carried away.

No one seemed to remember I was there, so I waited until everyone was gone. I took a moment to look at both sides of the backstage. The stage was bare besides the podium, speaking trumpet, and two small tables.

I hurried back to the kitchen, but Sid blocked the door.

"My office. Now."

I followed him inside, and he closed the door. "Will, how did you happen to be on the stage with the Supreme Navarch?"

"Jenkins had me stand against the wall when the Supreme Navarch and his men passed by. He stopped and chose me, I guess."

"There are hundreds of men here, and he chose you?"

"I was with Jenkins, delivering the food," I said. My voice had gone dry.

Sid looked at the door. "Didn't you work for Tompkins at the Air Loom?"

"Yes, Sir."

Sid leaned his back against the door. "How did you feel about killing him?"

"It is good to please the Supreme Navarch."

Sid moved closer. "Yes, but how did you *feel?*"

"I was raised by a peaceful family." I stepped back, my leg bumping a chair.

"How long since you passed the Blue Vial?"

Fear gripped me. Was Sid going to make me sniff the gas now? "It is good to pass the Blue Vial. I always am present—"

84

"Will, do you realize you have not answered any of my questions. You answer, but your answers skate around the question."

"Sorry, Sir."

Sid moved a chair and sat, almost blocking the door. He looked up. "Tompkins didn't show any sign of recognizing you. How do you account for that?"

I looked away and then tried to meet his eyes. "He was rarely there—for the night shift."

Sid gave me a weak smile, shaking his head slowly.

I looked at the door. If I tried to run, the door opened inward. Sid was huge. If I got outside, I had little chance of getting to the radio, contacting the *Silver Seed* or avoiding capture long enough to be rescued. Could I get to an aircycle?

"What is the third command? Word for word."

I tried to remember what the woman with the parasol had said to José while he held his breath almost two years ago. If given the gas, could I hold my breath long enough? "The Army of the United States does good. We should never interfere with the Army of the United States?"

"What am I to do with you, Will?" Sid gave me a crooked smile.

"I'm a good cook's helper. Let me stay?"

"You are not one of them."

Sid was still smiling. *Them.* Them didn't include either of us. Perhaps it was just a phrase.

Sid stood and turned his back to me, leaving a few feet for the door to open. I could bolt for the door and squeeze through. If I ran—down the long corridor, through the auditorium, back to the saloon, and then to the main entrance— No, the klaxon would be ringing. The gates at the entrance clanging closed. *He didn't repeat, "It is good to please the Supreme Navarch."* I took a deep breath.

"Neither are you." I stood my ground. I was taking a terrible chance, but the *Silver Seed* could not hover forever while I scrambled eggs.

Sid turned back slowly and put out his hand. "No."

We shook.

"How? Why?"

85

"Now is not the time. We will talk again—soon. For now, be careful. The Supreme Navarch may look for you. Stay out of his sight, if at all possible. But be ready if he should call you into his elite service. He takes some men on, like a puppy. But only for a short time. He also discards people. Tompkins, for example."

"But—"

"Not now. But practice holding your breath." Sid laughed. "I can hold my breath for a minute and forty-three seconds."

There were so many questions, but Sid opened the door. "And don't let it happen again!" He cuffed me on the back of the head and then propelled me out onto the floor.

Two kitchen men looked up and then went quickly back to their work.

I took the egg skillet from the pile of pots and pans and began to scrub. I took a deep breath and held it as long as I could.

Chapter 17

I was never very good at waiting. Impulsive, Laura had once said. I liked to believe that I was improving with age, but I couldn't get my mind off the possibilities. Wanting to know more about Sid. Wanting to tell the crew on the *Silver Seed*. Wanting to begin to make plans—what I hoped were the final plans.

I found myself thinking about others on the kitchen staff. Were there others like Sid? I realized that I had not bothered to look at or even pay attention to the people working in the compound. I had assumed them all dulled by the fog. I felt superior to them, as though they were not completely human.

And yet, even those in the fog were human. They had once had lives, hopes, and dreams.

As I helped prepare supper, I watched the others more closely. If I was to be of any use, I needed to know which men were with us and those who were dangerous.

When Jenkins came, I took carts to the Supreme Navarch's dining room. I skulked along like a rat in fear that the Supreme Navarch would appear in a doorway and recognize me.

"You OK, Will?" Jenkins asked.

The question was unexpected. I wasn't aware that Jenkins even knew my name. I supposed he learned it at the General Assembly. Was he in the fog?

"Yes, Sir. Just a little preoccupied, Sir." I needed to stop explaining myself.

"Stop wool-gathering and fetch the wine. Things are not good in there. The Supreme Navarch has gone to his lair, and The Twelve will drink a great deal when he is gone."

I turned the empty cart and started away.

"Will, not the good wine. Get the cases on the bottom shelf, on the right. Two."

"Yes, Sir."

As I moved down the hallways, it was unsettling trying to guess the nature of everyone I met. It had been easy when I assumed all were the enemy. It was still important to treat those I met as the enemy and not give any hint that I was anything but a

87

follower of the Supreme Navarch. The exception might be Sid, but only when we were alone and only when he brought up the subject.

I returned with two cases, and Jenkins smiled. "Good. I'll take them in. Go on back to the kitchen."

As I made my way down the hallways, I became more uncertain. Could I trust Sid? Or was he part of the Supreme Navarch's plan—a spy for his leader?

Sid wasn't in the kitchen, or at dinner. The crew finished cleaning up, and we left for the night.

I needed to get away long enough to send a message to the *Silver Seed*. If something happened to me, my friends needed to know there was at least one person in the compound not under the influence of the gas.

I considered writing a note and leaving it with the radio but decided against it. If the note were discovered before I could put it in the tree, it would end my efforts and Sid's as well.

The next day, after we served the midday meal, I went outside to stretch.

There were several men sitting and smoking. Five women were taking down the day's laundry. I wandered around and slipped behind a tool shed. I waited several minutes, but no one seemed to notice or care. It was one-fifteen.

The path was near, and I quickly entered the underbrush. I ran to where I could crawl out and watch the area below. The men were stepping on their cigarettes and moving inside. The women were gone. I took a last look and went to the tree José had mentioned. I found a small satchel lashed to the branch with a dark string. I quickly opened the packet and tested the code sender. It was one twenty-five.

BB WILL TO SS WILL TO SS

I waited, finger on the button. *Were they back from the fuel run?*

BB WILL TO SS WILL TO SS I began to fret the battery was spent. One thirty-five. I imagined the box was getting warm. I sniffed it and smelled nothing.

SS STOP

Relief washed over me. BB UNEXPECTED EVENT STOP SID HEAD OF THE KITCHEN IS NOT IN THE FOG STOP HE IS WORKING AGAINST THE FREEBOOTERS

STOP SUPREME NAVARCH IS INSANE AND MAY BE ILL STOP COLLAPSED AFTER GIVING A RAMBLING SPEECH STOP

I waited.

MR STOP ARE YOU OK STOP

BB YES STOP MUST GET BACK STOP WILL TRY TO COME OUT TUESDAYS AND FRIDAYS STOP LOVE TO LAURA STOP

ASLEEP STOP

I bundled the transmitter and tied the satchel to the limb. I fought the temptation to hurry down to the compound. Instead, I crawled out again to my vantage point for a look.

Several men were working on one of the gas bags. Two women went into a small building across the compound. Lazy smoke curled out of a chimney. They carried out several of the Supreme Navarch's uniforms on hangers. Halfway across the yard, a man met them. He inspected each uniform, brushing something off the sleeve of a coat. He raised his hand to the taller woman, shouting something. She shrank back, and he lowered his hand. He checked two more coats. When he was satisfied, the three went into the entrance.

When I reached the toolshed, a man came around the corner. "What are you doing back here?"

"Sudden need to relieve myself. Too much tea, I suppose."

He laughed. "It is good to drink tea."

"Yes, it is good to drink tea."

Sid stood at the door of a two-story shed. "Brush off your shirt."

I brushed and patted the dust away.

Sid reached out and pulled something from my hair. "Be careful, Will."

"Yes, Sir."

"While you are here, let me show you where we smoke liver."

I suppose my face showed that I had never heard of smoking liver.

89

"It's for the Supreme Navarch. The liver is sliced and smoked. He is convinced that smoked liver will cure him of whatever ails him." Sid picked up a tray by the door.

"What is wrong with him?"

Sid spoke in hushed tones. "No one is saying. Nothing that seems to kill him. He has doctors come from all over the country. Some kidnapped. The ones who please him stay for a while. After his fit at the General Assembly, some doctor may have been executed."

We went inside the smokehouse.

"How could you tell he was sick this time?"

"You will get so you know. He sometimes works his hands on the podium. We believe his fingers or hands are tingling."

"We? Are the more of us?"

"A few in each department." Sid adjusted a butterfly on the flue of a small square stove. Up the stairs, row after row of meat hung in the small windowless room. "Enough for now. We can never talk about this for long."

He took down a pole with meat hanging from strings. "This liver has been smoking for exactly twenty-eight days, coinciding with the new moon. We use only hemp string." He indicated a large spool on the wall.

He handed me a platter with the liver. "Don't drop that. 'It is not good to displease the Supreme Navarch' as you well know."

When we had the new batch hung, Sid closed the upper door. "I've misplaced my watch."

I looked at my pocket watch. "Three-eleven, Sir."

"No—it's the code we use. 'I've misplaced my watch, do you have the time?' is a way of checking, letting each other know we are still in control of our own minds. Make sure to say, 'I've misplaced my watch' before you ask the time. If someone, by chance, were to say, "'Do you have the time?' or 'What time is it?'—it means nothing. Bring the platter."

Downstairs, Sid stoked the small stove with square blocks of wood. "Piñon," he explained. "The Supreme Navarch insists they be cut into two inch squares. He believes it 'creates more surface area for the medicinal properties to be freed.'" Sid closed the door and

90

adjusted the chimney butterfly. "If you're sent to do this, only twenty-four blocks of Piñon. Not twenty-three, not twenty-five."

"Twenty-four, Sir."

"I'm serious. One time, the Supreme Navarch came and made us empty the firebox. He counted the blocks!"

Crazy.

Sid shut the door to the smokehouse, and we hurried toward the cavern.

"Sir, what is the tall spindly building called?"

"The Supreme Navarch calls it his Palace."

At the big kitchen stove, Sid showed me how to cook the pieces of liver in onions and oil. He let me try a small piece, and it was delicious. I realized I was hungry.

The Supreme Navarch was not in the meeting room that night, and Jenkins took the leader's special plate to another area. Then, the Chosen Few were served ham. *No liver for them.* Each time food was taken through the double doors, I stole glances into the room. Several of the men who were on the stage sat with others at the table.

They were laughing and drinking red wine. Jenkins sent me for several more bottles. The task suited me. I didn't care if they got so drunk that they fell out of their chairs.

I wheeled the carts back to the kitchen, and the carts from feeding the workers had returned. The kitchen staff sat down to eat.

"Did all go well at the meeting room?" Sid asked.

"Yes, Sir."

"Did the Supreme Navarch dine with the others?"

"No, Sir. Perhaps he was busy with important matters."

"Yes." Sid lifted his glass. "To the Supreme Navarch!"

"To the Supreme Navarch," came the chorus, and I realized it was impossible to tell who was under the influence and who was not.

A new man was polishing the counters, and I was tempted to say "I've misplaced my watch," but thought better of it. My watch chain was fastened to a belt loop on my trousers. I had to be very careful.

Chapter 18

I made it my habit to go out two days a week, as I had promised my friends on the *Silver Seed*. I never stayed long. The Supreme Navarch had not been back to the meeting room. I noticed lights in the upper part of the Palace and wondered if the Supreme Navarch was inside.

At the tree, I wrote a note for José and placed it inside the satchel in case he returned in the night.

The second Tuesday, I found my note still in the pack.

I turned on the transmitter.

BB OUT BUT CANT STAY LONG STOP

I paced, waiting for an answer.

WE ARE HERE STOP GOING SOUTH TOMORROW TO GET FUEL STOP

ALL IS WELL HERE STOP DO NOT WORRY STOP I WORRY ABOUT YOU ALL THE TIME STOP LL

LW

I packed the transmitter and made the satchel secure. I turned and was startled by Sid standing a few yards away.

"You must keep a close watch behind you, Will. I followed you. I have been watching."

"Yes, Sir." I knew the "Sir" was unnecessary, but I was embarrassed by my carelessness.

"We have a few minutes," he said. "Keep it brief."

The possibility of Sid being a spy—gathering information for the Supreme Navarch flickered in my thoughts. Time was not on our side. Right or wrong, I made the decision to trust him. "I have so many questions," I blurted.

"Yes, but answers first. How did you get here, and was that code you were sending?"

I explained about the radio and the *Silver Seed*.

Sid looked with wonder at the sky. "This ship. This craft is up there, now?"

"Somewhere. They are going to take fuel from the Freebooters. I am not sure when."

92

"The wagons left today," Sid said. "It takes two days to make the trip down and three coming back up the hill."

Sid looked around the area. "The ship lands here? Can it go up and down at will?"

"It can. It is a marvelous machine designed by Finn, our engineer. One of the Adjunct Commanders was constructing a levitating ship in California. We captured it."

"We heard rumors of a new ship the Supreme Navarch had designed. The story claimed it had been destroyed in a storm."

I kept my face neutral. "My friend José and I stole the ship right out from under their noses." I almost added that the ship was of poor design.

"How many are you?" Sid asked.

"Almost twenty of us have a safe place in the mountains." I decide to hold back Eagle's Crest's location. "We have a lab in another location, working on an antidote to the gas."

"I am guessing that a storm did not take down three of the Supreme Navarch's ships in the California desert?"

"We took them down, one at a time."

"And a flying riverboat? There have been newspaper accounts. Can I assume you are Captain Will Henderson, or is that another tall tale manufactured for the 'enlightened', as they think of themselves?"

I blushed. "Yes, I am Will Henderson, and there is a flying ship—modeled after a Mississippi steamboat."

Sid gazed into the underbrush. "And this is what defeated the army in California?"

"Yes. We thought the Freebooter problem was gone. But, here we are."

"We better start back. I will tell you some things you need to know."

"Yes." I regretted having told Sid so much about our work.

"Sixteen of us are in control of our own minds. There were eighteen, but two were transferred to the Air Loom project. The air is full of the gas, and it affected their minds. That's why I first suspected that you were not one of *them*. You did not appear to be affected, but…"

I shouldn't have claimed to be part of the Air Loom project.

93

"These two men are not true converts, but have received accidental commands."

"How can the commands be an accident?"

"One man turned into a gambler. Apparently, when he arrived at the Air Loom, the other workers were talking about a poker game—they were quite enthusiastic about the game. Our man now can think of little but playing poker. He has been locked up for causing trouble over gambling debts."

"And the second?"

"We had served a chicken dish. This fellow worked the night shift. The men there talked about the chicken dinner being delicious. One apparently said that we should eat chicken at every meal. Our man thinks of little else but chicken—breakfast, noon and dinner." Sid chuckled. "If it wasn't so sad, it would be funny. The poor fellow has gotten quite fat. He stole chickens and cooked them over open fires. They have him locked up as well. They plan to sober these two up and then re-instruct them. I am afraid they are lost to us."

We reached the end of the trail. Sid put out his hand, holding me back.

"We have one other problem. We pass the Blue Vial in a week. How is the breath control coming?"

Fear made my breath catch. According to my watch, I could only hold my breath for forty-six seconds. Not near long enough. "Not that good."

"Keep working. I may be able to pass the vial with the kitchen staff. It's done sometimes if we have a special meal to prepare." Sid looked at the sky. "Don't count on it. Practice. It would be a shame to lose you."

I didn't want to be lost. "Can't I just not be around during the passing of the Blue Vial?"

"They stamp the back of your hand with the Supreme Navarch's crest. The stamp lasts for about a week, and one of the commands is to be on the lookout for those without a stamped hand."

"We can't get a stamp?"

94

"We have tried. The Supreme Navarch is pretty paranoid. His delusions of grandeur are only outmatched by his paranoia. He believes everything and everyone is a potential enemy."

He's right about me. I thought of the Supreme Navarch, insisting that I walk beside him so he could test my will.

"Try this. Take several deep, I mean *deep* breaths."

I breathed in and out hard.

"Yes, but don't give yourself away. You don't want anyone to notice your breathing. Watch."

In the next few minutes Sid taught me to take several breaths and then breathe all the air out of my lungs before taking that last breath. My final effort was fifty-eight seconds. *Not good enough.*

Sid had been watching the sky. "Is that it?"

To the North, peaking out of a cloud, the *Silver Seed* was all but invisible against the afternoon sky. I blew a kiss up.

I blushed. "Sorry, but I know my wife, Laura, will be watching this time of day."

Sid shook his head slowly. "Never miss a chance to kiss your wife, Will."

I watched great sadness pass over him.

"Sally. Four years. She was lovely and a lovely person. Love of my life. We had an eatery in a town near Denver." Fire returned, and Sid gestured toward the compound. "I guess our good food made a reputation. They came, and I was brought here. Sally—Sally was killed. I guess he doesn't believe in women cooks." Sid worked his hands, making a fist and then stretching his fingers. "SL will be stopped."

I was confused. "The Supreme Navarch?"

"Simpering Louse." Sid drew himself up. "The little weasel will be destroyed, but we must destroy all his toadies with him."

At that moment, I became certain Sid was not spying on me. He looked as if it took all his willpower to keep from marching into the Supreme Navarch's quarters and strangling him bare-handed.

Fear of losing myself to the fog returned, causing my throat to go dry. "You have to keep me out of the passing of the vial."

"You are right—your breath control is not ready. I will plan a very special meal for the Supreme Navarch." Sid patted my shoulder. "Time to go. I will follow in a few minutes. Start five pots of water for potatoes."

As I walked across the yard, I could see several lights in the Palace, and men constructing yet another level of metal.

Chapter 19

The Supreme Navarch called three General Assemblies. The klaxons rang constantly. I sat with the others while he ranted and screamed, accusing and blaming.

Delusions of grandeur was his case exactly. During the second meeting, he spent much of his time quoting Bible verses.

"Thou shalt not muzzle the ox when he treadeth out the corn," he squeaked. "That means the worker shall be allowed his part. That is why I feed you. My enemies surround me. The Lord gives me my strength. But truly, I am full of power by the spirit of the Lord!"

He took a drink of water. "I am he who comes in the name of the Lord. All knees shall bow. I ride in the chariot of God for it says when thou goest out to battle against thine enemies, and seest horses, and chariots, and a people more than thou, be not afraid of them: for the Lord thy God is with me! I will bring God's reign to earth!"

The Supreme Navarch suddenly changed subjects, rambling on and on about fuel oil being captured. He made no mention of the *Silver Seed* or any flying ship, but there could be no doubt that the *Silver Seed* had been a success. I wondered if the crew had set upon the wagons with the ship safely harbored nearby or if the Supreme Navarch was avoiding the truth.

It made no difference, I decided. I needed to contact the ship.

The day before the passing of the vial, I managed to get to the tree and send a message.

BB OUT BUT MUST RETURN STOP

While I waited, I watched my surroundings carefully.

LAURA HERE STOP LAB HAS ANTIDOTE STOP MUST BE TAKEN BEFORE GAS STOP CLOUD QUEEN FLYING THIS WAY WITH SERUM STOP NO TIME TO CONTACT YOU STOP MY DECISION STOP L

GOOD DECISION STOP HOW LONG HAS CQ BEEN FLYING STOP

97

TWO STOP COULD ARRIVE IN SIX DAYS STOP
HEADWINDS STOP SHE IS SLOW BUT STURDY STOP
YES STOP I LONG TO SEE YOU STOP
I DIE TO SEE YOU MY LOVE STOP LL STOP
LW STOP

Too little, too late. I packed the equipment and lashed the pack to the limb. I was alone. If I went into the fog, neither Sid nor anyone else could help me. What bothered me most was the fear of what deeds I might do while influenced by the commands of the Supreme Navarch.

Sid announced to the kitchen that we would all meet for the passing of the vial after breakfast cleanup.

Cold sweat ran down my back and sides as I scrubbed egg skillets. Others were looking forward to passing of the Blue Vial. It was a sacred moment for those in the fog.

"Will, with me!" Sid barked.

We walked without speaking to the smokehouse. Inside, Sid whispered, "When we get back, you are going to start cooking a special soup. When it is time to pass the Blue Vial, join the circle with the rest. I will take it from there."

"Yes, Sir."

We took two large smoked hams, and Sid had them diced into tiny squares. He had others preparing a special sauce. He went from station to station, tasting and adding a pinch of this and a taste of that.

I started stirring the water in the biggest pot in the kitchen. Twice, Sid came by and said, "Not too fast, but not too slow. You have to prepare the water to receive the ingredients properly." His eyes twinkled.

I felt the heat of the stove. Sid adjusted the air twice and poured bowls and pots from other stations in my kettle.

"Attention, kitchen crew. It is the glorious time for the passing of the Blue Vial. Assemble!"

98

Immediately, the crew went to the side of the kitchen and stood in a circle. I followed. A man in a white uniform set a box on the counter and carefully lifted out a beautiful glass vial. A collective gasp came from the men, and several oohed and awed over the small crystal bottle. I could see nothing special about it.

He handed Sid the vial and a wide scroll with gilded handles and marched out of the kitchen.

"We now have the opportunity to re-dedicate ourselves to the glorious work of the Supreme Navarch," Sid announced.

"Re-dedicate."

I managed to join with "-edicate". The faces of the others told me no one noticed. All eyes and minds were on the vial.

Sid walked around the outside of our circle.

My head popped forward from a blow to the back of my neck. "Did I tell you to leave your pot unattended?"

"No, Sir. I just thought—"

"You'll get your turn, but that pot must be stirred at all times."

"Yes, Sir." I scrambled back to my place and began moving the big wooden spoon in a gentle circle.

"Not too fast and not too slow. This is for the Supreme Navarch's pleasure, Will. Do you understand?!"

"It is good to please the Supreme Navarch," I said.

I put my head down but turned my body to watch the circle. Sid joined the men and took the first sniff. A simple smile came across his face, and he fluttered his eyes. He presented the vial to each man in the circle.

When everyone had their turn, Sid brought the vial to me and put it under my nose.

I pretended to take a long whiff and then noticed that Sid had his thumb over the opening.

"Stay there and recite with us." Sid turned to the circle of men and lifted the scroll. "Recite after me. We live to serve the Supreme Navarch."

"We live to serve the Supreme Navarch" was repeated with conviction.

I joined the mindless echo.

"The only life worth living is the life I live for the Supreme Navarch!"

"The Supreme Navarch has the answers to all of life's questions, and yet he is not to be questioned."

I made sure I had a lovesick look as I stirred and recited.

"I will give my all, even unto death, to further the mission of the Supreme Navarch."

The instructions went on for several minutes. Near the end, these words gave me discomfort: "I believe the Supreme Navarch is the human manifestation of King Jesus, returned. Long live the king!"

Sid stepped out of the doors and looked both directions. When he returned he said, "I will obey Chief Cook Sid and never question Sid or Will being absent."

The men recited with glassy-eyed reverence.

Sid added steel to his voice. "Sid or Will may not be here some nights, but I will not talk to anyone about their absence."

I kept stirring while the kitchen staff repeated the commands.

Sid went to the inside of the circle and touched each man's shoulder. At his touch, each stretched out his hand. Sid took each hand, shook it, and then turned the palm down. "I place the Supreme Navarch's seal on you. Report anyone without this mark."

When Sid came to me, he touched my right shoulder, and I extended my hand. After shaking and putting the stamp on the back of my hand, Sid added, "Keep stirring!"

The image on my hand was smeared, but I could make out a bird's head and beak.

"All right, men. All back to work. We have a splendid meal to prepare and we do not want the Supreme Navarch to be disappointed."

The soup or stew was getting thick, and my arms were tired. Sid came over.

"What do you say, Will?" Sid looked directly into my eyes.

I kept stirring.

"So, are you feeling well, Young Will?"

"I am well," I said. "Thank you for arranging the passing of the Blue Vial."

Sid gave me a quick wink. He poured a canister of sugar into the soup. "The Supreme Navarch has a sweet tooth," he whispered. "This will ensure that he thinks this very normal soup is quite special. Keep stirring."

Sid lifted a bowl. "Attention, kitchen! This is the one that separates the chefs from the cooks. Mushrooms cooked with bits of sausage!" He dumped the contents into the pot. "Keep stirring, Young Will. Not too fast, but not too slow."

I had to grit my teeth to keep from smiling.

It turned out that the stew needed to be cooked the rest of the day. I had few breaks, and Sid often reminded me to "Keep stirring. Not too fast, but not too slow."

Chapter 20

Sid and I stood near the tree that held the transmitter. A week after passing the vial, we walked boldly out of the kitchen moments before the meeting room meal was served. None of the staff bothered to look up.

Now, it was almost dark, and none of the cooks questioned Sid when he said we were going outside for a breath of air. "If anyone asks, we have gone to get special ingredients for breakfast."

I could hear the whirr of the dynamos on the quadcycle and briefly uncovered our lantern.

The moment the cycle touched the ground, Laura wiggled out of the faring and into my arms. José waited a moment and joined her.

"Laura, José, I want you to meet my friend, Sid. He is to be trusted. Sid, this is my wife Laura and my best friend José."

José shook Sid's hand, and Laura smiled. "It is a pleasure to meet you," she said.

Mary and Addy remained in the quadcycle, ready to lift off if necessary. We moved closer.

Addy handed me a box through the faring.

"Twenty doses," Laura said. "That is all they could make so far. The *Cloud Queen* also brought the lab equipment and Professor Gruber. Finn is having him set up a laboratory a few miles from our camp. The camp is not Eagle's Crest but a haven for us. Oh, and Mr. Salsbury came! We got him a place in a canyon near Denver! He and his dog are quite content."

"Salsbury. Perfect." I thought of his refusing to fly. "How did you get him to make the trip?"

"After he had been under the influence of the gas, he said he could stand flying if it would get rid of the scoundrel who is behind it." Laura was enjoying the story. "At first, he would only sit in the middle of the front cabin, but he grew to like flying. He sat on the front deck for hours, watching the world go by."

Mr. Salsbury, aboard the *Cloud Queen*. I would be sure to tease him about this.

102

"Finn is setting him up as our scrounger. It cost some money for a cabin with a barn, wagons, and horses."

"It is worth it." I turned to Sid. "Salsbury is the best. He knows how to find what we need and how to keep his mouth shut and not raise suspicion."

Sid nodded his appreciation. "You have things well in hand."

"Where do we keep the antidote?" I asked Sid.

"I don't think we dare carry it into the compound. It should remain hidden out here," Sid said.

I agreed.

"You must take a dose at least four hours before breathing the gas. We are not sure how long it lasts, but at least several days," Laura said. "We don't have any more gas to test it."

José had shaved but his hair fell to his shoulders. "Do you want me to stay?"

"I think we are fine. It helps to have Sid. He got me through the Passing of the Blue Vial."

Sid laughed. "We made a special meal, so I could keep my kitchen staff with me. For hours, I had Will stirring water—to *get it ready* for the vegetables!"

Laura gave Sid a questioning look.

"The stew was nothing special, but I made a big deal out of how everything was to be done."

"I stirred water for two hours 'preparing it' to receive the ingredients! This guy works me down there."

"Awww." Laura pulled me close. "What is our next step?" she asked.

"We could poison the whole bunch, easy enough," Sid said, "but we are still trying to gather information about other compounds. You pretty well took care of California, but we must be certain there are no other Air Looms."

"Up to now, we have done our best not to slaughter those under the influence of the gas," Laura said. "They may not be innocent, but they are not in their right minds."

"What about the Leader? If we kill the queen bee, will the hive give up?" José wondered.

103

"When you stopped the Adjunct Commander in California, a replacement was dispatched," Sid said. "He was captured and sobered up before he got to the train." He smiled.

"How many make up the Chosen Few?" Addy asked.

"There are twelve in the compound, and several are eager for power."

"The Supreme Navarch thinks and wants others to believe he is Jesus, returning," I said.

"He believes he has a special connection to God," Sid added. "He never negotiates—because he is right. Never underestimate him. This man is extremely dangerous."

"How do we find out if there are other clusters, like California?" Laura asked. "We don't hear any code messages. Finn has been scanning the different frequencies, hoping to be able to listen in."

"The Supreme Navarch has been mulling over the attack. Recently, he reasoned that you have been listening," Sid said. "I just learned he is transmitting messages in code by telegraph. He sends men to Western Union!"

"So, we just wait?" José showed his frustration.

"Tell Finn to build a device to listen on the telegraph wires," I said. "Send a group to find which Western Union is being used. Find out where the messages are being sent. Listen to those messages."

"This is good," José said. He turned to Sid. "I am going to stay. Now that I have met you, I recognize your voice." He gestured toward the compound. "I put my tent around the vent from the kitchen. What you discuss, I pass to the ship with code."

"Spies spying on the spies," Sid said. "We are very careful in the early morning, but we never thought about someone listening in the vents."

"Sid, is there a safe place to put one of our transmitters in the kitchen?" I asked.

"Yes, but carrying it into the compound will be tricky."

"I will lower it down the big vent," José said. "Tomorrow morning. I will send the antidote down, too. Let me know when all is clear."

From his big smile, it was clear Sid liked José. "José, are you familiar with the 'Levee Song'?"

José shook his head.

"Someone's in the kitchen with Dinah, Someone's in the kitchen I know, Someone's in the kitchen with Dinah—" Sid had a fine voice.

"The Railroad Song." José's eyes flicked between Laura and me. "We learned it in school!"

"Good. I will sing when it's all clear."

Laura put her arms around me. "I miss you." She leaned into my ear and whispered. "I'm pregnant."

My neck and ears tingled. I whispered, "Oh, Laura. Are you all right? Are you feeling well? Should you be pedaling the quadcycle?"

"I am fine. You come back to me."

I held her at arm's length and looked into her big eyes. "I *will* come back."

Addy beckoned to me, and I leaned into the quadcycle. "Only José and I know. But we are happy for you." She squeezed my hand, and José slapped me on the back.

The three of us stepped back and watched the women take their places. The quadcycle lifted off, and was just a blur in moments.

Sid looked up until we could no longer hear the whirring of the dynamos. "You have a splendid team."

I wanted to tell him I was going to be a father. "I don't have them. They are part of me."

"I want to learn the code," Sid said. "You have much to teach us."

"I'll write out the alphabet. We will begin to practice."

I came early and cooked slices of ham to Sid's strong singing. Sid came to look at the large skillet. "Cook slowly—no burned edges." He looked across the kitchen. "Delivery was successful." He smiled.

105

Later when the crew had gone, he showed me a cupboard at the far end of the kitchen. "This is my personal cupboard. No one will look here. Not you either, if there is *any* chance of anyone being around." He opened the cupboard crowded with books and cooking utensils. He pulled a large cook book off the top shelf, and I could see the satchel tucked behind.

"You are needed to help get the fires started. I will come get you, tomorrow morning."

"Yes." I handed Sid a paper with the Morse Code written out. "Sometimes at Eagle's Crest, we talk with our hands. A slap for the dash, fingertips for the dots."

"Perfect, my friend. I will learn quickly." He studied the paper and then gave the countertop three taps, one tap, and a slap-tap-tap. SID.

I tapped out my name.

Sid ran his finger up and down the sheet. "Your name? I am guessing because you repeated the last two."

"Correct." I tapped it again. Sid would enjoy this.

Sid touched my shoulder the next morning, but I was already awake. We walked briskly to the kitchen. Two men I didn't recognize were there.

"Will, meet Jeffery and Sam. They will keep watch while we work." When both Jeffery and Sam gripped my hand they each gave four quick squeezes and then two. I returned, HI, to each man.

"I made copies of the code for all our men. As you can see they are studying hard. This will make our work much easier."

"We still have to be vigilant," Jeffery said. "The SL is a wily little rat."

"Sam is in charge of the guard detail. Jeffery works with the mechanicals that keep us warm and well-lit."

Jeffery and Sam took up their posts by the doors, and Sid began to sing the Levee Song while I got out the code box. In seconds, I heard "MR" echoing in the vent.

106

I turned on the transmitter. BB GOOD MORNING MY FRIEND STOP

GM STOP SILVER SEED IS HOVERING STOP WE WILL SEE IF THEY RECEIVE MESSAGES FROM YOUR BOX STOP

BB KITCHEN TO SILVER SEED STOP

I waited. BB KITCHEN TO SILVER SEED STOP

My box began to click, but it was José. BB WILL SENT MESSAGE STOP

José's box received NOTHING UP THERE STOP

The key on my box twitched, but it was evident that the mountain blocked the signal.

Sam leaned in the doorway. "Time's up."

Sid handed Sam two mugs of tea and turned to me. "Always create a reason for meetings. Explanations must seem natural."

I pressed the button. COOKS COMING STOP

I wrapped the code box back in the towel, and Sid stowed it in the cabinet.

Chapter 21

In the days that followed, when Sid came to watch my cooking, he often idly tapped the counter or the side of the pot I was using. He made mistakes, and I had to reply slowly, slap-tapping my answers, but he was learning fast.

One Saturday evening, we decided Sid and I would meet José on the surface by the transmitter tree. Others would join us if they could. The Supreme Navarch and The Twelve were on a retreat. Other than the Air Loom project, the workers had been given time off, and the saloon was packed. José waited at the foot of the trail.

Four men joined us.

After we were introduced, José asked, "Are we all here?"

"Yes," Sid said. "We won't be missed until morning. A new shipment of whiskey arrived, and the saloon will keep the men busy."

José pulled out his code box and tapped BB FIVE MINUTES STOP. We walked quickly up the slope.

"Why does he allow the men to drink?" José wondered.

"When the commands are given," Sid said, "the men don't completely lose their former personalities. Many in the compound are ne'er-do-wells. We reason that the initial idea was to convert a team of men who wouldn't be missed by anyone."

"The Supreme Navarch uses these nights as an enticement. Reward for doing well," a lanky man named Ira said.

Beyond the vents, we wound through a dark clump of trees. When we broke into a meadow, the *Cloud Queen* hovered ten feet above the ground, white paint gleaming in the moonlight.

"She's a beautiful ship," Sid murmured. "Hanging there—it's like something from a dream."

I agreed. I never tired of seeing the *Cloud Queen* hovering, the faint whine of the blower floating toward me.

Laura was in the pilothouse, and the ship slipped to earth, bells ringing faintly in the night air.

José turned to the men. "Anyone afraid of heights?"

108

Sid had chosen well. If anyone was afraid, he made no mention of it. They stood in awe as the grand ship eased to the ground.

Addy ran the front gangplank out, and we filed on board. Almost immediately we lifted high into the air. A fellow named Elmer stood with his back against the forward cabin wall, but Ivan peered over the railing in wonder.

I pounded up the stairs. Laura lashed the wheel and met me at the door. "How are you feeling?" I asked, almost afraid to hug her too tight.

"I am well. Don't worry."

The earth grew dark, and Laura navigated by compass. Lights twinkled in the distance, and she made a course correction.

Addy came to the pilothouse. "We dropped a line and are anchored to a tree. I'll lash the wheel and keep an eye on the engine."

"You have to see Finn's latest updates," Laura said. She led me to the engine room and I took note of a tank against the engine room wall.

I had missed the steady pulse of the engine, and admired the blur of the flywheel.

The three of us went across the breezeway to the table in the forward cabin where we shared a splendid meal. It was good to be with the original crew running the *Cloud Queen*.

"Sid says we must be back before daylight. We have to work fast," I said.

Finn spoke first. "The *Silver Seed* has gone south. We decided Mary would be best at getting information out of the locals. Nathan will accompany her at a distance."

I casually brushed the air to a doubtful Sid. "If anyone can take care of herself, it is Mary. There is a fire in her."

Sid didn't look convinced. "I'll have to trust you and your team."

While we ate, the four men told us about their lives and jobs in the compound. I admired their bravery and willingness to give up their former lives to join the opposition.

109

After we ate, Addy brought two pies to the table and played the stewardess, much as she had done when we were doing pleasure cruises.

"You keep servants?" Sam wondered.

I laughed. "No, Addy is as regular as the rest of the crew. But to make money for our projects, we give pleasure trips—mostly along the coast of Southern California. Addy is simply making you feel welcome." I reached up and touched the white cloth Addy had over her arm. "It is our way of making you feel appreciated."

I lifted my teacup. "To our friends who live like moles below the earth."

"And to Will, who is one of us," Sid added, "and to those who guard the skies."

"I worry more about José, camping each night while I sleep in a warm bed," I said.

"I am fine. You have not seen my latest tent. Finn got it for me. I have a cot and a small wood stove," José said. "And Sid sends up good food!"

"I give José a portion of the Supreme Navarch's special dishes. It only seems fair."

José gave Sid an appreciative nod.

"The Supreme Navarch is convinced that someone will try to poison him," Sid said with a wry smile. "I am to eat the food as a test. José gets what ever doesn't kill me."

José pushed his pie plate away. "Too bad someone does not poison him."

"We would like to try," Sid said, "but now that we know you and your airships are here, we have new hope of ending this nightmare."

Sam cleared his throat. "We have another problem before us. In spite of all our efforts, there are still parts of the cave system we haven't mapped. There's a machine shop deep in the mountain, and we have no idea what they build or which men work in it."

"I have walked the area over and over, and there is no vent that remains unidentified," José said.

"Could he be venting that shop through one of the existing vents or a natural fissure?" I wondered.

110

"And," Sid said, "there are rumors of a mother ship being built."

Sam sighed. "All our efforts to penetrate the teams working on these projects have met with dead ends. We are convinced that these men work under special commands."

"What *do* we know about the Supreme Navarch's plans?" Laura asked.

"Not much. He's brilliant and knows science. Who knows the extent of the instructions given at the passing of the Blue Vial? Lately, the Air Loom has been his focus. He talks of little else. More gas eggs are being made and prepared for dropping on the innocent. We believe he plans to bring the entire country to its knees, to put the government under his control."

"Has he increased gas production?" Laura asked.

Sid leaned back and gestured toward Ira. "Well, yes and no. He has adjusted the machine to produce more gas, but there have been a number of losses—tell them."

Ira leaned forward. "Sometimes, the tanks develop leaks." He chuckled. "So far, no one has had the nerve to tell the Supreme Navarch, so—life goes on."

"Is what you're doing dangerous?"

"We have developed a system. One man at a time works to sabotage the production. That man hides in one of the outbuildings for the rest of the night."

Sam laid down his fork. "We have come to believe the instructions must be given shortly after inhaling the gas. So far, no one has been hypnotized."

Sid continued to explain the underground plan. "The four of us are in charge of different crews. When it is time to pass the Blue Vial, we sometimes arrange for it to be done without a member of the Chosen Few being there. At these times, we give an added command."

Ira looked up and down the table. "In my case, my men are in charge of the tanks outside the compound. They now believe they should go out in the dark of night and add air to the gas tanks."

Sid tilted his head to me. "We haven't told you until now. We try not to have any one man know too much about our efforts in

111

case of capture." Sid slap-tapped IGNORANCE IS GOOD. "One good whiff and the command to 'tell-all' would be a disaster."

I shuddered.

Ira continued. "The Supreme Navarch designed floating roof tanks—a tank, upside down in another tank of water. The top tank floats up as it fills with gas. The tanks have small valves installed in the dome. My men open them each night, but no one notices because of the air we add."

"So his gas is diluted?" Laura asked.

Ira laughed. "Probably ninety percent air."

"Very clever!" Addy exclaimed.

"And I make sure we add enough air to make impressive measurements. The Supreme Navarch inspected them the other day." Ira pulled a small medallion out of his shirt. "I received an award for my management skills." He shook his head. "The little weasel is so sure we are under his control, he isn't worrying about anything but how *much* gas is being stored."

"And we store a lot of gas—well, air for him," Sid said.

When the last of the pie had been eaten, Finn took us to the tank in the breezeway.

"For extra fuel," Finn said. "And we are constructing a holding tank at our camp. We soon will have the fuel we need for battle."

The night was cold, and Finn led us into the engine room. We stood in the warmth of the boiler.

"How dangerous are the fuel raids?" I asked.

"There is little danger," Finn said. "We found a place where we can land. Now that the *Cloud Queen* is here, we take horses."

"You brought horses?"

"No, but we have plenty now. We have built a corral for them." Laura started toward the breezeway. "Sometimes we take more than fuel!" she said over her shoulder.

Sam slap-tapped. WE MUST BE CAREFUL "The next fuel run will have extra guards. The Supreme Navarch has been ranting about it for days."

Laura returned with a box. "Yes, but the men will be very sleepy." She removed the lid of a tin, revealing what looked like sugar. "The Professor brought these powders that will work well."

112

"How is it to be given to the men?" I wondered.

"Addy and I will make sure that happens."

I was alarmed and could tell José was too.

Laura patted my hand. "This formula is tasteless and has no smell. We have laced whiskey bottles with it and sprinkled it on damp tea leaves. Professor Gruber is certain it will work well."

Laura shook some tea leaves onto a cloth. "The professor tried the tea on himself." She smiled. "Probably the longest he has slept in months."

"We have been to the town where the fuel is stored. I have a tavern owner eating out of my hand. He will ensure the fuel detail gets the right whiskey," Laura said.

"We are not just a couple of pretty faces," Addy quipped. "We can be convincing."

I digested the information. The sky crew had been busy. Clearly, the operation was well planned, and was of less danger than an armed attack on the wagons.

"We are not depending on the fuel wagons for our supply," Finn said. "We are buying fuel. We will have almost three thousand gallons. If anyone knows how to gather supplies without arousing suspicion, it is Mr. Salsbury."

Laura put the powders back in the box. "The *Cloud Queen* has been flying almost nonstop, hauling fuel and supplies."

"Wait, so—you raid the fuel wagons just to disrupt?" Sid asked.

Laura half closed one eye. "Exactly."

The crew had been very busy, indeed.

We landed in the meadow after a few short hours of sleep. We hurried down the path, shivering. Sam's guards also had "special instructions" to allow anyone with Sid, Jeffery, or Sam to enter. The guards would not mention our coming or going.

When we slipped through the doors, the long hallway was dimly lit. We walked around and stepped over men who were too drunk to find their beds. Sid and I kindled the breakfast fires.

113

Chapter 22

The klaxon began calling a General Assembly. The kitchen staff had not finished breakfast, and there was confusion in the hallways. The fog did nothing to relieve fear, and I saw alarm in the eyes of the men. The klaxon stopped the call only to start again. It rang the call cycle three times. My ears were ringing by the time I found a seat in the auditorium.

The curtain was open, and the Supreme Navarch appeared shorter than usual. I realized he was sitting on a stool behind his podium. His gloved hands danced on the sides of the podium. Only six of the Chosen Few were present, and one handed him the speaking trumpet. The Supreme Navarch fumbled and finally was able to hold it.

"Get in your seats, you fools. In your seats." He gestured to our left and screamed, "If you can't find a seat, sit on the floor!"

The Supreme Navarch gestured to the one who had given him the speaking trumpet. The man came over and after a few words took the cone.

"In your seats. Our beloved Supreme Navarch does not have time in his busy day for this nonsense." He turned to one of the other Chosen Few, and the man hurried off the stage. The klaxon began blaring in the halls.

The last of the men hurried to find seats while some sat on the floor along the sides.

The Supreme Navarch reached for the speaking trumpet again. Holding it to his mouth, he began ranting, "Get in your seats, you fools. In your seats."

One of the Chosen Few brought the Supreme Navarch something to drink, and he downed it without stopping to breathe.

He looked across the auditorium, his eyes squinting into slits. The Supreme Navarch's voice became low and menacing. "Why are you sitting on the floor? Get up! Get to a proper seat!"

The men scrambled to their feet and stumbled into chairs.

The Supreme Navarch pinched out a smile. "That is better," he purred. "That is better."

The room fell quiet.

114

"You no doubt are wondering why we are gathered here." He looked back and forth, nodding. "There has been another attack on our glorious project. Our fuel wagons have been taken, our men drugged." His voice went up on the last word.

The Supreme Navarch's hand fluttered on the side of the podium, and he put it behind him. His voice returned to almost a whisper.

"You will be happy to know that this is a minor inconvenience to us. A minor inconvenience." He chuckled. "I am too smart for them. I know things before others. God has his hand on my shoulder." The Supreme Navarch's voice began to break and squeak. "When *ye* reap the harvest of your land, thou shalt not wholly reap the corners of *thy* field, neither shalt thou gather the gleanings of thy harvest!"

The Supreme Navarch's head sank, almost hidden by the podium. The speaking trumpet pointed into the air. "God has his hand on my shoulder," he whispered.

The room was silent. The curtain did not close.

The Supreme Navarch's head came up, and his fire returned. "I am the Supreme Navarch! Repeat, Repeat!"

"Supreme Navarch!" thundered in the auditorium.

"I have planned ahead. Our work will continue. Let the gleaners take the fuel oil. But woe to them that rob the storehouse. Woe to them. It would be better a millstone be tied around their necks."

"The Supreme Navarch stood. "But there must always be consequences. Consequences."

The Chosen Few had formed a semi-circle behind the podium and nodded.

"Oh, yes, always consequences." He held his arm straight, pointing around the room. "Always consequences. Spare the rod; spoil the child! And you are my children; you are my brood. I must teach you."

The Supreme Navarch let his arm drop to the podium. "Because the men drank whisky laced with sleeping draughts, the saloon will be closed this Saturday!"

115

An audible groan could be heard, but it died away when the Supreme Navarch wagged one finger. "Don't make me add more days," he said as if talking to a small child. The audience hushed.

"It hurts me more than it hurts you, don't you see? I am the benevolent one! I am the shepherd, and you are my flock."

The Supreme Navarch strutted away from the podium, only to come back and lean heavily upon it. "But there will be consequences. Even now, my men, my close comrades, are making a search of the stronghold. Yes, I have to know I can trust you, so I have my spies watching you!"

He turned and spoke to one of the Chosen Few, who hurried away.

The Supreme Navarch climbed onto his stool. He looked at the five remaining Chosen Few with irritation.

Seven men hurried onto the stage. One went to the Supreme Navarch and whispered in his ear. The Supreme Navarch's hands began to flutter, and he dropped the speaking trumpet. One of the Chosen picked it up and held it ready.

The Supreme Navarch pushed away the one whispering in his ear and grabbed the speaking trumpet.

The next few minutes were hard to follow. The Supreme Navarch was in such a state that he could hardly speak. One phrase was repeated over and over: "diluted Autogen gas."

I looked down the row to where Sid was sitting. His hand tapped his knee. NOT GOOD STOP IRA PROJECT MAY HAVE BEEN DISCOVERED

IS IRA HERE

FRONT ROW

One of the Chosen Few handed the Supreme Navarch another tankard, and he tipped his head back and drank.

When he began to speak, his voice shook. "Our Autogen has been compromised. It tests fifteen percent pure. Ira? Where is Ira? Ira! Bring Ira!"

Ira stood. "Here, Sir."

The Supreme Navarch showed his teeth in a sickly smile. "Come up here with me, Ira."

Ira went and stood to the left and a little behind the podium.

116

"Oh, no, Ira. You will stand next to me. I want to keep an eye on you."

Ira moved closer.

"No, Ira, on my right side. Like Jesus and God!"

The Supreme Navarch fiddled with something inside his coat, and I was afraid he would produce a pistol.

"Now, Ira, you are in charge of the receiving tanks for the Autogen. Is this not true?"

"Yes, Sir. I tend the tanks to further the glorious work being done here."

"Ira. You do good work. I gave you a commendation recently, didn't I?"

"Yes, Sir!"

"Ira, put your hand here, on the edge of my podium. Good. Now tell me about your tanks?"

"I personally check the levels daily, Sir. They are increasing at a tremendous rate."

"Increasing? But Peter tells me the gas in the tanks is not of the proper mixture. In fact, if the tests are correct, the gas is not sufficiently efficacious for my purpose." The Supreme Navarch raised his voice. "It is not efficacious for anything at all. I might as well be storing goat's breath!"

There was nervous laughter in the auditorium, but a wave of the Supreme Navarch's hand silenced us.

"Where is your medal?"

"I wear it around my neck as you instructed, Sir."

"Yes. Can I see it—no, don't take it off. Just lay it in my hand."

Ira leaned forward and placed the medal in the Supreme Navarch's gloved hand.

The Supreme Navarch rested his other hand on the podium, closed his eyes, and looked up. "God, give me a sign. Let Ira be shown to be a good and faithful servant—or a foolish servant."

With a loud crack, a spark jumped across the chain, and Ira went down.

The Supreme Navarch looked over the edge of the podium. "Ira, Ira. What am I to do with you? This sign from God says that you are a foolish servant. This does not make me happy." The

Supreme Navarch bent down and took Ira's hands. Another pop sounded, and Ira's body jumped.

The murmuring in the auditorium grew louder. The Supreme Navarch strolled in front of the podium. "You see, you can't fool me. God is watching you, and God shows me what he sees!"

A whisper drifted through the hall.

"Silence, or I will call on God's power to test some of you."

Seats rustled as men sat up straighter.

The Supreme Navarch gave us his malevolent smirk. "Anyone want to shake hands?" He reached out both hands to the crowd. "Anyone?" he screeched. "Anyone?"

He turned his back on us, and the curtain flew closed.

IS HE DEAD

Sid's hand patted his knee. NEW ONE STOP SOME SORT OF TRICK STOP

ELECTRICITY STOP FINN WILL KNOW

Chapter 23

Ira was in bad shape. There were burns on the back of his neck and both hands. He was not conscious. Hector Nuñez was in charge of the infirmary where Ira was taken. The news got to us via code, passing from one rebel to another. The news saddened Sid.

"Ira is a good man."

"Will he be released if he gets well?" I asked in hushed tones.

"He probably will be executed. You have witnessed one of those firsthand."

"There must be a way to get him out."

"Yes, but not until he regains consciousness. The big problem is that we have lost him and control of his crew. It has taken a long time to maneuver our men in positions of leadership."

I knew this event was a setback for our project. "Perhaps José can tell us what is happening at the storage tanks."

"Possibly, but I'm sure they will be heavily guarded from now on. We must assume the dilution process has stopped." Sid glanced around the kitchen as men came to their stations to prepare the evening meal. "I feel like singing!" Sid's strong tenor rang throughout the kitchen.

> O ye'll tak' the high road, and I'll tak' the low road,
> And I'll be in Scotland afore ye,
> But me and my true love will never meet again,
> On the bonnie, bonnie banks o' Loch Lomond.

Sid held the last note, his voice high and clear, tears rolling down his cheeks.

"Get to work, men. Tonight's meal must be perfect. The Supreme Navarch is unhappy with all of us."

I checked the potatoes. Sid clattered two kettles, large and small, thumping them with a wooden spoon.

BB NEED YOU TO WATCH TANKS STOP IRA CAPTURED STOP NEED DAILY REPORT STOP

119

Sid began to clatter with no particular rhythm but not so loud as for me to hear MR rattle on the vent. No one looked up from their work.

Would Ira awaken and be given new instructions? Would we all soon be under new orders? I slept uneasily.

The following day, after we ate, Sid addressed the kitchen workers. "You have done well. Everyone followed my instructions to the letter." He paused.

No one seemed to remember that Simpson had to be scolded for sneaking off and sleeping in the storage room. "You can all take fifteen minutes outside." Sid scribbled a hasty note. "If anyone should ask, show them this permission slip."

Sid turned a harsh eye on me. "Except you, Will. I found an eggshell in my eggs this morning."

"Yes, Sir. I will be more careful."

"You can be careful by not getting shells in the eggs!"

The men filed out.

We retrieved the code box, and I did the keying. José and I coded at breakneck speed.

BB LAST EVENING THE TANKS WERE SWARMING WITH MEN STOP FOUND VALVE AT TOP STOP VALVE REMOVED AND PLUGGED

THANKS STOP BACK TO COOKING STOP

"Did you get that?"

"Enough. Found-top-gugg or something?"

"Plugged. The tanks have been plugged, but you got the idea."

Sam put his head in the door. "Code from the showers. Ira is awake."

I felt a sense of relief. "Sid, what if we have him fake death?"

Sid turned to Sam. "Pass along to Hector—Ira needs to not get well. Play sick."

"Immediately." Sam pushed through the double doors.

Sid glanced after him and lowered his voice. "Once we are ready, Ira will fake dying. It's our job to make sure *they* don't get too close to Ira."

"How?"

"Can you skip eating after we feed the men at noon?"

"Easy."

While the kitchen men were eating, Sid and I went to the outside lockers. We entered a large icebox where Sid sniffed a ham. "Pretty gamey. I wouldn't want to serve this to anybody."

Sid cut the ham into strips and wrapped them in burlap bags. "I have a place we can put this so wild animals don't get to it. In a day or two, it should give us the smell of death. With luck, they won't want to look."

As we made our way back into the compound, a man sat idly in the hall, slapping his legs. He coded slowly. IRA GRAVELY ILL STOP WINK STOP SL INSPECTED IRA STOP IRA GAGGING AND MANAGED A BIT OF FOAM IN THE MOUTH STOP SAM CONVINCED SL IRA MAY HAVE SOME SORT OF FLU STOP IRA MOVED TO ISOLATION STOP

The ham did indeed smell rank. Ira was wrapped in sheets, with the ham strips lying alongside. The infirmary crew brought Ira out on a stretcher. I was to stand at the door. Jeffery was further inside. Sid was working in the smokehouse, keeping an eye on the procession. As a traitor, no one was allowed to attend Ira's burial.

A grave had been dug near the garbage heap, and as the body was laid in, Sid waved. I turned and motioned to Jeffery. Moments later the klaxon was sounding.

The burial crew started toward the caverns like lemmings. When they were inside, I joined Sid and Sam. We unwrapped Ira and made quick work of filling the hole. Even with a kerchief wrapped around his face, he leaned over and retched. José appeared at the trail and led him away.

We were finishing tamping the hole when the Supreme Navarch startled me. "And what do we have here?"

Sid turned and stood at attention. I saluted.

"Why was the klaxon sounding a General Assembly? I didn't call for a General Assembly. No one but me can call for a General Assembly."

Sid stood straighter. "I cannot say, Sir. We were attending to burying the traitor's body."

"All right, all right. I know that; don't bore me by repeating details."

"Permission to speak freely, Sir?"

"Yes, Sid. Speak."

"Sir, the burial party was made up of new men—men who need your instruction."

"Go on."

"Young Will and I were preparing some smoked liver for you, Sir. When the General Assembly call sounded, the men went in. Only Sam, the head of the guard, was left to bury the body. It was quite—ripe, Sir. Some gangrene, I belie—."

"Yes, yes. Don't include the seamy side of life. Get to the point. I am a busy man!"

"Yes, Sir. I'll be brief—I ordered Young Will to help. Ketterson, on my kitchen staff, will bring me up to date on your announcements." Sid sounded contrite. "I know I should have reported to the General Assembly."

"There was no an*nounce*ment!!" the little man squeaked, lifting on his toes.

"No, Sir. But I didn't know that, Sir."

"Sam, is Sid giving me an accurate report?" The little man leaned toward Sam, pointing with a long fingernail.

"Yes, Sir," Sam said. "I dismissed the burial detail, just as Sid said."

The Supreme Navarch poked his swagger stick at Sid. "Show me the smoked liver."

Sid led the way to the smokehouse. "Just starting another batch, Sir."

"Open it."

Inside, the little man stumbled up the stairs. Sid slid the bar and opened the inner door. Smoke billowed out. The Supreme Navarch strutted in and came out coughing. "Yes, yes. Lovely smoked liver."

Outside, Sid tried again. "I was hoping to surprise you, Sir. I believe celebrating getting rid of a miscreant like Ira would make you feel better about our efforts here. The liver is good for the blood, Sir."

The vain little man puffed up. "Well, yes." He turned to two of the Chosen Few standing nearby. "Don't just stand there. Find out why the AG was sounded. Now!"

He twirled back, locking his gaze on me. "I've got my eye on you, Young Will. You seem to keep turning up in times of trouble."

"I am eager to serve you, Sir, as a loyal kitchen helper."

"Hmm."

When they left, I asked Sid, "What will they find?"

"Shorted wires, I believe. Jeffery knows the compound like the back of his hand. We don't sit idle here."

No, you don't.

After breakfast the next morning, I was called to an Inquisition. When I arrived, Sid and Sam were in the Supreme Navarch's meeting room. *José will be listening.*

Sid was tapping one index finger on the other. STICK TO THE STORY

The Supreme Navarch took me into what looked like his office. He sat behind a large oak desk in a chair that made him look bigger. I realized it was on a raised platform. He was in one of his purring moods. I almost wished he were ranting and screaming.

"So, we begin with you, Young Will, as Sid has named you. Is there an old Will?" He smirked at his bad joke. "Why were you with Sid? Why weren't you in the kitchen? There were pots and pans to be washed. I went to see."

"I am learning to prepare the liver for smoking."

"And how is that done, exactly?"

I recited what Sid had shown me in the smokehouse, ending with the twenty-four blocks of piñon. I used my fingers to demonstrate the dimension.

"And that is what you were doing when the klaxon rang?"

I chose my words carefully. "Actually, Sir, I was at the entrance to the tunnels. I had a—" I paused and tried to look uncomfortable. "Nature call, Sir. A bit of indigestion, Sir."

"Yes, yes. Don't plague me with the vulgar side of life. What did you do when the klaxon rang?"

123

"I looked down the hall. I wondered if I should go, but Sid waved for me to come."

"Sid, waving? I thought he was in the smokehouse."

"I guess he heard the klaxon, Sir."

"Yes, yes. Then what?"

"Well, Sir, the directive is to follow our leaders. Sid was calling me and you were as well, with the horn."

"And?"

"I didn't want a reprimand, Sir. I went to my immediate superior. I like my job in the kitchen, Sir."

The Supreme Navarch coughed, a deep, rattling cough. He started to say something, coughed again, and waved me out.

We sat in the meeting room for twenty minutes. The racking cough drifted through the door. We developed various twitches in our hands and feet, discussing what I had said to the Supreme Navarch.

One of the Chosen Few stood in front of Sid. "Stop tapping your foot! You are making me nervous."

"Sorry. I feel guilty. I should've come to the General Assembly. One should always obey the Supreme Navarch."

We echoed the sentiment.

The door to the office opened, and Sam was taken in. The meeting was short, and Sam tapped NOTHING NEW as he walked to his chair.

In the end, the Supreme Navarch was not pleased but could find no sign of craft in our story. Nevertheless, he assigned each of us to extra duty: I was to shine shoes for the Chosen Few, Sam to dig the ditch for a new cesspool, and Sid to wash all the pots and pans for three weeks.

The Supreme Navarch began to appear when least expected. The Twelve were constantly in and out of the kitchen. Sam overheard two laughing over the fact that the Supreme Navarch planned to preside over Sid, Sam, and I when we passed the vial.

The morning of the Passing of the Blue Vial, Sam and I met Sid in the kitchen at two in the morning.

"Will, get a fire kindled in stove number two and put a large pot on to boil. If asked why we are here in the middle of the night, we are making a special stew with a combination of hog, steer, and

124

deer bones. It is very good for the blood and strengthens the constitution. Sam, watch the hall."

Sid lifted down the antidote from his locker and dropped a pill into my hand. I chewed as the fire kindled, a bitter taste spreading in the back of my mouth. Sid pulled face as he chewed his pill. He went to the door and gave Sam his dose.

I fried potatoes when the stove was hot, and time lagged. Two of The Twelve came into the kitchen. The tall blond beckoned for the three of us to follow. Outside the swinging doors he said, "Hustle it up! It is never good to keep the Supreme Navarch waiting."

"Never good to keep the Supreme Navarch waiting."

We fell in behind him, and my stomach tightened. This was the big test. I didn't like the thought of what failure might mean.

The Supreme Navarch sat in a chair raised several feet above the meeting room. He was pale, but he was rarely outside—I could only hope that he was becoming more ill as the days passed.

"Now, gentlemen," the Supreme Navarch cooed, "I will perform the special Passing of the Blue Vial Ceremony." He laughed. "I may have some special comments for you." He laughed again.

The tall blond presented Sid with the vial. Sid removed the stopper with reverence, leaned forward, and inhaled for a long time. We each took the vial in turn, and when it was my turn, the gas had a sickly sweet smell, and I coughed. I looked at the Supreme Navarch and gestured toward the vial. "May I?"

He nodded, and I took another sniff, letting my face go blank. He smiled.

I couldn't feel any difference. Was I going to drift into the fog? I found myself reciting the times tables in the back of my mind. *Six eights are forty-eight, six nines are fifty-four.* Feeling silly, I thought about destroying this place, the Supreme Navarch's plans.

The bottle was returned to a varnished wooden box.

"Now, Will, Sid, and Sam. You are pleased to be my special helpers."

"Pleased to be your special helpers."

"You are sorry you remained at the gravesite during a General Assembly."

125

We echoed the words.

"It is not good to think—to take initiative. You are only to follow orders. The orders of the Supreme Navarch."

I kept my voice flat and dull as I responded.

"You are to support the Supreme Navarch at all times and in all ways."

"You will be on the lookout for spies."

We repeated the commands.

"A spy is anyone doing anything not allowed by the stronghold rules."

We recited in unison.

"If you see any furtive action you are to report it to me, directly."

I stumbled on the word furtive, and the Supreme Navarch gave me an almost kindly smile. "Poor Young Will. Your education has been lacking. Furtive means sneaky or secretive. Do you understand?"

"Yes, Sir. Furtive. Sneaky or secretive."

The little man wiggled in his chair, a chuckle gurgling in his throat. "You will eat with your knife—never use a *fork*," he squeaked gleefully.

When the ceremony was over, the Supreme Navarch gave a quick nod, and one of the Chosen Few entered and led us out. Apparently, there was a way for the men outside to see into the room.

I took a deep breath and coughed, but the smell of the Blue Vial stayed in my nose and throat. *I am my own man. I am my own man. I will do everything in my power to destroy the Supreme Navarch's plans.*

126

Chapter 24

José reported that Ira was growing stronger. Ira had been able to slip down one night to check the levels in the gas tanks. The gas was building rapidly. We began to worry that one of the ships would be loaded and take its poison to Denver.

It was frustrating that so much was being accomplished on so many fronts, yet we could never sit down to talk and discuss plans together. We decided to have a meeting with as many as could safely attend.

A report came that the Supreme Navarch and the Chosen Few were on another special retreat. They had told Jenkins that they would not be served meals that day. They only wanted tea. No wine, no food.

Sid said this was not the first time this occurred, and in previous times, everyone had been given the day "to reflect on the glorious project." Of course, for many that meant drinking, but even that was quiet. No one wanted to chance disturbing the Supreme Navarch's contemplations. By evening, the day's drinking and relaxing had taken its toll, and many went to bed early.

At dusk, we were able to leave the compound without question. Six of us made our way through the trees to the clearing where the *Cloud Queen* hovered.

We boarded quickly and lifted off. I went to the pilothouse where Laura guided the ship at night. She wore her long coat and hat with goggles and smiled when I came up.

"Hello, Love," she said. "It's a dark night, so I have to keep my wits about me."

She watched the compass and the stars. "Our headquarters are only a few miles North East, but we don't want to drift off course." She leaned toward the speaking tube. "Call for two blinks."

In the distance, I saw two faint blips of light. Laura eased the wheel to port.

We sailed silently, and I felt safer each moment. I realized that while our life in the compound had become routine, there was always danger. Here, high in the sky, the threat became distant.

127

"How are you feeling? No pains?" Before, Laura had harsh pains before she slipped a baby.

She turned for a moment. "I feel very good. I can even eat breakfast now."

I put my arm around her and watched the front lights blink twice. An answer came to our left, and Laura made another correction.

"The breeze has come up, but the air will be still in the meadow," she said.

Laura brought us over a large clearing with corrals and fuel tanks. The *Silver Seed* sat on a flat, and I felt a wave of homesickness for Eagle's Crest.

We touched down and immediately went to the *Silver Seed*.

The *Cloud Queen* lifted off with Mary and Nathan as crew, hovering with a tether.

"We have added a few trusty guards," Finn said, "but we don't keep both ships on the ground. We keep pressure up in the *Cloud Queen*. It wastes fuel, but we cannot lose either ship."

Dolph hurried down the hall. He had grown but still had the same boyish face.

"Dolph, I didn't know you came!"

"I wanted to surprise you."

"He's been on the *Silver Seed* installing the code recorders," Finn said. "We can tell you much more in the meeting." He led the way to the rear salon. The long table was inviting, and it felt like I was home.

"Let's begin with the Supreme Navarch's compound," I said. "Ira, tell us about gas production."

Ira was thin. "The report is not good. They are making gas in greater volume than before. It's as if a second Air Loom is running."

I looked to Sam. "Do we have any idea where it would be?"

"No. If there is one, it's a well-kept secret. I assume the Chosen Few would know if there is another machine."

José said, "I listen to the meeting room. There has been no talk of building a second machine."

"We must find out," Sid said. "That will be at the top of the list for us in the compound."

128

Ira put a small bottle of blue liquid on the table. "The stopper has been wired shut. I was able to get it from a tank storing the liquid after it's converted from gas."

"I tell Ira to be careful. He is still weak from the shock," José said.

"I'm careful." Ira squared his shoulders. "We had to have a pure sample. This is important to Professor Gruber's experiments."

"Ira comes from a cattle family near here," Laura explained. "We have created a lab in one of their storage sheds. It's remote."

"Professor Gruber is attempting to create a blue liquid," Finn added. "It will smell and look like the real thing, but not cause mind control."

"How long?"

"Days, he says." Laura chuckled. "I am not sure how he knows days from nights. He rarely comes out."

I slid the bottle to the center of the table. "Let's talk about Ira being shocked. How did the Supreme Navarch do that trick? Did he have the podium wired?"

"I believe it is a condenser—a device that can store electricity and then release it quite quickly," Finn said. "Sid, I am betting the Leader doesn't always wear gloves?"

"No. Only that day. Does he now have the power to shock at will?"

"Yes and no. Condensers are not like a battery. They store a large amount of voltage, but it is all released at once."

"Ira was shocked twice. Would he need two of these devices?" I asked.

"That is my guess. But after two shocks, he would have to recharge the condensers."

I thought back to the stage at the General Assembly. *He asked if anyone else wanted a shock. A bluff?* "Wait. The Supreme Navarch fiddled with something under his coat before he approached Ira. Could he wear these condensers?"

"Condensers come in all sizes. The Supreme Navarch is a clever scientist. It's hard to imagine the design of condensers he might create."

The Supreme Navarch walking around with the ability to electrocute frightened me. "We went to his meeting room to pass the Blue Vial. He didn't wear gloves that day," I added.

"My men have been watching," Sam said. "He has only worn gloves the one time."

Addy, restless, stood. "So, he is especially dangerous when he is wearing gloves?"

Sam sat back in his chair. "He is physically sick and mildly insane, but never underestimate this man. He is evil and cunning. He is always a danger."

"How many have been given medallions for good work?" Finn asked.

Sid and Sam each pulled an emblem out of their shirts.

"And you are told to wear them?"

"At all times," Sam grumbled.

Sid removed his medallion, and Finn studied it carefully.

"This is a silver chain. Very conductive." Finn fingered the links. "It will take some doing, but I believe I can find a chain that will look like this but doesn't carry electricity."

"If the Supreme Navarch is planning to shock, the person will already be in big trouble," I said.

Addy slipped out, bringing back a tray of pies. I smelled apple.

"Yes, but he is a man who likes routine." Sid reached for his medallion. "The medallion was part of his demonstration to the General Assembly. It was effective; I would guess he would want to pull that stunt again. If you didn't receive the shock he thought you would, it might give a man a chance to escape or play dead."

Sid accepted a piece of pie from Addy. "If you didn't fall to the floor, the Supreme Navarch will have a fit. He doesn't like to fail, and he is so sure this works that he will want all in the General Assembly to be reminded of his power."

"But if he takes your hands?" I asked.

"I fear that causes the most damage. Electricity passes through the chest. The electricity could stun the heart."

"I lived," Ira said. He held out a shaky hand. "Nerves are jumpy, but I am alive."

"Addy, I should have you work for me in the kitchen," Sid remarked. "Why can't you make pie like this, Will?"

"I'm lucky to scramble eggs."

I made a decision. "Finn, find replacement chains, but that is not a top priority. What about the code interceptors?"

Finn washed his pie down with a swig of milk. "We have discovered that messages are being sent to the east. We have one of our code recorders capturing messages. Mary found that one message was going to Kansas City. It's a big country out there to look for a compound." Finn nodded to Dolph.

There were deep circles under Dolph's eyes, and I knew he probably wasn't sleeping or eating unless reminded. He wasn't having any trouble with his pie.

Dolph indicated three books next to his pie plate. "We know where the message is being sent but there are many messages. These are Western Union lines. I have tapped the wires. Mary was able to learn *when* a message was being sent. She radios and I turn on the recorder. We are pretty sure we listened to one of the messages, because it makes no sense—was in code."

I was more tired than I thought, and it took a moment for this information to sink in. "Wait, you were out there by yourself, Dolph?"

He laid his fork on his plate. "I am almost fifteen, Will. You were flying the *Cloud Queen* when you were seventeen."

Dolph's steady gaze made me realize that he was no longer the round-faced lad that had tagged after Finn in the lab at Eagle's Crest.

"I have several cipher books." He tapped the volumes. "We know certain letters are most popular, such as 'E', but so far—no luck."

"Dolph has been tireless," Finn said. "We have stopped intercepting any more messages until we crack the code."

"I should have cracked it by now. Ciphers are not that hard once you know the algorithms."

Algorithms. Dolph was indeed growing up fast.

I looked at Sid. "Any ideas?"

"None."

131

Dolph gave us a big grin. "I will get it. Finn buys me lots of books."

"And he studies them," Finn said.

No doubt.

The men from the compound were smiling and nodding between bites of pie. It was good to be able to hear these things all at once. Our communication by code was effective but sometimes left us with partial information.

"We need to hear from Mary," I said.

"I'll call the *Cloud Queen*," Laura said.

We stretched our legs, enjoying a peaceful moment.

When Mary came in, every man from the compound looked up. Like Laura, she wore a long duster and a stylish hat.

After introducing the men to her, I asked, "Mary, how dangerous is it to find out when messages are being sent?"

Mary laughed. "Don't worry, Will. I'm in complete control of the silly fellow at the telegraph office. I also have the men coming down from the compound eating out of my hand. And—" She swept her eyes around the table. "It's necessary."

I cocked my head, looking at her through my eyebrows.

With one quick move, Mary pulled a knife from her cloak and held it to José's neck. José hadn't seen the weapon coming.

With a twist, she had José out of the chair, and on his back, a small pistol pointed at his head.

José gave her a sheepish grin and held his hands up, palms toward Mary.

Mary stood, the knife and gun disappeared, and she reached a hand out to José and pulled him to his feet. "Besides, Nathan is never far."

No one spoke.

Mary stood tall. "Look. We all know this is dangerous. I want to beat these people as badly as the rest of you." She looked at each of the men in turn. "I lost a husband and baby to this freak. I am not in any more danger than you, the men in the compound, or Ira and José."

I met her eyes. "You're right, Mary. I should never have doubted you."

Later back in the wheelhouse of the *Cloud Queen*, Laura said, "Will, don't worry. She practices all the time. She has two knives, a pistol, and a Derringer when she is out."

"All at once? Where are they?" I was immediately embarrassed.

"When you're shaped like Mary—well, never you mind. She manages. Finn provides lots of ammunition for practice. She doesn't miss." Laura shook her head in wonder. "She can throw her knives, too." Laura reached behind her apron and flicked a six-inch knife, backhand, into the window frame. It hung, vibrating.

She raised one eyebrow. "The first few weeks you were in the stronghold, we hovered for days at a time. We don't play darts with darts anymore. No more talk about helpless females."

But are we ready for what lies ahead?

133

Chapter 25

The General Assembly had just begun, and my ears were still ringing. We were taking a big chance. Sam stood outside the Supreme Navarch's office while Sid and I searched for a code book. Other opposition members were in the hallways leading to the Meeting Room.

The door was unlocked, and we slipped inside. My hands were cold and clammy. I forced myself to take time to study the contents of each drawer of the desk, so I would leave everything as it was.

Sid searched a cabinet against a wall. "Anything?"

"He's very tidy."

The top drawer on the left side of the desk held an engraved wooden box. Setting it on the desk, I opened the lid. "Sid, look." I lifted out one of the Supreme Navarch's Crest stamps. "What do you suppose the symbol means?"

Sid handed me a blank piece of paper from a pile on a table. "Stamp it in this corner. We can study it later."

I opened the ink pad, rocked the stamp into the surface, and carefully pushed the stamp onto the paper. When I lifted the stamp away, the crest was clearer than when stretched on the back of a hand. Sid blew on the ink, carefully folded the paper, and put it in his pocket.

I closed the pad and started to replace the stamp. I reconsidered and wiped the inky face with the inside of my shirt tail and carefully laid the stamp beside the ink pad.

Before returning the box, I reached into the drawer and slid my fingers above. A sheet of thin wood created a slot along the underside of the desktop. I was able to feel a piece of paper and pull it out. Three paragraphs were carefully written in a foreign language.

"Sid, look!"

We had no idea what we were seeing, but we began copying the paper word for word. Sid wrote the first paragraph, and I tackled the last two.

134

While I finished my second paragraph, Sid looked behind cupboard doors, drawers, and pictures. I laid the paper on the desk to dry. When the original document was in its hiding place, I closed the desk drawer. I put the pens back in their slots and closed the ink well. The rest of the drawers seemed dedicated to bottles of elixirs and bullets. The top right drawer held a silver revolver and a derringer with an inlaid pearl handle.

Sam rapped on the wall from outside. ASSEMBLY ABOUT OVER

Sid drew my attention to a large painting of the Supreme Navarch hanging on the wall over a sideboard. The picture had an ornate gold frame. The Supreme Navarch appeared younger in the portrait. "These walls are thick. Perhaps a safe is behind this?" Sid stretched to lift the picture down, but the nail pulled out of the wall and fell behind the credenza.

"A plague of all cowards, I say," Sid grumbled, "and a vengeance too."

TWO MINUTES

"Will! Help me!" Sid started to pull the credenza out.

"Wait. Don't make marks on the carpet. Maybe I can reach under." I flattened myself on the floor, squirming my shoulder under the front lip. I reached, batting back cobwebs, feeling for the nail. "We skinny guys are good for something. I have little monkey hands."

LEADER ON THE MOVE

My stomach rolled. I squirmed further and felt the nail. I touched the nail, trying not to push it further away. It lay against the wall, and I played with the head, trying to roll it toward me.

"We're going to have to lift this out," Sid said.

"Almost." I wedged my shoulder into the wood, my shirt tearing. "Got it." I stood and worked the nail back into its hole. "Go, go!"

Sid made two attempts to hang the picture.

TWENTY YARDS TO THE FIRST TURN

Sid grunted, reaching out, and the wire caught on the nail. He adjusted the picture while I stood back, guiding his moves. When it was hanging straight, I started for the door we had come in.

A panel slid open, and Sam poked his head in. "This way."

135

Sid eased the secret door closed behind us until he heard a click.

I grabbed Sid's arm. "The papers we wrote are on the desk!" I turned, fumbling with the latch on the door. It clicked and I dashed to the desk.

"Get his tea on his desk," came from the other room. "Make it snappy!"

I stuffed the papers in my pants pocket, and hurried to the secret panel. Through the crack as it closed, I saw Jenkins open the office door, carrying a silver tray with a teapot, cup, and saucer. I didn't bother to latch the panel.

We followed Sam down a narrow passage. A room with a commode was to our left. Sam slipped to the door at the end of the hallway. He eased it open and squinted through the slit between the hinges. He opened it further and stuck his head out.

"Clear. Hurry, but don't run."

A man hurried past us, slap-tapping his chest. LESS THAN A MINUTE

I followed Sam into the hallway, with Sid close behind. Sam let us catch up, and we walked three abreast. We were at the doors where the food carts were delivered when the clomp of feet could be heard. Then came that unmistakable whine.

"I am tired of being told No. I am the Supreme Navarch. Without me, none of this would be possible. It is *my* intellect, my superior intellect and scientific prowess that makes this all possible."

"Yes, Sir."

Sam started to turn back.

"Wait! There are closets here," I whispered. I pulled the first door open and was met with shelves of linens. The second held cleaning supplies, and we crowded into a small room with mops and a sink. A bucket started to tip toward the hallway, and Sid grabbed it. Sam pulled the door closed, but it hit my shoulder and didn't latch.

I caught the knob and pulled it slowly, leaning hard to my right. I was against a basin and put my hip up on the edge.

I held my breath. Something cold was hitting my right hip. *Water!* I twisted, feeling for the tap. I turned it the wrong way and cold sloshed on my side.

"What's that?" Sam was alarmed.

136

"Water tap—it's off."

"And I am tired of 'Yes, Sir'." The Supreme Navarch stopped to cough. It sounded as if he was just outside the door.

"Do you want your special wine, Sir?"

The Supreme Navarch took a long, wheezing breath. "What I want are *real* answers."

There was a short scuffle. "Get away from me with that. I said I don't need that now. What I need is to get rid of this cough. I'm certain I caught it in that vile kitchen from one of the scullery men."

"They are a vile lot," someone said.

"Stop repeating everything I say! Why are we just standing here? Move, men, move!" There was another cough that rattled deep and the sound of spitting. "Ah, my first deep breath of the day. See, I am better already. Get someone to clean that up!"

I tightened my grip on the handle, and it wiggled in my hand. "Someone has locked the cleaning cupboard."

"Yes, yes. I don't mean now. Why should I stand and watch someone cleaning the floor!"

"Yes, Sir. I'll find a key and attend to this later."

Footfalls began to recede but didn't get far when another spasm of coughing began.

"Do you want me to get your rolling chair, Sir?"

"No, No. What I want is to clear my lungs and get my breath,' he wheezed.

"Perhaps I should order your special liver for tonight, Sir?"

"Yes, Albertson, go to the kitchen straight away. I want liver and smooth mashed potatoes. Get that lazy Sid and his crew started on an early meal. I don't want any lumps, tell them. Smooth."

"Yes, Sir."

"Where was I? Why am I constantly being interrupted? I will not tolerate interruption. I was saying, I am going to prepare a memo to Greyland saying I want my fleet ready in two weeks' time. I dema—" The voices faded as the meeting room doors swung closed

I eased the closet door open. "All clear."

Sam looked both ways. "Stay together. In front of me. Move fast."

137

In the hallway, we could hear the Supreme Navarch was not pleased. We slowed long enough to hear, "I don't care if they just got back. Send the message just as I have written it. Don't stand there, man. Move!"

Sam hurried us around the corner.

"Let me walk between you. My pants are soaked!"

Sid slapped the back of his neck as if he had a mosquito bite. DID JOSE OR IRA HEAR THAT

YOU CAN DEPEND ON JOSE

When we were nearing the sleeping quarters, I paused, taking a deep breath, trying to shake away my fear. "I need to change."

Sid glanced up and down the hallway. "Hurry! Sam, you better head back to your guard detail. Will and I are expected in the kitchen."

I pulled my extra pants out of my duffle. My efforts were hindered by the wet pants sticking to my legs. When I peeled them off, I felt a wad in my pocket. *The paper!* The corner tore, and I resorted to turning the pocket inside out. A blue wad fell out, and the ink had stained the pants.

"Will, come on!"

I tugged clean pants on and slipped my feet into my boots. I wadded the paper up, uncertain what to do with it. I clenched it in my fist and went out.

Sid grabbed my upper arm, and we walked quickly together.

"What took so long?"

"The paper we copied got wet—it's a purple mass."

"No time to fret."

When we got to the swinging doors, we could hear voices inside. "Ready?" Sid asked.

"Yes."

He grabbed me by the collar, pulled me through the swinging doors, and threw me to the ground. "Don't let me ever catch you trying to sneak off to your bed. Are you a baby that needs a nap?"

I scrambled to my feet. "No, Sir."

Albertson stepped forward. "Where have you been?" he said to me.

138

"I—I felt sickly, Sir. I think I'm coming down with a cough." I made a weak effort to wheeze.

"Maybe you need to have a talk with The Twelve, Boy. What happened to your shirt? The Supreme Navarch doesn't tolerate slovenly dress!"

"I grabbed him by the shirt." Sid got a firm grip on my upper arm. "Let me handle this. I'll give him a taste of my razor strop. That'll cure any cough he might think he has."

Albertson seemed uncertain.

"If the boy is sick, I wouldn't want him in the meeting room. We must protect the Supreme Navarch."

"It is good to protect and serve the Supreme Navarch," voices murmured.

Albertson looked directly at me. "Watch it, Boy, or I may take more than a strop to you."

A drip of purple water hit the floor. I slid my foot over it.

Albertson squared off in front of Sid. "The Supreme Navarch requires an early meal. Liver the way he likes it, and mashed potatoes." He surveyed the kitchen. "Smooth potatoes, understand. Smooth—no lumps—understood?"

"No lumps," we droned.

I pulled open the closest firebox and tossed the wet paper in, along with three sticks of wood.

Albertson shoved his way through the swinging doors.

I swished my purple fingers in cold wash water. The stain would stay for a while.

Sid turned toward the stares around the kitchen. "You all look sleepy. Maybe we all need a klaxon in here to help everyone attend to their duties. Here!" Sid handed me a large pot and a wooden stir. "Bang on your drum, boy. Keep these men awake!"

BB SUPREME NAVARCH SENDING MESSAGE TO GREYLAND STOP NOT SURE WHAT GREYLAND MEANS STOP FLEET TO BE READY IN TWO WEEKS STOP

Sid's head snapped around as I banged out the final STOP. "Keep drumming, drummer, until you think everyone has heard your drum."

I hammered out my message again. As the pot's ringing stopped, I heard a faint "R" being tapped. José wouldn't dare chance

139

sending code when the kitchen was quiet, but a small leaf floated down the vent.

"Everyone has heard and is awake, Sir. Permission to finish cutting potatoes."

"Yes, and cut small pieces. When you mash, put your back into it. I'll add extra milk and butter."

I swept the leaf aside with my foot and went to work. It helped to be doing something normal.

Jenkins paced in the hallway as I pushed the cart toward the meeting room. When I drew close, there were three gunshots, and I ducked behind my food cart. There were shouts, orders, and general confusion inside. When it was quiet, we stood at the door, waiting. One of the Chosen Few came to the door.

"The Supreme Navarch went into his office, and a painting fell when he slammed the door. There was a crash of breaking glass. He shot through the door several times."

"Was the painting ruined?" Jenkins asked.

"It was his portrait. Apparently, it jarred loose when he shut the door. It will be repaired."

Screaming came from the meeting room. "I want a carpenter, now. I cannot have a door with bullet holes in it. Tell them to clean all this up!"

One of the Chosen Few came out of the far door.

"The Supreme Navarch will especially appreciate tonight's meal," Jenkins offered. "The cook has prepared his favorite, smoked liver and onions. The potatoes are extra creamy."

"Good. He has a great deal on his mind, commanding this huge operation. Tell Cook his efforts are appreciated."

When Jenkins opened the door, I caught a glance of the Supreme Navarch slumped in his large chair at the head of the table. Jenkins and one of The Twelve carried the platters into the meeting room.

140

When it was finally time for the cooks to eat, we did not have smoked liver and onions. Our fare was beef stew, but I was hungry, and it went down well.

After Sid finished his pots and pans, he called me to his office and closed the door. He raised his voice. "You will not ever sneak off to your bed again during the work hours." Sid slapped the strop against the floor four times.

I held out my left forearm. Sid gave me a questioning look. "The work is too hard in there!" I shouted.

The end of the strop slapped and wrapped around my arm. For a moment I thought, *That's not too bad.* Then the burn started, turning to fire. I watched the red welt become brighter as Sid slapped the floor. "Don't ever backtalk!" He slapped the floor two more times.

Sid pointed to the floor. LAY DOWN came in quick slap-taps.

I laid down, making sure my left arm was toward the door.
STAY DOWN

At the door Sid said, "Silly boy fainted. Bring tea, and get to your beds."

Fredrick, a helper under the influence, brought a tray. "Is he going to be OK?"

"You let me worry about Will," Sid said gruffly.

When the kitchen was quiet, Sid checked outside, latched his door, and said, "I have been looking at the Supreme Navarch's crest. Is this a two-headed dragon?"

I got up and sat at Sid's small table, resisting the desire to look at my arm. "Or bird? We need to get this to José and on up to the *Silver Seed*. Dolph and his books will work it out."

"If we go back to the kitchen, will José be listening?"

"I think José is always listening." I sometimes wondered if I would be so devoted if José was in the compound and I was camping above.

Sid turned the lights back on and sang the Dinah song. I joined in just for something to do.

"Count the eggs for tomorrow. We'll need fifteen flats."

Right. Always have a reason for being here.
IRA HELE STOP

141

Ira was still learning.

BB LET DOWN THE STRING STOP

Sid went to the Supply List and used the ink pen to write a note on the back of the crest. The string came down.

"Better check the corridor while I do this."

I stood at the door, but the hallway was empty.

After the note had been delivered, I found my bed, making sure the rough blanket didn't rub on the welt. Being a spy was hard work.

Chapter 26

"The Supreme Navarch has chosen me to sail on his flagship as chef." Sid looked out the rear window of the *Silver Seed* salon. "I have no choice."

"And we do not even know where it is," José added.

Only Sid and I had come from the compound. He felt it necessary to tell those above in person.

"The Supreme Navarch may have it come to the compound—to load supplies," Sid guessed.

I paced back and forth. "He's cagey. We can't count on who might be aboard. This guy hides behind the innocent. Until we are certain who or what he has aboard, we should not destroy it."

"There are going to be casualties," Sid said. "On both sides."

"Professor Gruber has a supply of antidote." Laura sat a sack marked "Ginger" on the table. "He didn't make it into pills. It is a fine powder. He mixed it with another chemical to kill the bitter taste. It tastes like chalk and is slightly pink."

"For the food!" Sid's admiration showed. "Clever. No one in the kitchen would know what to do with ginger. Will and I will make sure everyone in the compound begins to get a dose."

"Here is the recipe Professor Gruber suggests." Laura pointed to a list. "There are two. Start with the light amount for a week and then increase the dose to this quantity. He says it mixes well with mashed potatoes."

I couldn't help smiling. So much progress was being made while I was in the caves.

Dolph came rushing into the salon. "Albanian!" He plopped a book on the table. "Sorry to interrupt. This is a book of flags and crests Mary 'borrowed' from the library."

"I have a card." Mary gave us an innocent smile. "However, I may be unable to return the book on time."

"I didn't start looking at this book until moments ago. I was interested in the books about creating codes." Dolph sat heavily. "I'm guessing the messages are in Albanian."

"Good work, my friend. You should get some sleep."

143

"After you go—but I need an Albanian dictionary. We could have Mary back in the library by tomorrow afternoon."

"Agreed. Finn, does the *Silver Seed* have enough fuel for another round trip?"

"Yes, but I would like to fill the tanks. We don't know how long we may need to stay in the air."

"Tell Addy to bring us down and start pumping fuel. We are almost done here."

Sid tapped the flag in the book. "Two-headed eagle."

"That might mean something," Finn said. "Does he have two ships or two compounds making gas?"

"Or maybe he just used his country's flag," I said. "Dolph, compare the stamp image to the flag. He may have inserted symbols that have special meaning."

"In the meantime, we can't let Will be brought into duty on one of the ships." Sid crossed his arms. "He is needed up here."

"But I *am* going back with you tonight. Business as usual. We don't want suspicion aroused."

Laura did not look happy, but she gave me a quick nod. I wished she were smiling.

"So, we won't have Sid in the Compound when the Supreme Navarch is gone." I turned to Sid. "Do you think the remaining opposition can handle the sobering process? The 'enlightened' won't all come out of the fog at the same time. Some will be surly. Some will want to go home immediately. Some will want to fight those who no longer support the Supreme Navarch."

"They will have to," Sid said.

Ira's pale face looked troubled. "I have discovered large containers that hold twelve demijohns. I'm guessing he may be shipping the liquid to other compounds. But trying to understand the mind of the Supreme Navarch is like trying to guess what a mad dog is thinking."

"If he is shipping the fluid, this may be the only place it is manufactured," Mary surmised.

"Agreed," José said. "If there was an Air Loom in Sacramento, they could have restocked when the Adjunct Leader's huge ship was being repaired."

144

I felt the ship settling to earth. "We need to learn the destination of those boxes."

"I would be the one to get that information," Mary said. "I'm also the one with library contacts. Which is more important?"

"We have to break his code." Dolph stood. "Will, we have to know what orders are being given."

I agreed.

"I have some minor maintenance before the ships go out." Finn hurried down the hall.

I kissed Laura. "We should go now."

"Will, I want to hide two of the original aircycles above the compound," José said. "And one of the quadcycles. I will teach Ira how to pedal. It will keep him warm." He grinned at Ira.

"Excellent. If things go upside down, an aircycle may give us a way to escape—especially at night. I'll help you load them on the *Cloud Queen*."

José waved his hand. "Already being taken care of."

I should have known the idea man would make careful plans.

The *Cloud Queen* approached the clearing, and I took off from the deck on an aircycle. I wanted to practice flying, and it felt good to be in the air again, under my own power. I found my legs were rubbery. I would need to get ready for peddling again. I was spent when I landed.

The *Cloud Queen* touched down, and Sid and I unloaded the quadcycle.

"I hid my aircycle on the left as you come out," José said. "I shoved it deep in the brush."

We stood in faint moonlight when Sid spoke. "I will try to get the Supreme Navarch to see me. I'll suggest that Will stay on as head cook."

My head snapped up. "How will I know how to plan for meals?"

145

"I will make some notes for you in the next few days." Sid paused. "If you don't see me at breakfast, you can assume the meeting did not go well. Be on the lookout. If you have to, make a break for it."

José said, "We will be ready for a fight up here. If you can get out in the open, we can protect you."

Addy walked down the gangplank with three rifles. I started to protest, but José turned one palm up, giving me a resigned smile.

We said our goodbyes at the kitchen vent, and Sid and I made our way into the stronghold.

I slept fitfully and went to the kitchen very early. Jenkins was there.

"Will, the kitchen will not prepare food for the meeting room or the Supreme Navarch. You are to start the fires today to feed the workers."

"Where's Sid?"

"The Supreme Navarch and a Special Few have gone to his glorious ship. Sid went with them."

I tried to hold my face calm. *Was the ship outside?* "Of course. The Supreme Navarch will need a good cook."

"Yes. It is good to please the Supreme Navarch."

"...Supreme Navarch. What do you do now, Jenkins?"

"I am packing the meeting room service."

I could see Jenkins was disappointed to be left with such a lowly job as packing the silver and china. "Do you want me to bring you breakfast?"

"I will eat with the kitchen men as I regularly do."

When Jenkins left, I quickly looked out into the hall and moved back under the vent. "Did you get that?"

"Yes, I heard. Addy has gone to the bluff."

There was a long silence. Then, muffled, excited conversation as Addy's voice became clearer.

"Will, there has been a low cloud—we couldn't see thirty feet. The Palace—is gone! José ran to look."

Gone! "The Palace *is* the ship!" *How did we miss this? It's been right under our noses.*

José was breathing hard. "It is gone. The connecting tube has been pulled back somehow. Will—two more gas bag airships are

146

arriving." He took a deep breath. "I cannot believe that huge metal tower can fly."

Levitrite. When we first saw the Cloud Queen, we didn't think it could fly. Light metal. Open spaces. "Call the *Cloud Queen*. They must give chase. He cannot get away."

"Addy is sending a message.

"There is more," José said. "A huge electric cord is stretched across the ground. It wasn't there before." There was a long pause. "It comes from a big area—fifty feet across. Camouflaged doors in the mountain. The rocks and dirt slid into piles when it opened."

"What do you think?"

"Impossible to tell, but the doors are sealed now. No way in."

"Give me a second." I looked in the hall again, my anxiety increasing. "Back. Not much time."

Addy's voice trailed down the pipe. "The *Cloud Queen* is refueling, and a bearing on the left airscrew must be replaced."

My throat went dry. *Why now?*

"Finn heard it rumbling when the ship came in last night."

"How long?"

"Half a day."

I paced in a circle under the vent. "Nothing can be done, I suppose. I have to start the fires."

"I will get Ira," Addy called. "He is listening at the meeting room vent. I am sorry, Will."

"This is no one's fault," I told José. "I am just frustrated that we can't follow them. I hoped we could destroy the ship before Sid went on board."

The Supreme Navarch was craftier than I had imagined. Somehow, the massive ship had been constructed right under our noses. *The men working on the ship must have had special instructions.*

José sounded resigned. "I will send a message to the *Silver Seed*. They need to know the Supreme Navarch is on the move and what his ship looks like. Perhaps they can intercept her."

There could be no confusion if anyone were to see that tower of a thing flying in the air. *I saw a new Jerusalem coming out of the sky.* I lit the stoves and started on the ovens. I missed my chance to

147

see Sid before he left. I realized how much I depended on him in the compound.

I went to Sid's private cupboard and noticed several of his cookbooks were missing. The code sender was gone as well. *Smart man.* I smiled, thinking of him packing his things, stuffing the satchel in with the books.

A note was attached to the recipe board. It had the Supreme Navarch's crest stamped on the bottom. "Will, Sid will accompany me as my special cook. Sid had one more week of pot and pan cleaning duty. You are to do his job. Make everything shine, Will."

The note was signed *Supreme Navarch, the World's Future.*

Chapter 27

A slight, sour man, Simms came into the kitchen. He had always been around but kept to himself in the pantry and store rooms.

"I have an announcement."

Only one of the other cooks was there.

"Our glorious Supreme Navarch has appointed *me* the chief cook in place of Sid." He almost spit the word "Sid."

Another cook I didn't know came in, and I gave him a look of caution.

Simms raised his voice. "There will be some changes in this kitchen. I don't believe in coddling the scullery people. Sid ran a loose ship." Simms only needed the Supreme Navarch's swagger stick to complete the picture.

"I believe in discipline, and we will have discipline! Will!"

"Yes, Sir."

"Will, you seem to be one of Sid's favorites."

I wasn't sure yes sir would be the correct response, so I looked straight ahead.

Simms leaned close, but had to look up at my face. "You are not one of *my* favorites."

His breath was foul.

"You will do the pots and pans for the rest of the week!"

I tensed my jaw to keep from smiling. "Yes, Sir."

"You will come early and fire the stoves and ovens."

"Yes, Sir." *Who do you think lit them this morning?*

148

"Yes, yes." Simms seemed unsure of any other directions to give me. "Yes, yes. Well, good." He looked around. "So, it is time to start preparing breakfast."

I realized Simms had no idea what came next. "Alright then, let's get biscuits and gravy started," I said.

Simms spun and gave me a look. "I will give the orders! Yes, don't just stand there. And make the gravy—thin. Those fools don't deserve good fare."

Simms went back to the storeroom. I suppose it was a safe place for him. I stirred in the first dose of the antidote.

WHAT WAS THAT ALL ABOUT STOP

I looked up, and a new man stirred a pot, tapping quietly on the side. GIVE SOMEONE A LITTLE POWER AND IT GOES TO THE HEAD STOP

WERE YOU REASSIGNED STOP

SAM DID SOME FANCY PAPERWORK STOP KITCHEN IS THE HUB STOP

WHAT DO WE HEAR OUT THERE STOP

NOT MUCH COMMUNICATION STOP THE NETWORK MUST BE REBUILT STOP

HOW MANY WENT TO THE NEW SHIP STOP

MAYBE TWENTY STOP AT LEAST FOUR OF THE CHOSEN FEW ARE STILL HERE STOP

Simms came and looked at the gravy. "Yes. Maybe more pepper."

I shook pepper and stirred it in.

"Yes."

I tapped out a final message. I WILL MEET THIS AFTERNOON WITH MY FRIENDS ABOVE STOP WE MAY HAVE TO STEP UP OUR PLANS STOP

While we were eating, Simms made another long speech, reminding me I was to do the pots and pans.

There were sly looks of disapproval. The fog did not shield them from displeasure. Perhaps it was that the Supreme Navarch was no longer in the compound. Or maybe they didn't want to be led by a fool.

After breakfast, I was left alone with my pots and pans. I took a chance and talked to José through the vent tube. I reasoned that if someone came in the kitchen and realized someone was outside, José, Addy, and Ira could be long gone before anyone could get to them.

"They are pumping blue liquid into the eggs. The work is going quickly. Twenty are filled," Ira reported.

"There has been no mention of it in here. Communications must be broken, or the Supreme Navarch is taking extra safety measures. Kitchen is clear." I realized Sam hadn't come for coffee that morning.

"The *Cloud Queen* is hurrying to fix the bearing," Addy reported. "Laura is afraid more of his ships with side dumps will be coming to pick up the blue liquid. They are gearing up for a big attack."

"Ira managed to damage some of the gas bags," José said. "Any smell in the caverns?"

"No."

"Probably because a crew of men have been working with a device that patches the holes. I am going to let down more of the antidote pills in case. We have already taken our doses. It stinks out here. Professor Gruber wants the opposition in the caves to take pills. The powder in the food will not have time to provide protection."

"Drop them."

The small parcel fell easily into my hands. "Got it. I better start finding out which of our opposition members have been taken. That is probably why news isn't traveling."

"Be careful."

I chewed a pill, urgency growing in me.

Simms came back when I was putting the last of the pots away. He looked in one and cuffed me on the back of the neck. "Shiny-ER! Just getting them clean is not enough. I want all these looking like the day they were made!" He turned toward the kettles on the shelves. "In fact, take all these down and scour them as well. Make that copper shine!"

Simms was going to be hard to take.

150

José and I stood on the hill above the stronghold. The balloons were being inflated on the new ship, the *White Dove*. Two smaller ships were docked beyond the compound. The first was the *Golden Hawk*. The second ship had been christened the *Golden Eagle*.

"How long will it take to fill the balloons?" I wondered.

Ira took a turn with the spyglass. "They have been working on this for a while. I'm thinking it will take at least a day."

I studied the devices and machines. "How many years has this been going on—this compound?"

"At least twenty. Freebooters were the second phase."

It was mind numbing.

Shouting from the compound interrupted our thoughts. Guards spilled out of the mouth of the cave below. They had rifles and ran straight for the shed and the trail beyond.

"Not good." Ira was already moving. "How did they know?"

"Not sure." But I was sure. The new man in the kitchen was no friend. I realized what a fool I had been.

We ran to José and Ira's camp by the big vent.

Addy handed each of us a rifle and gave the radio to José. "They are having a fit down there!"

Shouts told us the men had crested the hill, and we retreated into the brush.

I glanced at the low clouds. "quadcycle. We can't chance being separated."

José stopped and opened his pack. In moments he had a quarter stick of dynamite lit and threw it in a high arc.

Ira tugged on the quadcycle. A pedal was caught on the trunk of a small pine. José lifted it out of its hiding place. With shaking hands, Ira and I arranged our weapons and two packs as quickly as possible while José watched in the direction of the shouting.

The charge went off followed by silence. Dirt and foliage rained on us, followed by more shouting.

Addy took the second seat, José the front. I sat behind Ira.

WE HAVE BEEN DISCOVERED STOP Addy coded. ON QUADCYCLE STOP ENEMY SWARMING STOP

I strained to hear CANT FLY, and my breathing constricted.

151

The dynamos began to spin, and I joined in, giving my best effort. We lifted off, and immediately José gave us forward propulsion.

"Amazing," Ira said. "Amazing!"

"Haven't you been flying with José?"

"No, just pedaling for practice."

I wished I had been practicing. We were probably one hundred feet in the air, but not moving very fast.

"Up," José panted, "into the mist."

Gunshots popped below, and José and Addy stood in the pedals.

The rifles sounded weak at this range, but I knew they could kill. My legs were already feeling weak, but I put on more speed. The propeller tube's whine dropped to nothing; José had put all power into the lifters.

A bullet ripped through the faring behind me, and I redoubled my efforts. The faring was torn above my head, dangerously close to the main Levitrite box.

I closed one eye and sighted down the handlebar; we were not drifting back.

The shooting continued but grew fainter. The wispy cloud began to envelop us, and for some reason, I thought of the cozy heater in the pilothouse of the *Cloud Queen*. Normally, flying in clouds was cold, but we had no need for heat.

When we could no longer see the ground, José added forward thrust.

"How do we know where we are going?" Ira gasped.

"I have a compass." José breathed hard. "We will fly lower when we think we are out of range of the guns."

"José, I am not in good shape any more. I have to slow down."

"You and Ira both can rest for a minute. We are fine."

José pumped like the steam engines in the airships, and Addy never broke cadence. I shook first one leg and then the other and began a slower pace.

Ira began pedaling as well, and I could hear the thrusters increase their speed.

152

"How far is the camp?" I was embarrassed that I had not bothered to pay attention during our flights.

"Ten miles," José breathed. "Hills—steep—jagged—nearest place."

I felt despair. The quadcycle had never flown ten miles per hour, and I was already winded. Ira stopped pedaling, and I tried to increase my speed.

"Good," José called. "Rest one at a time."

Ira and I spelled each other for the next few minutes. José and Addy eventually agreed to rest while Ira and I did our best. Each time I resumed, I tired faster than the time before.

"I am going to bring us lower. Will, look back to be sure we have left them."

I hoped José would tell us we could slow the cadence, but instead, the propulsion tubes whined higher. I was in agony.

When we came out of the mist, we had not floated back over the compound and were not over the open meadow where the *Cloud Queen* usually met us. I strained to look over Ira's shoulders, but water drops covered the front faring.

José's breathing was labored. Maybe he did get tired after all. "There is a small clearing. Should we stop for a few minutes?"

"Please!" Ira groaned.

"Rest, but be ready to pedal hard if we need more power to land."

Ira and I sat quietly. His shirt was soaked with sweat, and I could feel mine clinging to my back.

At fifty feet, I could see we needed to go forward. I joined José and Addy, trying to keep their pace. Ira began as well.

The propulsion tubes increased their speed, and we glided into a tiny clearing.

I walked back and forth near the quadcycle, trying to get my legs to calm down.

"We cannot stay long," José said.

Back in the air, José kept us near the ground, but the hillside became steeper. "We have to climb over an escarpment," José said.

I wasn't sure what escarpment meant, but was afraid it involved harder pedaling. "Any chance of a rest before?" I puffed.

153

"No sense losing the height we have. Go!' José increased his cadence, and I followed suit. A sheer wall of rock loomed no more than twenty feet in front of us.

"Thirty feet more. Keep the pace."

My legs were on fire. I put my head down, concentrating on turning the pedals evenly. Ira paused.

Addy was out of the saddle, pumping with a vengeance.

The cycle crested the shale. "Give it all you have. We—do not want to—start again!"

The propulsion tubes began to whine, and I felt the increased drag in my dynamo. I stood.

The front wheel bumped an outcropping, and my heart lurched with the machine. Even Ira was spurred into a frenzy of pedaling.

"Almost!" José's voice was a breathy whisper. "Do not— stop now."

We moved forward, over the top, and came to rest on a sheet of rock. We flopped ungracefully and lay panting in the faring.

José began to move. "Everyone OK?"

Addy mumbled something, and we struggled to open the flaps and set the quadcycle right.

Ira lay flat on his back, breathing hard. "Sorry. Still so shaky sometimes."

"Not to worry." I moved next to Addy, looking out over the terrain below. Her cheeks glowed, and her dark eyes were piercing. *No wonder José's in love.*

"One of the reasons we chose the location of our camp is because this ridge runs for miles. Anyone following on horses would have to go almost ten miles east to get around this." She pointed west. "Further, that way. Not a problem for the airships."

Big problem for the quadcycle—or at least me.

José joined us. "No damage. The faring has a tear or two, but we do not have to walk."

I wasn't sure walking wouldn't be easier.

Addy passed a small flask of water. "Just a swallow—we didn't want any more weight than necessary."

154

We landed five or six more times. Night was upon us, and José had Addy call for a signal. When a faint light blinked far to the west, José swung to port, and we all made an extra effort.

In the end, Ira and I were of no help, and we landed several hundred feet from the *Cloud Queen*. Ira and I crawled out and started to walk. Without our added weight, Addy and José flew the quadcycle to the front deck and helped Ira aboard. I felt as if the ground were moving under my feet.

Laura walked me up the gangplank. "You are exhausted."

I could only nod.

Chapter 28

In the forward cabin, we drank water by the tumbler full.

"My mistake. Big mistake." I set my glass down a little too hard. "A man came into the kitchen. He told me he had been reassigned. We were code talking at the stoves, and I—" I paused, irritated with myself. "I assumed he was one of us. He did give me some information, but now I question whether anything he said was true." I shook my head in disgust. "I was a fool."

"What did he look like?" Ira asked.

"Young. Tall." I thought for a minute. I remembered him tapping on the kettle. "Part of his left pinky finger is missing."

"Patrick O'Malley. He was on the communications team—not one of us. One team we were never able to penetrate."

"How do we tell the others he is not part of the opposition?"

"No problem there. They know O'Malley. He simply took advantage of the fact that you don't know everyone on the opposition."

That guy probably tried code on many. I wasn't sure I felt much better. The ship shuddered and lifted. "Is the propeller bearing fixed?"

"Not quite, but we shouldn't stay on the ground," Laura said. "We don't know if they are searching for us."

"They would have to ride around the cliff." I didn't add we almost didn't get over it.

Addy took a long drink and set her glass on the table. "For all we know, they might follow in one of their airships."

Prickles slid up my spine.

"Finn is making the final adjustment to the chain drive," Laura continued. "We are tethered. When the airscrews are ready, we can cast off."

"What about our camp? The fuel?"

"We have both ships full. We have the extra tank in the breezeway full. But we are hoping they never find our camp."

I was too tired to do anything but trust their decisions.

156

"There are two kettles on the stove and soap—clean clothes. You are—well—clean up. I will contact the *Silver Seed*."

We let Addy go first and then made short work of our own washing. I picked up the green shirt and pants, ready to toss them overboard when Ira stayed my hand. "Wait. We might need them."

The Engine Order Telegraph rang, and the airscrews started.

Finn came forward. "The ship is ready, but we'll stay tethered for the night."

Supper was a fine time with the old crew back together. I took the first shift tending the ship and stumbled to bed at midnight.

As I drifted off to sleep, I felt the pedals under my feet, the swaying of the quadcycle. Laura said I hardly moved all night.

"We need to check their progress with filling the airship gas bags. Do you think we can get high enough to not be noticed?" I asked.

"The elevation here is five thousand feet," José said. "The clouds are high today. The air will be thin if we go up another six thousand feet."

"Do they know we have airships?" Laura wondered. "Did they see you leaving on the quadcycle?"

"They shot at us." The bullet ripping through the faring flashed in my mind. "We can hope they won't connect the quadcycle with airships. They might be expecting clumsy balloon ships."

The code key began clicking, BLUE VIAL LIQUID A SUCCESS STOP SMELL AND LOOK ARE IDENTICAL STOP EASY TO MAKE STOP ONE GALLON NOW STOP TWO BY TONIGHT STOP

Finally, a little good news. "This changes everything! How do we get it?"

"I want to see Professor Gruber's processes. I can go on horseback," Finn said.

"Neither Will nor Ira can take the liquid in to the compound," José said. "I am the next choice. I have been the closest, listening."

157

It was a dangerous mission. "How would we get him in, Ira?"

"If José joined the auxiliary crew he might not be noticed. There are a number of men being brought in every week."

José said, "There are lots of Mexican-looking people there. I can fit in."

Addy got up and went to the stove.

"It will be OK," José said.

"I know, but I don't have to like it."

We landed near the corral. Finn threw a saddle on a beautiful gelding. "To the lab and back takes four hours."

I helped him put packs on a second horse and trotted to the airship. It felt good to stretch the sore muscles in my legs.

"Laura, take us up. High as we can stand. I will go to the engine room when I hear bells."

In the forward cabin, Ira unrolled a large piece of paper on the table with circles where the vents were located. "OK, this is the large tunnel at the opening."

We began to add all the passageways and tunnels we could remember.

"I'm going down with him," Addy announced.

The steel in her voice surprised me. "I am not sure that's a good idea."

Addy squared herself, looking up at me. "Will, we have been over this before. I lost my father and my brother. When I had my leg shot, this man saved me." She shook José's shoulder. "This man. I'm not letting him go into the caves with those animals and not be near."

José pulled the corner of his mouth back, squinting.

My left ear throbbed, and I worked my jaw to try to relieve the pressure. "OK, but you must take a code box, and if things go bad, you get out of there."

Addy crossed her arms.

José leaned on the doorjamb. "Will is right—if I am captured, you cannot help."

Addy opened and closed her fists. "I know, but—"

158

When the telegraph rang for Slow, I went to the engine room. The gauge told me we were at eleven thousand feet. We were in a mist, but the ground below was still visible.

Laura rang for Stop, and the *Cloud Queen* hung high above the earth. We moved to the front deck.

It took a moment to get my bearings. Laura pointed to our left.

We took turns at the telescope. Wagons were moving gas eggs toward the nearest ship. A second had been moved closer, and the third waited nearby. The first ship's balloons were full, blocking our view of the eggs being hung on the sides.

Laura looked at the watch pinned to her apron. "It is four o'clock. I doubt the first ship will sail tonight."

"Yes, but José and Addy must be back on board before we can follow." Our efforts were being squeezed by time. *I* felt squeezed by time. "Take us back to camp."

Laura wheeled us around. I wished the *Cloud Queen* could skim down like a bird, but we had no wings. We ran the propellers at Flank speed, all the while descending.

AT CORRALS STOP

I sent MR

The deck pulsed from the steam engine, and the new bearing spun silently.

Finn watched us land. He and José carried two packs up the gangway.

I opened one pack to find more than a dozen Blue Vials stowed neatly inside, wrapped in cloth. "Where did the Professor get so many bottles?"

"They were on one of the wagons," Finn said happily. "The spoils of war."

"Do we need anything from the camp?" I asked. "One ship is loaded and ready to launch soon."

"No, let's go." There was urgency in Finn's voice.

"If we are not coming back, we need to let the rest of the horses loose," José said.

"I suppose." Laura seemed uncertain. "They are fine animals."

Finn pulled the saddle off his horse. "They may find their way back to Professor Gruber's lab."

Laura and I took the halters off the rest of the horses and carried the tack to the back storage room of the *Cloud Queen*. We slapped their rumps, and the horses trotted a few yards away. The bay looked back and nickered. They turned and moved into the night.

I felt no affection because I had not been around the animals. Those who had been at the camp watched wistfully.

I broke the silence. "Laura, get us in the air. José, prepare for a quick stop. You will have to hike in."

Addy had two packs and her long coat. "We are leaving one vial on the ship. If the *Cloud Queen* were to be captured, the enemy may use it to indoctrinate her crew."

"Excellent thinking," I said.

Ira joined us in the forward cabin, and we went over the map of the interior of the stronghold again. I struggled to remember every detail that might help José survive. "Jeffery's the best man to receive the vials."

A sliver of moon created a shadowy scene when we hovered over the high meadow. José and Addy each chewed one of the antidote pills. The *Cloud Queen* slipped in, and the two hopped off the front deck.

Laura stood outside the pilothouse and gave a brief wave as we slowly rose. José went to the side of the trail and pulled an aircycle out of the brush. He pushed it back and hurried to the other side. When he pulled out the second, he clasped his hands above his head in victory. He and Addy picked up their packs and gazed up.

I raised one hand and prayed it was not the last time I would see them.

Chapter 29

I went directly to the pilothouse. "Hover for a few minutes." I watched the clock and paced back and forth.

"They are at the vent," Finn announced through the speaking tube. "Apparently, the enemy didn't take the tent down. None of José's things are missing."

He won't have to wear Ira's greens.

"Finn, set us for a steady climb, set the airscrews at Slow, and have everyone come up, please."

We stood, looking out over the shadows below. "Do you suppose that the gas makes people lazy—slow to move?" I caught Laura's eye. "If you don't have your own mind to drive you, it makes sense that some of your—" I struggled for the word.

"Initiative?" Laura suggested.

"Yes. Initiative—drive. Without instruction, a person might tend to be idle. The biggest problem the Supreme Navarch had was the lack of production. He was driven, but the men lacked motivation." I thought of Jenkins, who when his job was gone, seeming rather puzzled by the situation.

I had been blinded because of my feelings of superiority. I felt smarter. Better. "Unfortunately, a lack of motivation does not make them any less dangerous."

Laura put her hand on my arm. "If anyone can fool them, it is José," she said. "He is quick and strong."

In the engine room, the code key began clicking. DOLPH HERE STOP HAVE DICTIONARY STOP SYNTAX MAKES TRANSLATION DIFFICULT STOP

WILL HERE STOP HAVE FAKE BLUE LIQUID TO ELIMINATE THE FOG STOP JOSE DELIVERING STOP

GREAT NEWS STOP

MR

My ears were popping as I went forward to the telescope. Bright lights showed all three ships remained.

We went to the forward cabin and settled around the table. Laura had the cook stove chimney red hot. I spoke first. "We have two problems before us. He is using the Albanian language in his

161

messages. This makes me think there are other compounds, and we must be sure."

I sighed, thinking of the ruined paragraphs Sid and I had copied. "Second, we must stop the Supreme Navarch's ship."

"And we must make certain the root of this awfulness is stopped, once and for all," Laura said.

Finn looked up from a journal. "The first will depend on Dolph and his ability to decipher the Albanian code. The Supreme Navarch cannot be stopped until we can be certain about other strongholds."

Laura tapped the table. "What if we had Dolph send a message? Maybe we could help figure out the code."

"It's worth a try." Finn went to the keypad.

DOLPH SEND A MESSAGE IN QUESTION

NJE PRAPA Z MDV NJE KFSVTBMFN PESE... The message went on.

There was resignation in Laura's voice. "Absolute gibberish. Without a dictionary, we have no idea if we are even close."

So close and yet so far. On the paper was what the Supreme Navarch was planning, and we were powerless to unravel the puzzle.

That evening, the code key began clicking.

DOLPH HERE STOP MESSAGES ARE ENGLISH STOP FIRST WORDS OF MESSAGES ARE ALBANIAN NUMBERS STOP NJE TRANSLATES TO NUMERAL ONE STOP PRAPA IS BACK STOP SIMPLE ALPHABET OFFSET STOP NJE PRAPA MEANS ONE BACK STOP WORK ON THE MESSAGE I SENT STOP MANY TO DECODE HERE STOP

Dolph sent the Albanian words for the numerals, one to five.

I watched over Laura's shoulder as she numbered the alphabet. "It works! I know this one," I said. "This is one of things the Supreme Navarch says in his rambling speeches. He's quoting the Bible. It's in Revelation."

Laura reached for the Bible. "He's quoting from Revelation 21. 'I saw a new Jerusalem, coming down from God out of heaven, prepared as a bride adorned for her husband.'"

I sighed. "Not much help. We know he built the Palace to look like a city in the sky. He wants the world to believe it is the beginning of the new heaven and new earth."

Finn tossed the message back on the table. "This is his command when the gas is dropped—telling people they are seeing the new Jerusalem, and like lambs, they will believe."

The mind of the Supreme Navarch sickened me. "The gassed will see the Palace ship and think it is from heaven. He thinks or wants them to think he is Jesus."

I began to think out loud. "Does this mean he intends to be present at every gassing? If so, does that mean there are no other adjunct compounds and that his armada will travel together to the areas to be poisoned?"

Laura murmured, almost to herself. "When we take a ship down, gas will be released."

"Will, message from Dolph," Finn said. "Come listen."

In the next few minutes, Dolph explained that the ships at the compound were not all going to the same place. The *White Dove* was headed to Denver, as we expected. The *Golden Hawk* claimed to be on course to Pueblo.

"Pueblo?" I had not heard of the town.

Dolph explained that there were iron and coke works there —the Supreme Navarch probably wanted control of steel production.

Dolph lamented he had lost time translating one message. Mary had been the first to realize that one of the words was not the name of a third town but the name of the Supreme Navarch's ship —the *Celestial City*.

The ego of the Supreme Navarch was hard to comprehend. *Celestial City*! The ship was huge but not as big as the ego of the little despot who controlled it.

We held a quick counsel and decided the *Silver Seed* would take down the gasbag ships. Denver and Pueblo had to be saved. The *Celestial City* would be handled by the *Cloud Queen*.

NO COMMUNICATION STOP MUST HAVE CHANGED FREQUENCIES STOP TAPE RAN OUT STOP SORRY DID NOT HEAR THE CHANGE STOP

We sat around the table in the forward cabin. The *Cloud Queen* hovered at ten thousand feet, and I had a headache. We had spent most of the day at high altitude because Finn hoped it would give us a greater listening range.

"How do we know where this guy is?" I wondered out loud.

"A needle in the haystack," Ira said.

Exactly.

Finn stayed up all night, scanning code frequencies. At four in the morning, he tapped on our door.

"Found the frequency," he whispered, "near the end of our radio's capabilities."

Laura slept soundly, and I slipped from our cabin. "What do we know?"

"He looks forward to seeing the sun rising over the Chicago Peaks in the morning!"

"Chicago?" I felt failure closing in on us.

"Will, you're half asleep! Chicago *Peaks* are the mountains around Denver! We have him. He's close!"

It's a big sky.

"He wants to watch the 'glorious subjugation of the masses.'"

He'll be watching as the ships drop his villainous payload.

Laura came into the engine room in her night-rail and long coat. "Why didn't you wake me?"

"I wanted you to be more beautiful than ever." She was lovely, hair tossed and cheeks rosy from deep sleep.

We tried to rest until morning, but the excitement proved too great.

BB JOSE HERE STOP EASY STOP GREENS I STOLE WERE STILL IN THE TENT STOP JEFFERY WAITING FOR ME STOP WAITING ALL WEEK STOP GOOD MAN STOP

?VIAL STOP

JEFFERY CAN TAKE CARE OF IT STOP TWELVE OPPOSITION REMAIN IN COMPOUND STOP NEXT VIAL

164

PASSING THIS WEEK STOP COMPLETE SOBERING SOON STOP

ON OUR WAY STOP

I made a quick decision. "Ira, can you go back down? You know the compound vents. You can listen and report. I need José and Addy with me."

Ira did not hesitate. "I'd rather be on the ground. I mean you no offense, but this flying does nothing but give me headaches and indigestion."

BE READY TO BE PICKED UP STOP IRA WILL TAKE YOUR PLACE STOP LEAVE EVERYTHING FOR HIM STOP

READY

The thought of having the old crew together again gave me new hope. We had beaten the Freebooters twice before. The only bitter pill was Benny's death.

"Let's start down. We'll land in the meadow just before dawn." I went to the code key and told José and the *Silver Seed* our plans.

Now, the Celestial City. But how do we destroy her without Sid and any others of the opposition dying?

We ate an early breakfast in preparation for a long day.

"Ira, you must be careful down there," I said.

"I will. But we all know the dangers. I have devoted years to stopping this lunatic."

Finn handed Ira a new code box. "I have modified this key coder. There is a switch on the side. I didn't have time to put fancy labels, so I scratched Us on the up position. The other is their frequency. Never send on their frequency."

"Got it."

"Take your pill."

Ira winced at the taste of the pill. "I will be in touch."

We sank quietly into the small meadow, and José and Addy carried one of the aircycles to the *Cloud Queen*.

"Ira, you should practice on the other aircycle," José said. "Just go up a few feet. Spin the pedals, and the left grip is for up and down—the right is for forward movement. Your life may depend on it."

165

"Understood." Ira shook hands with José. "Will, Laura—" He looked around the forward deck. "It has been a pleasure to know and work with you. The men below are encouraged just knowing you are here." Ira shook hands with Finn and me. He tipped his hat to the ladies. "Godspeed."

"And to you, Ira," Laura said.

We lifted off a few feet and waited until Ira went into the copse. We lifted to five hundred feet to watch and listen.

"So, your mission was a short one," Laura said to José.

"Yes. Jeffery was on the lookout for me, leaning against the wall, tapping code. I was only in the compound for a few hours, but code is being tapped with feet, hands, and fingers. I never had to talk."

"So where are the Blue Vials?"

"I brought the packs down the trail behind the smokehouse. They are well hidden in the bushes."

"I was afraid you would have to stay longer." Laura put her arms around him. "I'm glad you are back!"

Addy and Laura went to the forward deck.

"Jeffery said they are watching very closely, looking for spies, and that I should get out before someone brought me to one of the Few."

I was comforted knowing the opposition was still working in the compound.

The code key began to click. BB AT CAMP STOP ALL IS WELL STOP SAFE JOURNEYS STOP

BE SAFE STOP

I rang for Slow. "Finn, take us to ten thousand. We don't want these guys hearing the airscrews."

When we were high and to the east of the compound, I rang for Flank.

166

Chapter 30

It was cold even though the sun was making the decks of the *Cloud Queen* glisten. We came lower, and Addy and Laura took turns at the telescope looking for the *White Dove*. When the sun drew high, they spotted her, plowing along miles to the east.

We took turns studying the ship. The propellers lacked the size to move the great balloons through the air at any speed. She had made no more than twenty miles since her launch. Apparently the Supreme Navarch had not learned much about airships.

TO SILVER SEED STOP FIRST BALLOON SHIP WHITE DOVE IS MAKING SLOW PROGRESS TOWARD DENVER STOP NO HURRY STOP IT IS MOVING LIKE A TURTLE STOP

GOING TO CAMP TO TOP OFF FUEL

"Do we wait in the air or put down somewhere to save fuel?" I wondered.

"We have plenty of fuel," Finn said. "With the tank in the breezeway, we can fly for three weeks. I would like to empty that tank and get rid of it."

The tedious part of this battle was the waiting. Laura and Addy gave me a lesson in knife throwing.

TO CLOUD QUEEN STOP CELESTIAL CITY HAS SIGHTED WHITE DOVE STOP GREAT JUBILATION STOP

MR

We began scanning the horizon. Because we were not sure of the altitude, we started low, watching toward the east. We then raised the telescope a few degrees and scanned again. We saw birds and clouds but no ship.

On the third day, we spotted her. She lifted out of a cloud, deck after deck appearing with lights glimmering. My stomach became more uneasy with each moment.

"Oh, my," Laura gasped. She began to count decks as the ship rose from the cloud.

Finn took a turn at the telescope and then snorted. "That is like trying to fly the Eiffel Tower! I believe he is suspending the whole mass from above the dome."

167

"What I don't understand is there were no propellers at the compound. How is it flying?" I refocused. "There was no glass dome! Is it the same structure?"

Finn's voice became resigned. "He built it under the hatch in the mountain, flew it with the electric cord over to the Palace, connected it, and took off."

Why didn't I realize that? After all this time, the magnitude of the Supreme Navarch's plans dizzied the mind.

Finn continued. "I believe propellers slide out from the sides. He has used some sort of shiny metal. It must be fairly light." Finn went to his cabin and returned with a book. "I have been reading about aluminum. It's very new—light and strong. The Supreme Navarch must have perfected pouring and shaping this metal."

The second workshop.

"So, it is lighter than it looks?" Laura asked.

"It's tremendously heavy but much lighter than if made of steel or wood."

"I don't think he has seen us," I decided. "Without the telescope, they are just a speck in the sky, and we are tiny by comparison. But let's go up. I don't want to take any chance of him knowing we are here."

We leveled off at eight thousand feet and matched the speed of their ship.

"Faster than I thought," Finn remarked. "He must be using a tremendous amount of oil to run all those propellers."

Laura leaned over the front drop. "He has seen us! Finn, take us higher. Fast! Up fast!"

I got the spyglass and looked down the rear drop port. Tiny specks were coming out of the sides of the *Celestial City* like flies off a horse flicking her shoulder.

Bells rang, the *Cloud Queen* began to come about, and the propellers churned faster and faster.

Finn studied his gauges. "José, bring the pressure to one-seventy."

I went to the speaking tube. "Set up a zig-zag. No pattern. Laura, how much time do we have?"

168

"They are rising quickly, and they fly fast." She leaned back over the drop port. "They are two-man pods. Cigar-shaped—with some sort of gun on the front."

I went to the speaking tube. "Addy, work your way north."

"Two are almost level with us!" Laura cried.

"Some sort of large bullet whizzed past," echoed in the speaking tube.

"More altitude! We have to keep the hull between us and them." My ears were already beginning to ache. Finn pulled the lift lever to the maximum.

Too high. "What if we dropped suddenly? Fall?"

Finn watched out the back drop port. "I am pretty sure they could fall as fast as we can."

The sound of wood splintering was sickening, and from the back hall, I could see a shot had torn through the upper structure of the left propeller cage. The airscrew continued to turn. *I'm not losing this ship.*

"Finn, let us down as fast as you dare. They are trying to take out our propellers."

The drop was sudden. It felt as if I would lose my footing.

"They are above us," Addy called down. "I think that surprised them."

I slipped out the engine room door and looked up. There were five cigar shaped pods above us.

José came out with three rifles. He lay down on his back and began firing his rifle. "Trying for the propeller."

Laura and I took our places next to José. I worked the Winchester lever with careful precision. Addy was firing from the pilothouse.

"The gun on the front does not have much swing—cannot shoot up or down," José said. "When they are level with us, they will shoot again."

The little pods were falling fast, gaining on us. Two headed to our port. A driver peered over the side, and the craft began an arc toward us. A small chimney boiled black smoke.

I rolled over and crawled into the engine room. "Finn, go back up. Now!"

169

"Good shot," Addy called through the speaking tube. "A propeller blade is wobbling."

Rifles continued to fire in rapid succession as the *Cloud Queen* rose. I went from fearing I would float off the deck to being pushed against the boards. The *Cloud Queen's* timbers groaned in protest.

Laura, José, and I staggered to the breezeway, and flipped up the deck shield. I lay on my stomach, chancing a look.

José began to reload. "One to our port. Co-pilot has a rifle."

I shot once before something hit behind me. Oil dribbled down the side of the spare fuel tank.

"José, take my gun."

I crawled to the door of the engine room. "They've punctured the spare fuel tank!"

In the breezeway, Laura was reloading for José. Only one pod was to our port, the pilot's head above a shroud. Black goggles covered his eyes.

The second man stood, holding a longbow sideways. My shot missed. He was back behind his cowling, but a flaming arrow struck the railing, its shaft vibrating. Fire flickered around the tip. The bowman was lighting another arrow when a shot rang. He slumped over the cowling. José shot two more times at the pilot, and the pod dropped below us.

I worked the arrow left and right until it came out of the wood. The oiled wad fell away.

Finn inspected the hole in the tank. "Laura, use a demijohn cork." He ran back to the engine room.

We were rising faster than the pods, and my left ear felt as if it might burst.

Laura came with the cork, but it was too large. I whipped out my knife and whittled at the cork. When it fit the hole, I hammered it in with the butt of my knife.

"They're below us," Finn called. "Come to the engine room."

Laura and I gathered the rifles and shells and followed José.

"One is back!" José shot from the front drop port.

I glanced at the altitude gauge. We were at twelve thousand feet and climbing.

170

"One has a damaged propeller, and another's heading back to the mother ship. Three are following us up," Laura reported.

José fired again. "One is under us, Finn. Down! Down! Slam him."

Finn closed the lift lever, and an awful grinding noise rumbled under us, and then all was quiet. José went to the side door, shooting.

"They are following us down," Laura cautioned. "Ten seconds or so."

Finn had opened the lift lever, and I felt my feet pushing into the deck and staggered sideways. "The *Cloud Queen* is quick to rise and fall, but these small pods react much faster."

"Two toward the stern," Laura called, "rising fast."

José and I went to the propeller cages and each took a side. It was clear that they wanted to disable our propellers. I held my breath and squeezed the trigger. My shot hit near the rear of a pod, and fluid began to be whipped into the air by the pod's propeller. I held my breath again and took careful aim. The shot hit the rudder, and it flopped sideways.

"The rudder, José, aim for the rudder."

"No need. Mine has a jammed propeller."

We began to sink again, and the *Cloud Queen* was coming around. Addy had the rudders hard over. One pod retreated, falling away fast and making great speed toward the *Celestial City*.

Our fall stopped, and the deck became solid under my feet.

"Will, José, to the bow," Addy yelled out the pilothouse door. "Finn's going to scoop up a disabled pod!"

Wood splintered as we reached the front deck. The pod skidded and stopped against the starboard light pole, narrowly missing the front gangplank. The railing lay in pieces on the front deck. José held a pistol to the head of a blond man who poked his head out of the pod. I recognized him as one of the Chosen Few. He opened a flap to make room for his shoulders and crawled out.

"What about the other pods?" I yelled.

"One is behind us but aimed the other way," Laura called. "He has lost his steering. One has gone down."

"Down as destroyed?"

"No. He controlled his descent."

171

"Come! We have a prisoner!"

Laura reached for José's pistol, and they took the man away. The second Freebooter was dead.

After the pilot was out, the two-man ship teetered, and I put my full weight on the front.

José came with rope. We lashed the pod to the pole, making sure knots.

A large shell crossed the bow, making a "whooff-whooff" sound.

Addy came to the side of the pilothouse. "Will! Shots from the *Celestial City*. They have big guns!" The ship came about.

I moved quickly to the engine room, noting the propellers were still running at Flank speed. "Large guns! They can shoot almost straight up and, I assume, down."

"We will have to move up and down to elude their aim," Finn said. "No pattern."

We fell and held on to the railing around the engine as the *Cloud Queen* plummeted. The flywheel spokes were a blur. Finn pulled the lift lever, and we started to climb. I had staggered halfway up the stairs when we began to fall again.

In the pilothouse, Laura scanned the skies behind us with the spyglass. Addy spun the wheel hard over.

"Any sign of more pods coming?"

"No. One of the two left is halfway back to his ship. He is beginning to sink."

I worked my jaw. The *Celestial City* floated at quite a distance below us. They gained altitude but not as quickly as the *Cloud Queen*. I went to the speaking tube. "Finn, keep climbing. I don't think there is much chance they will hit us at this distance."

"Straighten us out, Addy," Laura said.

The propellers were running faster than Flank, and I knew Finn must have a terrific head of steam. "How much pressure?" I called down.

"One-seventy. Two-hundred-eighty revolutions."

"Can she do it?"

"Either that or get blown out of the sky. Those big guns can penetrate our deck!"

172

I found Laura on the deck behind the pilothouse. Addy had the back window open.

Laura cupped her hands. "Two shots—hard aport."

The distant thuds of the guns were impressive. "How long before you heard the report?"

"Four seconds. I think we are out of the worst of it. Straighten us out, Addy, straight north again."

"Finn, level off," I said into the speaking tube. "Let the pressure drop some. Let's not damage anything."

"Throttling back."

Laura watched for another ten minutes. "I think we are safe." She handed me the glass. "They have stopped shooting."

The enemy ship appeared small at this distance. I couldn't tell if they were trying to give chase, but I knew we were the faster ship. I handed the spyglass back. "I'm going below."

I caught a whiff of smoke coming from the front drop port. I leaned over, drawing a long breath through my nose. A second sniff stung my nose. I cupped my hands and cried, "Fire! Fire!"

Back at the port, I poked my head down as far as possible. No flame was visible, but the smoke smelled of burning oil.

José joined me with a bucket of water.

I pointed down. "They must have shot a flaming arrow at the hull."

"Maybe more than one," he said. "You could let me down in a sling like we did when we dynamited the side of the mountain."

"Hard to fight fire from a sling," Finn said.

I made a quick decision. "We have to land—hover to see what is burning and what damage has been done."

I stood. "Laura, I want you in the pilothouse. Finn, start down."

173

Chapter 31

José and I watched for open ground through the drop ports. The area was heavily wooded.

We agreed on a meadow. From the lush trail of grass meandering through the field, we reasoned there was a stream. Occasionally, smoke curled into the engine room.

I stood. "Stop the air screws. Let down the landing cable."

Finn eased the ship down, stopping a few feet from the ground.

"Do not flatten me," José quipped. He slipped through the port and landed lightly on his feet.

He went forward and brought back an arrow, the wad of hemp still burning lazily. "Only one. Hand me the bucket."

Finn brought a second bucket, and I started to hand it down.

"No need," José said. "Only a small area, and the flames were gone when I got back. I doused it to be safe." He gripped the edge of the port and snaked himself up in one quick move.

Finn pulled the lift lever, and we hovered at twenty feet. "Will, Laura says to go to the bow."

Addy crouched, the telescope trained at a sharp angle. "The *Celestial City*."

"Any sign of them launching pods?"

"No."

"Maybe they will think we crashed?" I hoped.

We followed Finn to the captured pod and lifted the dead man out. "I don't think we have time to bury him," Finn said.

José wrapped the man in an old sheet and dropped the body over the side. "May your soul find peace," he said and crossed himself.

At the tiny pod, Finn opened a square hatch to reveal a small steam engine. "This whole ship is made of tin—to reduce weight. No wonder we can damage rudder and propeller so easily."

"Do you think one of these things could come this far?" I asked.

"It is doubtful, and they would never make it back; the fuel tank is small. I'm studying the water recovery system, and I believe these ships were designed to do just what they did. They are meant for quick attack. That is why the two remaining pods turned back."

"Like hornets," Addy said.

"Good name. Hornets. Good at the quick attack."

"Before you go, I want everyone to see this." Finn pointed to a small radiator under the rudder. "This cools the steam to be used as makeup water. It is very sophisticated—little copper tubes with these fins. If we hit this, the makeup water will escape."

"I was shooting at the rudder and saw something spraying in the propeller wind."

Finn nodded. "The engine wouldn't run long after he began losing water. Probably why the one decided to land."

"Finn, if you're sure nothing is going to explode in the Hornet, let's get underway. Addy, don't let the *Celestial City* out of your sight—José and I will have a chat with our prisoner."

We went behind the rear cabins. José had done his usual superb job of securing the man.

The blond fellow squinted, a smug look on his face. "I know you. You were on the kitchen crew."

I gave no sign of recognition.

"When you were told to kill the traitor, I watched you. I knew you were a rat."

I looked at José. "See to the engine." I made my voice harsh and uncaring.

José stepped away.

"Yes, I was one of the unenlightened. I am the captain of this ship." I stepped closer. "I came to the compound and was working to destroy the Supreme Navarch's mission. Then Sid—" I put a simple look on my face. "Then Sid led a Passing of the Vial. I now understand that it is good to support the Supreme Navarch. I must defeat the opposition. At all cost."

The man looked unconvinced.

"I'm to take the Blue Vial today—to reinforce my orders. If I take the Vial in front of you, will you believe me?"

The man looked away.

175

I went to the forward cabin. "I think I can convince this guy that I am under the influence of the gas. Please get me the fake Blue Vial."

Addy was back in a moment with the bottle.

"We are sure this does nothing?"

"Professor Gruber has tried it on himself. He said it stinks like the real stuff but has no effect."

I put the vial in my coat pocket and returned to the prisoner. I pulled the vial out and put my hand on the stopper. "How do I know you won't give me a command? Sid gave me commands for this mission. We cannot interrupt this chance to destroy the opposition."

"I won't countermand your orders."

I opened the vial, took a big whiff, and put a vacant look on my face. "It is good to support the Supreme Navarch."

"Scratch you palm if I say peach."

I was disappointed the prisoner did not trust me more, but his command was simple. I slowly returned my focus to him. "Convinced? Want a whiff?"

"You are a peach."

I absentmindedly scratched my palm.

His lip curled into a partial smile. "Why did you fight the *Celestial City* and the Stingers?"

With no emotion, I said, "I am to take out the opposition's big ship. I must bide my time. The silver ship that destroyed many of the Supreme Navarch's glorious ships must be eliminated. It is good to take out the big ship of the opposition." I slowly turned to the Freebooter, leaning close. "The better question is, why did the *Celestial City* attack this ship? Is Sid not on the *Celestial City*?"

"Sid is there, but he said nothing about you."

I turned quickly toward him. "I am not sure I can trust you." I raised my voice. "Why would they put this ship in danger if its mission is to get close to their silver ship and destroy it?"

The man shook his blond head as if explaining something to a small child. "You are an underling. Do not question me. I am one of the Chosen Few. I am one of The Twelve!"

"Captain Will," José called. "You are needed in the pilothouse."

176

"In a moment." I turned to the prisoner. "You must say nothing. Do not give me away. Give me away, and we both will be dealt with. I don't want to be tossed overboard. It is a long way down."

I slipped the vial into my coat pocket and stalked up the hallway between the back cabins.

José stood in front of the controls in the engine room. "Finn wants you at the bow."

I handed José the vial. "Please give this to Addy. I don't think my plan had much effect on our prisoner."

On the front deck Finn pointed inside the Hornet, showing me the rather flimsy frame. "The rear man tends the boiler. The pilot controls the ship and, of course, the gun. But here is the real gem." Finn pointed to a code keypad. "Tuned to a new frequency. The Supreme Navarch has been quite chatty."

I smiled. "And?"

"Mostly demanding that the Stingers—that's what he calls these small ships—Stinger's destroy us. A few minutes ago, ordering this ship to report."

"Any chance we could use their own gun against them?"

"Perhaps we could lash the Stinger down in front and use the gun. The problem is ammunition. They only carried fifty shells, and this one had used half of that."

"Is the gun worth fiddling with?"

"A breach loader. Also hastily made. The designs are good, but the workmanship is shoddy, and they cut corners." Finn stood and stretched his back. "It's strange that the equipment used by the Freebooters is not well made."

"The whole time I was in the compound, the Supreme Navarch pushed the men to work faster."

"These things are a death trap." Finn turned. "I'll send José."

Laura called from the deck above, "We are at six thousand feet. Only about a thousand higher than the ground."

"Good. Let's run at Dead Slow. No sense getting too far away from that hulk. Best to keep it in sight."

José came and put his hands on his hips. "You want me to fix the front railing?"

177

"Leave it. We may try to use the Stinger's gun. It's aimed in a cockeyed direction, but who knows?"

José gave the Stinger a light kick. "The prisoner is one of the Chosen Few. Why would he be sent on a suicide mission?"

"Maybe he was to lead the others. Or—maybe the Supreme Navarch is dissatisfied with him. He has sudden changes of mind and heart, according to his lights." I thought for a moment. "Let me have another go at him."

When I reached the prisoner, I grumbled, "Fools can't do anything for themselves."

The man half-closed one eye.

"It is *your* turn to gain *my* trust. I know you are one of the Chosen Few." I leaned forward. "The Stingers are not built for long sustained flights, and the pilots of Stingers are expendable. Why were you sent?"

"There are times when the Supreme Navarch is ill. He makes sudden, rash decisions. They are not good for him and sometimes not good for the glorious work. As his number one, I try to counsel him. It's my job."

His number one has fallen from the little man's favor. "Is counsel part of your commands when the Blue Vial is passed?"

"Peaches."

I scratched my palm and put a vacant look on my face. Was he avoiding something? Were the Chosen Few not under the influence of the Blue Vial? Certainly, the Navarch's paranoia would not allow anyone to be in control of their own mind.

I rubbed my eyes as if to clear my thoughts. "So why were you in the Stinger?" I pulled out my pistol. "I am not sure I can trust you. Perhaps you gave me commands when I was susceptible."

"I told you to scratch your palm when I said peaches."

I scratched my palm.

"The glorious leader and I had a disagreement, and he became displeased. I was sent on the mission."

"What is your name?"

"Svend."

"Hmm. I will be watching you, Svend. I must leave you now. It will be cold tonight. I will tell them to bring you a blanket."

Chapter 32

We sat down to a fine meal around the table in the forward cabin. Twilight turned to dark and the air was cool. Addy had lashed the wheel and made several trips to the pilothouse to true the ship. Occasionally, I heard the propellers start.

"The *Celestial City* is miles away, lit up for all to see. It's not coming closer," she reported.

"What about the man we captured?" Laura asked.

"I tried to gain his confidence by taking a sniff from the fake vial. The silly fool told me I would scratch my palm when he says peaches—so I've been scratching my palm for him."

"Is he convinced?"

"Not totally, and I'm not sure it makes any difference. The good news is that I sniffed the vial and didn't automatically do what he ordered. I feel no compulsion to scratch my palm."

"Is he of any use?"

"I doubt it, and we can't keep him with us," I said. "We don't have time to keep an eye on him."

"How many blankets does he have?"

"José took him one."

"Two," José said, "and I let him relieve himself."

Laura gave José her smile. "Thank you."

José was quick to get us back to the problem at hand. "Jail. Like before, put him in jail?"

"Mr. Salsbury," Laura said.

I had almost forgotten Mr. Salsbury was with us in Colorado. "Perfect!"

Finn put one of his charts on the table and made some measurements. "I reckon his place is no more than a couple of hours. But hard to find in the dark."

"Then we spend the night here and start in the morning?" José wondered. "Are we sure the *Celestial City* will not sneak up on us in the dark?"

"I will take the first watch," I said. "I suggest we all try to get some sleep."

179

Mr. Salsbury heard the *Cloud Queen* and waved us down. His coding was still limited. but he was a great help to us.

When we touched down, he came near. "What brings you kids here?"

"We have a prisoner tied up in the back, and we don't have the manpower to keep him with us," I said. "He is high up in the Freebooter's leadership. He must *not* escape."

Mr. Salsbury laughed. "Let me show you my system." We walked to a small barn behind the main barn. "I had a fellow try to follow me when I was getting supplies. I—well—look."

A man was chained to a stake driven deep into the ground. "I am getting to know the sheriff," Mr. Salsbury said. "He isn't crazy with the gas. I was gonna take this one down to jail—but I am sobering him up first."

"How long?" Laura asked.

"He is half in the fog and half out. Typical. Pretty ornery in the morning, and by evening he is almost his normal self."

"What's your name?" I asked.

"Brian Zigler."

"Where are you from?"

Brian thought hard. "Denver—yes, Denver. I am—was a—" He squinted. "Why should I tell you," he snarled. "You are the ones fighting the Supreme Navarch." Brian stared at the wall. "Watchmaker. I—" His chin went to his chest.

"So, can you handle one more?" I asked Mr. Salsbury.

"Of course. I have a little help. Hope you don't mind? A young buck, Charles Witt. Met him in town. He is to be trusted."

"I would like to meet him."

"He's in town, getting some gear oil Finn ordered. We buy from different places. Never too much in one place."

I shook hands with Mr. Salsbury. "Thanks. This all helps."

Salsbury turned away from the prisoners. "I am wondering. Once these men are sober, good and sober—can't they be released? When Brian is himself, all he wants to do is get back to his home. He has a wife and family."

"Let him go. He won't bother; in fact, most folks out of the fog have a true grudge against the Freebooters."

"I'm their worst enemy," Mr. Salsbury grumbled.

I looked around the shed. There were eight more stakes in the ground. "You getting ready for company, Mr. Salsbury?"

"Never hurts to be prepared. I don't have time to guard any Freebooters I take prisoner. Can't be bothered with that," he laughed.

José and Addy fixed the chain around the Chosen One's neck to the stake furthest from Brian. "That should hold him, but be careful, Mr. Salsbury."

Mr. Salsbury patted his pistol. "Always careful. Can't be too careful."

"Is your money holding out?" Finn asked.

"More than plenty. You youngsters always pay in advance and pay well. You gonna need more fuel oil? Got three hundred gallons here."

"Keep it here. But we will top off our tanks," Finn said.

We moved to the front cabin to eat lunch, and Charles Witt joined us. Both men were anxious for news about the battle.

The code key clicked. The *Silver Seed* had the *White Dove* in her sights. The *Celestial City* stood sentinel at a distance.

"We must go." I was sorry to say goodbye to Mr. Salsbury, but we launched, sailing toward the mammoth ship.

"How do we take down that monster?" Addy wondered.

"If he launches more Stingers, we could try dynamite," José said. "But they would need to be below us, and it is hard to judge the fuse length. I think it has little chance."

"How high can they go?" Addy asked.

"Good question. As high as we can. But going to high altitude takes fuel, and I don't believe they're meant to fly more than thirty minutes," Finn said.

The code key clicked slowly.

BB SID STOP CC EAST OF DENVER STOP

CLOUD QUEEN SOON ABOVE YOU STOP HOW MANY STINGERS LEFT STOP

RESTRICTED AREA STOP SL RANTING ABOUT LOSING FOUR STOP

181

GOOD STOP

SL HAS HOSTAGES STOP MAYOR DENVER STOP WIFE STOP CATHOLIC PRIEST STOP NINE TOTAL STOP

HOW DID HE CAPTURE THEM STOP CC HAS NOT BEEN NEAR DENVER STOP

FREEBOOTERS BROUGHT THEM TO COMPOUND STOP

MR

We stood around the code key. The Supreme Navarch's operations had many fingers. We had tried to monitor all that happened in the compound, and yet he had prisoners brought to him, and we missed it.

José was concerned about the Stingers, and we knew that even one was too many. I had to accept the truth; the *Cloud Queen* was no match for them. It was like batting at flies.

"And the little weasel plans to hide behind the innocent," Laura said.

The rooms of the *Cloud Queen* were warm, but outside, it was bitter cold, and we were in and out of the clouds. Finn was concerned about the ice forming on the decks, making us top-heavy. He drew up a schedule of rotating watches. We took turns with a small sledge to break up the ice and shovel it overboard.

When the *White Dove* wallowed into sight, it was twenty miles north of Denver. The area below was uninhabited. The time had come for battle.

I went to the code key. TAKE THE WHITE DOVE DOWN STOP

Laura smiled her approval.

We breathed in gasps, but I asked Finn to take us higher. My head ached, and the others probably felt the same. We went to the front and trained the telescope on the *White Dove*. It took several minutes, but Laura's sharp eyes spotted the *Silver Seed*. She moved across the sky toward the slow-moving scow. I knew she was flying at a terrific speed, but at this distance, she inched across the sky.

The *Silver Seed* slid over the *White Dove,* and the forward balloon was torn open. The ship began to founder and sink, spinning like a leaf in a whirlpool. We watched the ship fall toward the earth. The crew dropped some of the bags of blue gas in an attempt to lighten the load.

I trained the hand glass on the *Celestial City,* watching the cannon along the west side firing. They had little chance of doing any damage to the *Silver Seed.*

WELL DONE SILVER SEED STOP ONE DOWN STOP TWO MORE COMING STOP

MR STOP WILL INTERCEPT STOP

YES STOP WILL KEEP AN EYE ON CC STOP

MR DOLPH HERE TRANSLATING INTERCEPTED MESSAGES STOP

Chapter 33

Mornings were beautiful on the *Cloud Queen*. The weather had warmed, and ice was no longer a threat. We kept our distance, watching the *Celestial City*. We had worked the messages until the wee hours of the morning, splitting up the work. There were almost sixty in all, and the *Silver Seed* had sent enough to keep us busy until our eyes were bleary. But work has its rewards.

We learned the *Golden Eagle* was much closer than we thought possible, and Mary decided to keep the *Silver Seed* a few miles from the high mountains above Denver. The Supreme Navarch was livid. He railed at the captain of the *White Dove* who was still sending messages. I was relieved some of the crew survived. Under the influence of the gas they were the enemy—puppets of the Supreme Navarch.

José had been watching the horizon through the telescope, and when he joined us in the wheelhouse, he was shivering. "They are coming. The *Silver Seed* is ready to attack at any time."

I put the hand glass to my eye. The morning sun glistened off the airship. Dew gave the bags a golden sheen. The balloons had shrunk in the cold and black smoke followed the ship as the crew worked to heat the bags and run the engines.

"Will, small ships," Laura warned.

I turned the glass to the south and José went out the door. "Clever."

Two of the Stingers appeared pulling balloons. I handed the spy glass to Laura.

She studied the craft. "Are those little gondolas they are towing?"

"I think so, carrying extra water and oil." I went out on the deck in front of the wheelhouse and called down, "José, what do you make of them?"

"They can move faster than the *Cloud Queen*, but towing the balloons slows them."

Finn joined us.

"Do we go higher, or do we run?" I asked.

Finn took a long look. "The gondolas are balanced for this altitude—won't rise, so they will have to leave them."

184

"Raise the boiler pressure. Let's go up for now."

"Watch closely," Finn said. "The moment the Stingers cast off from the gondolas, they will be able to destroy." He went back and immediately we began to rise.

The pods were still some distance, but I estimated that in thirty minutes they would be able to leave their supply balloons.

The fireman worked a pump from time to time, probably moving fuel or water to the Stinger. The pilots hunkered low, their goggles making them look like large owls.

In the wheelhouse, Laura took us west. The *Silver seed* was closing on the *Golden Eagle*, and while I wanted to watch her take the *Golden Eagle* out, the Stingers were of greater concern.

"Are they rising with us?" I asked Laura.

"No. Finn's right. They will leave the balloons and supplies behind when they attack."

"If they leave them close enough we might destroy the balloons when we descend."

"Will!" José pounded up the stairs. "The first Stinger is coming."

I went down with José and we leaned out over the bow, holding tight to the right light pole. A Stinger was flying fast toward us, rising rapidly.

I signaled for Laura to take us down and felt my feet grow light on the boards.

Addy was at the steam gun, and Laura turned us toward the Stinger.

We plummeted past the Stinger and a shell tore into the wheelhouse shield. Laura waved she was alright, but I could see a large dent in the metal shield.

When we were level with the balloon carrying Stinger supplies, Addy shot twice, a cloud of vapor rising in the air. As we fell past, a man in the gondola shot back.

The Stinger above us was dropping fast and José took careful aim and shot twice. The Stinger continued to drop.

"Second Stinger is loose!" Laura called. "Second Stinger is loose!" She went back in the wheelhouse, and I felt the boards press against my feet. It was clear we could rise faster than the little crafts.

We rose past the first Stinger, and José shot once.

I rested my rifle on my leg. Trying to hit the balloons at this distance, as we went higher and higher, was probably a waste of ammunition.

My ears were aching, and I was starting to shiver. "How much time do you think we get from each climb?"

"Just minutes. They rise with us and when we can go no higher they have us."

I ran to the engine room. The gauge needle was at its limit of twelve-thousand feet. "Finn, what do you think? Do we keep climbing?"

He was watching the Stinger from the front drop port. "The *Cloud Queen* can stand it, if we can."

I yawned, and I steadied my rifle on the back drop port. "Level off."

The Stinger was staying under the *Cloud Queen*. "Do you think he knows we have ports underneath?" I asked.

"I don't know. He is rising under us. Perhaps his plan is to pop out one side as he comes close."

"Don't shoot. I'll watch the boiler and you get José."

The Stinger was about one hundred feet below and lurking like a cat under the bow of the *Cloud Queen*. It was hard to get the angle I needed for a clean shot. The second stinger came into view. José joined me.

"I think they plan to slip up beneath us. They may not have noticed the drop ports. They probably want to pop up and attack."

"One on each side," José said.

"I think I see an angle. When they rise to our level, they will have to fly out from under us. That forward gun won't be pointed at us until they turn. That is our moment."

"*Silver Seed* closing on the *Golden Eagle*," Laura called.

I went out and trained the hand scope on the *Golden Eagle*. The *Silver Seed* closed the distance like molasses dripping from a bottle.

The *Silver Seed* cut the forward balloon as before, and the *Golden Eagle* spun in. I went to the engine room.

"Here they come!" José looked up from the range finder.

The angle remained bad and they were rising fast.

"Down, Finn, down!"

186

Almost immediately we began to fall. All hope of the *Cloud Queen* striking one of the Stingers was lost.

Several pistol shots were fired from the pods and bullets whined off the shields. One pod managed to turn, and a loud crack came from above us.

"Laura! Laura!" Finn called into the speaking tube.

There was no answer, and I took the stairs two at a time.

Laura was lying in the wheelhouse, blood oozing from a wound on her forehead. Panic overtook me, and I pulled her up. It didn't look like a gun shot.

I laid her back. "Laura is hurt! Laura is hurt," I called toward the speaking tube. I rang for Full and spun the wheel to port. The Stingers were dropping with us but not quite as quickly as we fell.

José's rifle was firing in steadied even shots. Someone was shooting from the other side of the *Cloud Queen*.

Finn came up and carried Laura down. I spun the wheel to starboard and rang for Flank. It took a minute or so for the Engine Order Telegraph to answer.

I turned the wheel back to starboard.

I saw a Stinger above us, on the port side. Vapor was boiling out of the rear of the pod. José had done his job with his rifle, but the Stinger's propeller was still spinning. On the other side Addy was firing steadily, in slow cadence.

I was mad with fear for Laura, but began spinning the wheel to port. We had to either destroy or escape the Stingers.

187

Chapter 34

We were climbing again and I turned the wheel to starboard. The *Cloud Queen* groaned in protest. Wood splintered over the Engine Order Telegraph. On the bow, José threw small logs with dynamite lashed to them. They arched high. Almost immediately charges began exploding. The *Cloud Queen* rocked with the concussions as we started to turn away from the Stingers.

A single chuff came from the steam gun. The balloon of the supply gondola whipped but the shell did not hit squarely. The bag was unharmed. Addy reloaded and tried a second shot.

All four Stingers turned toward their supply balloons. The damaged craft seemed to make fair speed and the smoke had disappeared. I brought the wheel to center.

"How is Laura?!" I called into the speaking tube. "How is she?"

"She was not shot. She has a bruised head."

I lashed the wheel and ran down the stairs. Addy met me.

"I missed. I had one chance when we turned."

"They are refueling. We have some time," I said. "Tell José to head away from their supplies. We must make them fly further from their fuel."

José took the pilothouse steps three at a time.

Laura was on our bed. Addy put a damp cloth on her forehead. Laura was pale.

"The bullet broke a hinge off the shield and it swung and hit her in the forehead. I think it is only a bruise." She lifted the cloth and there was a knot growing above Laura's left eye.

"I'm awake," she whispered. She started to sit up.

I reached for her hand. "No. Lie back. They are refueling. We have some time."

She sighed.

"Stay with her. If she begins to feel better, come forward. We are in the battle of our lives."

In the engine room the pressure gauge showed we were near the limit. The propellers were chopping the thin air. I went out and

188

tested our speed with my hand. We were flying fast for the *Cloud Queen*, but she was not built for speed.

José called down, "They are still refueling."

Addy came up the hallway. "Laura's OK. Dizzy."

Relief flooded my whole body. "Thanks. Go up and send José down."

Finn and I went to the stern. The Stinger's supply balloons were receding into the distance, but they were still within striking range.

"They like to come up from the bottom. We need to foul their propellers," Finn said. "A net or something."

"Blankets?" It was foolish, but I was casting at straws.

"I have light line in the back. Perhaps we go fishing." José brushed the dust off his hat and put it back on. "Maybe we put a weight on the line, drop it and tangle the propeller?"

It was worth a try. "Get it ready."

In the engine room, Finn handed me a message from the *Silver Seed*. SHIP DOWN STOP THIRD SHIP CLOSE STOP DO WE COME TO YOU STOP

The question in my mind was, do we wait for the Stingers, hoping they come from below, or do we have the *Silver Seed* come to help?

Addy called down on the speaking tube. "Another Stinger, towing supplies."

"Tell the *Silver Seed* to come. I don't think we can survive four of those contraptions again." I went to the wheelhouse.

The *Silver Seed* became a slit as she turned toward us. I knew they would fly fast, but we were very much alone for the next half hour.

It took another fifteen minutes for the first Stinger to leave the supply balloons. The damaged Stinger flew toward the *Celestial City*.

The second Stinger left the balloons and made great speed. To encourage an approach from below, I had Finn take us up.

In the engine room, I put a box of shells near both drop ports and leaned the rifles near.

José was coiling his line neatly behind the rear drop port. I checked the rifles and my pistol.

189

We watched as the Stinger took its place under the *Cloud Queen*. "Level off, Finn," I said.

As was his custom, José waited patiently. He had a gear tied to the end of his line.

The Stinger eased up below us, its propeller turning slowly, keeping pace with the *Cloud Queen*.

I took measurements with the range finder. "Seventy-five."

The pod was almost directly below the forward drop port. "Move to Flank!"

The propellers spun up and the pod began to drop behind. The size of the *Cloud Queen* may have given the pilot a sense of security because he let the Stinger slip to our stern.

José stood calmly, a slight smile on his face. With one casual move he dropped the gear and let the line play out through his gloves.

Coil after coil rose off the deck, straightened and slid through José's fingers. I remembered seeing a picture of a man fishing through a hole in the ice.

José grabbed the rope, wrapped it around his left hand and pulled. The rope went tight and he staggered toward the drop. Addy and I grabbed him and for a moment we were motionless.

"Let go, Friend, let go."

José got his feet under him, and with a tremendous grunt, he gave a mighty pull on the rope and it inched toward us.

José took a step back, let the rope slacken and then pulled.

"You have his propeller snarled," Finn reported.

"Come to me, big fish," José growled. He jerked the rope again and the pod swung around, its rudder toward us.

José made a quick tie, and I peeked over the edge.

The Stinger tried to break the rope by dropping but was hanging at an awkward angle. The boiler man opened his hatch, crawled out and sawed on the rope with his knife. He lost his grip, clawed at the pod surface and fell away.

The driver turned awkwardly in his seat, a pistol coming up. A single shot from José, and the man slumped back into the cockpit.

"I want that Stinger," Finn growled. "It's a valuable weapon."

I went to the speaking tube. "How close are the other Stingers? In minutes?"

"Maybe ten," Addy said.

"*Silver Seed*?"

"She is pulling alongside."

I nodded to Finn. "Tell them what to do."

PULL SLOWLY UNDER THE POD HANGING BELOW US STOP COME UP UNTIL IT IS RESTING ON YOUR UPPER DECK OVER THE CABINS STOP TEN MINUTES TIME STOP

I went to the speaking tube. "Addy, keep a close watch on the Stingers. Remember that gun can shoot farther than a rifle."

We watched as the *Silver Seed* moved into position. The periscope swiveled as did the propulsion tubes. The ship was beautiful.

Nathan's head appeared in the rear hatch, and he stepped out onto the upper framework. He had a rope tied to his waist as there was no railing or footholds. His shirt ruffled in the breeze created by the propulsion tubes.

"Finn, stop the airscrews." The nose of the Stinger touched the *Silver Seed*.

Nathan made his way to the front of the Stinger and checked the pilot. He looked up, shook his head, and wrestled the man out. He carried the body easily to the side of the *Silver Seed*, paused for a moment, and dumped the corpse.

Back at the pod he lifted the nose. The periscope swiveled, and the *Silver Seed* slowly rose until the Stinger was lying on the upper sheeting.

"I'm going down," Finn said. He tied a rope around his waist.

I clicked the telegraph, and the *Silver Seed* eased up below us.

"We have five minutes to get that pod aboard," Finn said. "I can fly it. If it has no steam, I will stay on the *Silver Seed*."

I nodded my OK. We were all taking big chances.

I hung over the front port and watched as Finn's feet touched the *Silver Seed*. Nathan came over, and they had a quick conference. Nathan unsheathed his knife and began untangling the propeller.

Finn quickly climbed into the rear seat of the Stinger and worked a lever. A steam cloud came out of the small vapor tube and then began flowing in puffs. Finn made an adjustments and the pod lifted off the deck. The propeller tried to turn, the blade hitting the rudder frame.

Nathan started to bend the propeller blade, but Finn put out his hand.

Nathan made a quick cut, and the line around Finn's waist fell free. The Pod floated, and the *Silver Seed* dropped away.

The *Cloud Queen* made a tight turn. The Stinger hovered in the inside of the circle ten feet away.

"Two minutes!" Addy called from the wheelhouse door.

José tossed a rope to Finn. Finn caught it and nodded. José gently pulled the rope, hand over hand.

"Time is about up!" Addy's voice was hoarse.

When we could reach the pod we pulled it to us and walked it forward. It floated eerily in our hands. I could feel the mass of the thing as we maneuvered it along the side of the deck. José backed into the breezeway.

The pod settled to the deck, Finn scrambling out.

José made his way to the engine room, and immediately the deck pressed under my feet. Fifty feet higher than the closest Stinger, we leveled off.

Chapter 35

The *Silver Seed* rushed toward the closest Stinger. I went to the front deck.

The forward gun on the Stinger puffed smoke several times and the pilot started to descend but not soon enough. The *Silver Seed*'s blade swung down and caught the pod midships. The pod rolled sideways, steam and smoke billowing out, and it fell away.

THIRD SHIP DRAWING CLOSE TO CITY STOP MUST INTERCEPT AND DESTROY STOP

I tapped GO and went to the breezeway.

True to Finn's nature, he was still fiddling with the Stinger's steam engine with only thoughts of the mechanical. "Finn! Get to the engine room! We're fighting a Stinger!"

In the pilothouse I went to the wheel. "Go below, use a rifle!"

The Stinger was below and rising fast, the crew crouching low. The little ship came level with the *Cloud Queen,* swinging toward us. José, Addy, and I fired with precision, intent on keeping the crew from putting their heads up. Once again José's accuracy paid off, and vapor trailed in the propeller turbulence.

A loud shot popped. Addy was in the dead Stinger lashed to the light pole. The craft was canted on the deck, but undeterred Addy tossed the casing out and fired again.

The pod turned sluggishly, its bow coming around.

I hauled on the wheel, turning the *Cloud Queen* to give Addy a better angle.

After the third shot, the enemy pilot began to descend rapidly. I thought the ship was losing power, but the descent was planned. I supposed even the indoctrinated had their limits when it came to life and death.

I trained the hand scope on them. The little ship slipped into a small glade and the men clambered out. *They won't bother us now. They may find water and be able to fly, but their range will be limited.*

Addy and José scanned the skies for the fourth Stinger.

I went to the stairs, intent on checking on Laura, and met Addy. "Quick thinking, Kid. Good shooting!"

193

"I missed."

Finn looked up from the Stinger. "Only one propeller blade is bent, but I believe we can salvage this. José can help me straighten it."

"Finn, you can't keep leaving the engine room."

"I just came for a moment. We are rising and running at half."

"Do you think we can use it to attack the *Celestial City*?"

"Or fight any pods that come our way."

José came from the bow. "No Stingers in sight. Finn—the propeller wings are bolted on. I think we can use two from the wrecked Stinger on the bow."

"Good thinking. I will leave you to it. I need to work on the boiler on this one. I believe I can double our range if not more."

I fought the desire to order Finn to the engine room. Instead I went to the main controls. When I was sure all was well, I eased the levitation lever to stop our climb.

I leaned toward the speaking tube. "Addy, I'm going to check on Laura."

Laura was lying quietly on our bed. "I'm OK, really. Just dizzy when I move my head.

I pushed her curls back and inspected the red knot just below her hairline. "Well, good thing we humans have hard heads."

"Are you saying I have a hard head?" Her eyes twinkled. "Treading on thin ice, Mister."

I put my hand on her shoulder. Neither eye was dilated. "I love you."

"And I love you."

We were hovering, the *Celestial City* distant in the afternoon sun. Addy had lashed the wheel and was tending the engines. I helped José unbolt the propeller blades when Addy approached.

"Will? José? Sorry. There's been trouble. The *Silver Seed* has been damaged. The balloon ship went down, but a Stinger was there. They hit one of the propeller tubes. The ship cannot be driven straight."

In the engine room, the code key was clicking. The Stinger had been destroyed.

"How?"

"When they were hit, they went up fast. Nathan was in the rifle pod and shot both the pilot and the fireman. They went down."

Finn joined us.

Addy gestured toward the clicking key. "They can fly, almost sideways and are retreating from the area in case there are more Stingers. I'll be in the pilothouse."

Finn was deep in thought. "The one air tube will tow them sideways. I am not sure how fast they can fly."

NATHAN INSPECTED STOP MOTOR NOT DAMAGED STOP TUBE DENTED BY LARGE SHELL STOP PROPELLER CANNOT TURN STOP IN TIME WE CAN REPAIR STOP

We're on our own.

The *Silver Seed* reported that the *Celestial City* was on course to return to the compound. Dolph was translating the messages quickly. Apparently he had made a wheel that could be turned to the offset, and Mary was becoming good at translating without the wheel.

"We must plan carefully. The *Celestial City* must be stopped. If it gets back to the compound, even if we disable it, we are back to where we started. The Supreme Navarch has hidden there for almost twenty years, and I am sure he has engines of destruction we haven't discovered."

My stomach growled. "We can fly much faster than that scow. Let's take a few minutes to eat and think," I said. "I will check on Laura."

Laura was sitting up when I came in, and held up one hand. "I know, but I really am doing better."

"Are you still dizzy?"

"Yes, but not as bad. I am not sick to my stomach—in fact, I'm getting hungry."

I checked her eyes. *Pupils look fine.*

"OK, let's see how you do standing."

195

She stood. "I got whacked in the head, not shot."

Arm around her waist, I walked her to the front cabin. "At least sit down—please."

In the wheelhouse, Addy stood at the wheel, the hand glass trained on the *Celestial City*.

"Lash the wheel and come down. We all need to eat and rest. We must be strong for what we have before us."

Finn insisted on finishing improvements to the Stinger's condenser. He worked quickly with the torch, while José tightened the last of the bolts on the propeller.

They were shivering. "Alright, enough for now." I pulled on Finn's arm. "Inside. Let's pretend for a moment that we are normal people."

I went to the wheelhouse to keep us aimed toward the *Celestial City*. I watched the evening sky with the hand scope for several minutes. The air was clear with no sign of Stingers. I lashed the wheel again, went to the engine room, and set the propellers to Slow.

In the forward cabin the wood stove was warm and the room smelled heavenly. I held out my hand, watching my fingers tremble. I couldn't remember when we had last eaten.

José and Addy put the food on the table. Laura jumped up to help, and I insisted that she sit in a chair and rest.

"So, Finn, can you fly the Stinger?" she asked.

"I believe so. I will hover in the breezeway until I am certain."

"We could go down for a test flight. If you fail, no sense falling thousands of feet," Addy said.

"True." Finn treated us to one of his rare laughs.

The code key began to click.

SID TO WILL STOP SID TO WILL STOP SORRY STOP FIRST TIME SAFE TO USE TRANSMITTER STOP SL IS FUMING STOP HE STANDS ON THE BRIDGE AND SCREAMS STOP

WILL HERE STOP GOOD TO HEAR YOU ARE SURVIVING STOP HOW MANY STINGERS ARE LEFT ON THE CC STOP

196

I AM GUESSING ONE STOP DAMAGED BUT MANAGED TO RETURN STOP IT IS BEING FIXED STOP

In the next few minutes we found that the *Celestial City* had twelve crew members plus the Supreme Navarch. Sid and Sam were the only two who were part of the resistance. There were also ten innocent hostages on board.

Sid told us the hostages were kept on the third level, in the interior of the ship, before his transmission was cut short.

SN IN TOP DOME ST was the last we heard.

We sat in silence.

"Finn, can you get me to the top dome?"

Laura started to protest and then bit her lip.

"Yes. If there is only one Stinger, I think we can draw it out. While it is fighting with us, we take the captured Stinger to the *Celestial City*."

"What about the *Celestial City's* guns?"

"I have been studying those guns. The ship carries heavy cannon, not made to fight Stingers." Finn paused. "We stand a chance."

"José, if we miss the Stinger, how will you take it down?"

"I am going to turn the damaged Stinger toward the front. Between the steam cannon and the Stinger gun, we can do it."

"We will need some shells with us, and you will need some here."

"It is your decision."

"I don't think so. We have to think carefully."

"Half and half?" José mused.

"Two thirds for the *Cloud Queen*. One third for the Stinger I fly. We may not need more than a shot or two. We cannot risk hitting the innocent."

"I don't want to risk losing you or Finn," Laura said.

"And we don't want to risk losing the *Cloud Queen*."

The keypad chattered a quick message. BB TOMORROW MORNING SLEEPING POWDERS IN CC CREW FOOD STOP

José handed me a pack in the breezeway. "Lengths of light line you will need to tie Freebooters. I fastened a hook on the side of the Stinger."

197

"Tomorrow morning we will attack from the east, just as the sun rises. I want them squinting."

Chapter 36

I rubbed ice from the tiny windshield. My hands were clammy in my gloves. My job was to drive the Stinger and shoot. Finn climbed into the second seat to operate the boiler and engine. We had taken our antidote pills.

We moved slowly away from the *Cloud Queen*. When we were halfway to the huge ship, Finn shut down the propeller, and we waited.

"There," I pointed. A Stinger moved away from the fourth deck of the *Celestial City*. *Why aren't the cannon shooting?*

"I am going to Full," Finn said.

The enemy Stinger closed rapidly. When it was fifty yards away, I made two shots with the gun. It was a clumsy weapon, and it shook the entire craft. I watched the other pod and could tell my flying experience gave me the advantage. The other pilot's moves were sluggish, and he bore straight ahead while I moved left and right, up and down.

I pushed the control forward, making a sudden dive and turned to the port. The Freebooter pilot began a slow turn.

In that time, I turned back toward the Stinger and shot from below as it passed. "Start bringing us up!"

I fired the clumsy breech loader as rapidly as possible. My third shot cut through the tail section. The entire rudder and propeller fell away. Steam billowed into the cold morning air.

The Stinger spun, hanging on its nose, and slipped away. The craft retained some levitation and fluttered like a leaf in the breeze.

When I turned back toward the *Celestial City*, one deck gun was firing. It was cocked at an odd angle, and I couldn't tell if it was aimed at us or the *Cloud Queen*. I dodged and bobbed, being careful to keep my movements random.

As Finn predicted, the deck guns were large and awkward, designed for long-range. It was the rifles we were most worried about.

199

I shot toward three Freebooters who were positioned along a railing, but they were not shooting with any regularity. Two were leaning on the railing. The third shot wildly and then sat down. Sid's sleeping draught was working.

"Let's glide." All was quiet.

"This looks too easy," I said to Finn.

"If Sid did his job, this might be easier than we thought."

We eased the Stinger forward, and it came to rest on the bulkhead. The three riflemen lay on the deck. Finn took their guns and ammunition, and we trussed them securely.

BB SID STOP WE ARE OUTSIDE THE SEVENTH DECK STOP

Finn reached into the Stinger and pulled out our bag of ammunition. I looked over the railing. The *Celestial City* was still under power, the propellers whining like bumble bees. Heavy bollards were attached to each parapet.

BB SID STOP WE ARE OUTSIDE THE SEVENTH DECK STOP

When there was still no answer, I slung my pack over my shoulder and grabbed the rifle. We crept along the bulkhead and came to a ladder that led to the next level.

"Do we go up?" I wondered.

Finn looked over the edge of the walkway. "All we need is one man who skipped breakfast, and we could be done."

"Guard me." I put my foot on the rung and began to climb. As I neared the top of the ladder, I slowed and lifted my head to deck level. A Freebooter was lying on the narrow deck, inches from my face. He slept soundly. The only access to the inside was from a door on the side of the bulkhead.

I signaled for Finn to follow. Above, the glass dome gleamed in the sunlight.

I slipped across the deck and peeked inside the metal door. The area was vast and empty. On the left, a staircase went up to the next level. Near a large support column in the center, stairs with railings led down through an opening in the floor.

The ship's interior was a series of girders and buttresses laid out in triangles. The floor under me was solid, and the ceiling was probably the observation deck.

200

Finn put his head in the door, and I motioned for him to stay. I pointed toward the staircase, and he slipped back. A shot hit just outside the door and whined away.

I ducked behind a girder, pressing my back against the outside wall.

"Young Will, I never liked you. I should have had you killed long ago."

I waited.

"Did you think I am so foolish as to eat when everyone else eats?!"

I dashed to the ship's center post and slipped behind it

"I wait to eat my meals until hours after everyone else has eaten. Ha ha!" The Supreme Navarch's whiny voice sounded hollow. "No, I am not as foolish as you might think, Young Will." Two shots rattled around the interior.

I realized that I could easily be hit by a ricochet. Finn had the door open a crack, but it swung out in such a way that coming through the door would put him in plain view from the top of the stairs.

"You have no place to go Young Will." A shot rattled the railing and whined until it clattered against a wall. "I have you like a mouse. My men will begin to wake up, and then—I will have you thrown off the ship to your miserable death."

I couldn't see the Supreme Navarch, but the bullets came from above. I didn't waste a shot in his direction. Finn swung the door open, and a shot hit the deck outside.

I extended the hand scope and tossed it up the stairs. It toppled back down, bouncing and clanking.

Three quick shots hit the railing. *He's shooting at sound.*

"You think you have defeated me, but I will destroy you. We have crippled your shiny ship, and we will destroy your steamboat. I will prevail." Another volley of shots sprayed in different directions.

He's loading between bursts of shots. Six-shooter?

Where were Sid and Sam? I ran to the railing around the staircase and took a quick look over the edge.

Staircases crossed back and forth, down toward the bowels of the ship, the center column extending toward the base. Around

201

the sides, there were other decks to be seen. I had become used to heights, but I found the view dizzying.

A swishing sound in the ceiling made me jump. Above was a long polished tube, swiveling a periscope lens. It stopped, watching me. I scrambled back to the other side of the center column.

Laughter drifted down from a speaking horn above me. I saw two other periscopes behind me. I watched, and when they did not move, I knew. *He's alone.*

A thunderous noise echoed from the ceiling. Was he jumping up and down, trying to scare me?

The periscope to my left began to swivel. I moved behind the protection of the post and dashed to the staircase. I could see no movement below and went down. It was awkward, the rifle banging on the handrails.

At the next level, a catwalk wrapped around the inside of the ship. I felt like I was a bee inside its hive. A man was lying in a doorway. I nudged him with my foot, but he was not waking up soon.

I returned to the edge, cupped my hands, and shouted, "Sid!" A slight echo responded, and I stood listening.

There was a steam engine running along with other whirrings and clankings. *How long can the ship fly with no one attending the engines?* "Sid! Sam!"

I went to a porthole and saw our Stinger outside. Finn appeared and tapped, PROPELLERS HAVE BEEN SHUT DOWN STOP

NO ONE TENDING THE BOILERS STOP

I MUST COME IN STOP WE ARE TOO HIGH STOP ENGINE STOPPING WILL MEAN DEATH TO EVERYONE ABOARD STOP

WILL COVER YOU AS YOU COME STOP STAIRS TO LOWER DECK CENTER THIRTY FEET FROM DOOR STOP I SHOOT YOU RUN STOP

I left my pack and climbed the ladder with my rifle over my shoulder. I put my hat on the end of the rifle and slowly raised it above the deck. When I was sure it was safe, I moved to the center support, leveled my rifle, and put a single bullet on the highest step I could see.

Finn sprinted across the deck and pounded down the ladder. I fired another round, ran to the steps, and slid down using the railing. The butt of the rifle caught the railing, and the barrel clipped my jaw.

Finn stood next to me as I rubbed my chin. "We have to get to the engine room and make steam. Any idea where it is?"

I pointed down.

We began pounding down stairways, back and forth. My ears were starting to feel the loss of altitude. The sounds of the machinery grew louder with every tier we passed.

I had counted seven decks when we felt warm air. Finn stepped over a man, and I followed him into the engine room. The boiler was massive. The heads of the cylinders came through the floor, rocking as the connecting rods below cranked.

An engineer lay on the deck. I gave him a nudge with my foot. He didn't grunt, and I leaned closer. He had no color and was not breathing. "Finn, I think this guy's dead!"

Finn tapped the water level sight tube. "We are out of water."

"Maybe heart. He vomited a little bit."

"Will! It won't matter if we crash! Follow the water pipes!"

I traced the line to a tall tank. No water showed in the sight glass. Two more tanks were mounted in a semicircle around us. I closed the valve on the first tank and opened the second tank.

Finn peered into the firebox. "This will be tricky. I am going to lower the fire. We don't want to melt or crack any tubes."

The cylinders slowed, and I felt the floor falling away.

The injector pump pulsed, and Finn twiddled the flame control. The engine wheezed and turned faster.

"Will, we are at seven thousand feet, but how close are we to the mountains?"

At a side port the trees were closer than I hoped. "Finn, better get the lift back. We are going down fast. Maybe five hundred feet!"

The injector pump pulsed again, and Finn added fuel. The pressure gauge hung at twenty-eight pounds. The engine continued to turn, but the lights were dim. Then the floor pressed against my feet.

203

The port hole showed we were still falling. "Now, Finn, or we are done for."

Finn adjusted the flame until it roared. The injector pump rattled and then went back to work. "Air, in the line," he called. "It is pumping water now."

The pistons gained speed, and the lights brightened. Water rose in the sight tube, almost to the top.

"Still falling, but slower," I reported.

"We may have damaged one of the tubes. We should be making steam by now."

The cylinders knocked twice, and Finn turned the water injector off. "Too much," he said. "Water got into the cylinders. We don't want to lock the engine with a slug of water."

We were falling again, and Finn eased open the flame control. The engine turned faster, and water began to fall in the sight tube. He started the injector and the engine knocked again.

"Give me one of our boilers any day, "Finn said. "I can't seem to strike a balance."

The deck felt solid under my feet. "I think we are level."

The engine knocked again and recovered.

"I don't understand. It's as if the injector is too large for the boiler." Finn alternated turning the injector on and off.

We were probably only a hundred feet above the trees outside the port. I could feel the lift strengthening and weakening. Each time the engine knocked, the lights dimmed.

"Will, how many turns was the valve open on the tank you turned off?"

"I was able to turn it off quickly, but I had opened the new tank's valve all the way."

The engine hammered hard and the lights dimmed.

"Turn the valve down!"

I ran to the valve and started turning. "How far?"

The injector pump rattled.

"About there."

We stood watching the engine. The sight glass steadied at the halfway point.

"This is foolishness—poor design."

204

The engine was turning steadily, but the lights were not as bright as they had been. We were very close to the ground. The tip of a pine was even with my window. The ship shuddered but felt solid under my feet.

"Give me a half turn—no more," Finn said. "We must be on the side of a mountain. This ship will tip over if we cannot maintain lift."

I opened the valve a half turn, and the injector pump responded with a solid pulse. The engine began to turn faster, cylinders rocking in a steady cadence. The ship righted herself. Water in the glass sank low.

"There, that's about right."

The tip of the pine remained at the same level. "We are not rising."

"We're not making enough power to provide lift, and he's not running the propulsion propellers. Give it another quarter turn."

The ship swung like a pendulum, and the pine slipped away. "A little more," Finn said.

I gently opened the valve, and the engine turned faster.

"I think I'm getting the hang of this."

"Yes, thank you," the Supreme Navarch croaked through the speaking tube. "I didn't think you had the brains to do it, Young Will."

The sound of his voice gave me the creeps.

"And who is your friend?"

Chapter 37

I searched the bulkheads and girders above. A glass eye was pointed toward me.

"Yes, here I am, Will. I see all, know all. I am all!"

Finn was out of sight of the periscope, and he picked up a rag. He put his finger to his lips and pulled a ladder near.

I watched the single lens. I imagined seeing one of the Supreme Navarch's evil eyes watching me. I reached for my rifle.

In a quick movement, Finn tied the rag around the periscope. It twirled and twisted and then tried to pull up into the overhead deck. The rag bound in the opening, and the twisting stopped.

I almost laughed, thinking of the Supreme Navarch struggling to lift the periscope. Perhaps it was powered with gears and motors, but I enjoyed thinking of the little man tugging on handles.

Finn tapped the altitude gauge and opened the water a quarter turn. A power gauge hovered at ninety percent. A hum echoed down from above. The engine made it difficult to identify the sound, and I moved toward the center ladder.

Finn pointed to the speaking tube and spoke in quiet tones. "He has started the propellers."

The gauge said we were flying at six thousand feet. *A thousand feet above the mountains.*

Finn moved the ladder toward the speaking tube and stuffed another rag deep in the mouthpiece.

I went to the stairs and climbed into the inner structure. "Sid! Sam! Sid!"

"Coming!"

I could hear someone clattering down staircase after staircase. At last, I saw Sid three levels up, moving fast.

We shook hands on the level above the engine room and then went down to join Finn.

"We have stopped the Supreme Navarch's spying on us. Finn plugged the speaking tube. I suppose by now he knows you are part of the resistance."

Sid chuckled. "He knows and has threatened me with every kind of unpleasant death."

"He told me he would throw *me* off the ship."

Sid patted my shoulder. "That is nothing. I am to suffer a slow death."

"Where's Sam?"

Sid's face darkened. "One of the Chosen didn't eat breakfast. Sam was shot. I killed the Chosen One and tried to stop the bleeding. I failed." Sid drew himself up to his full height. "Sorry for the delay in getting to you."

My breath caught. Sam had a wife and three children in Kansas but had devoted his life to destroying the Freebooters.

"Have you been in the control room under the dome?"

"No. Only the Chosen Ones are allowed. His right-hand man, Svend, fell from favor and was sent to pilot one of the Stingers."

"Yes, we have him. He is not happy but safe."

"The ship hasn't had the Blue Vial since before we launched. He will begin to sober up."

"I think I have the boiler stabilized." Finn poured oil into the engine cups. "Unless the fool at the controls does something silly, the ship should continue to fly."

We told Sid about the damaged *Silver Seed* and began making plans.

We moved up the ladders, stopping to bind the hands and feet of all we found. Finn tied a rag over every periscope and plugged the speaking tubes. Sid knew all the crew by name and marked them well.

On level four, we explored the Supreme Navarch's cabin. We had to break open the door but found a luxurious set of rooms. There was even a fireplace with red velvet upholstered chairs and couches. There was no fire, but the wood was laid, and bellows ready to kindle the flame.

At the detention area on level five, we found the hostages sleeping soundly. "The silly fool didn't make them sniff the Blue Vial. He said he had no need of them other than insurance." Sid scribbled a note explaining the situation.

We were on level six when we tied the next-to-last Freebooter.

"Have we been to every area?" I asked.

"Yes. One man remains." Sid looked up. "I fear he is in the wheelhouse. One of the Chosen Few. A taciturn man named Phillips."

"We have to get up there, take control. Land the ship safely so we can get the hostages off."

"We don't know how soon Phillips will begin to revive," Sid said.

"Keep him up there, wondering what we are doing until we can figure a way in." I pulled out some twine and a hand scope out of my pack. "Not much here."

Sid ran down a level and brought two pots and a few utensils. We carried our collection to the level under the dome, and Finn quickly plugged the speaking tube.

Near the center column, we made a big production of putting the pots down and knelt, blocking a clear view from the periscope.

I took out my knife, making cutting motions in the large pot. Sid "handed" me objects from the other kettle. The periscope never moved.

Sid handed me a Blue Vial. "Be careful. This is the real thing," he whispered. The stopper was secured with wire. I laid it carefully in the pot.

The periscope remained aimed in our direction. I made a face as I pretended to tighten something in the pot. "We need José. Get out the code box."

Sid blocked the periscope view with his back, bringing the device out of his pack. He held the button, and I keyed the message.

BB JOSE CAN YOU GET TO US ON AIRCYCLE STOP ALL GUNS SILENCED HERE STOP NEED DYNAMITE AND BLASTING CAPS STOP WEAPONS

ON MY WAY STOP CLOUD QUEEN ABOVE STOP BRING CODE BOX STOP EXPLAIN LATER STOP

Two shots hammered my ears, one bullet glancing off the center post. *How many bullets does that guy have?*

Sid gave a disgusted grunt, ran to the periscope watching us, and wrestled it up and down. It only moved up and down inches, but the impact above could be heard each time Sid jerked it down. The shooting stopped.

I continued to hold the power button down. Minutes passed.

BB ON THE DECK BY POD STOP

Sid bounced the tube up and down, swiveling right and left.

TAKE LADDER UP STOP DOOR SWINGS IN STOP DANGEROUS STOP WE ARE THIRTY FEET FROM DOOR STOP SAFE FROM HIM HERE STOP BE CAREFUL

I beckoned to Sid, and he joined me. We took careful aim at the staircase.

The door swung wider, and five shots rattled and ricocheted at the top of the ladder. José's rifle barrel pulled back from the crack at the hinges, and he ran across the room, keeping low and firing a single shot toward the stairs with his pistol. He slid down next to us.

There was a whistle of air, and the rag fell out of the speaking tube. "Young Will, you cannot win. When my men awaken, we will rain down destruction. You will see what happens to people who go against God, and God has his hand on my shoulder. God is starting His final reign, and I will burn the chaff!"

"He does not know God," José mumbled. "He uses God as a club,."

Finn kicked the rag on the floor. "José—how high are we?"

"High, but descending."

Finn stood. "Something's wrong. I have to go back to the engine room."

The speaking tube purred, "Yes, send your engineer. It's about time one of you remembered—without the engines, this ship falls out of the sky. Perhaps I should put an end to this all!" The deck gave way under my feet and then pressed back.

Finn made a dash for the staircase and started down. José drove the rag into the speaking tube with the butt of his knife.

I doubted the Supreme Navarch had the nerve to ruin his ship and himself. I had seen many sides to this man, but bravery was not one of his strong points.

209

Chapter 38

I picked up the Blue Vial. "We're going to give him a taste of his own medicine. Cover me. Then tie a rag around the periscope lens."

José fired a shot toward the upper staircase while I went down. I took the steps two at a time to the Supreme Navarch's quarters. I grabbed the bellows and met Sid on the stairs.

"I'm gonna check on the men we tied. I will try to wake up the prisoners."

"Good." When I peeked my head up, José fired another shot to keep the Supreme Navarch cowering, and I hurried to his side.

"We're going to use his own gas on him. You chewed a pill?" José nodded.

I opened the Blue Vial and poured several splashes of the liquid into the bellows' air intake. We tested the bellows by pumping it once, and the smell of the gas was almost overpowering.

I carried the bellows to the speaking tube. The periscope didn't move. I removed the rag and called, "Supreme Navarch. It's Will." I lowered my voice. "I have a proposition for you."

I shoved the bellows into the speaking tube, and José held the rag around the nozzle. I pumped the bellows ten times.

"Supreme Navarch," I murmured. "I have a—" I let my voice dwindle. I put the bellows back and pumped ten more strokes.

In a firm voice, I said "You will not harm Will or his friends. You will cooperate with Will. Will is to be protected. You will stand close to the speaking tube and listen. Breathe deeply."

I pumped the bellows a dozen times. "You will cooperate with Will."

José held the rag against the tube. "But is he listening?"

I pulled the bellows back. "Supreme Navarch, what is your plan?"

"To support Will."

"This is Will, telling you to come down the stairs."

We waited.

The Supreme Navarch descended the stairs and turned toward us.

I looked into his eyes. His expression was blank, as if gazing at a distant landscape.

"Lay down your rifle."

He placed his rifle against a beam and stood simply in front of me.

"Tie him up," I said to José.

José took a rope and reached to tie the Supreme Navarch's hands behind his back. A loud crack of electricity caused me to jump back, and José fell to his knees and slumped to the floor.

The Supreme Navarch held a gun to José's head. "Don't move, Will. Move one inch, and I will blow your friend's brains out."

We stood, considering each other. "Don't shoot him. I will put my pistol down."

José was unconscious, but his chest was moving. I bent over to lay my gun on the floor. The Supreme Navarch's pistol remained pointed at José's head when I threw myself forward, tossing my pistol at the Supreme Navarch's face and ramming my head into his stomach.

He flinched, putting one hand over his face to protect himself, and his pistol clattered to the floor. I slammed into the arm, trying to rip off the glove. I grabbed his other forearm. It was easy to hold his arm back, but he squirmed and wiggled. I clawed at the glove, but he had his fist balled.

We struggled for a moment and he staggered back a step, trying to make contact with both hands, but he was no match for my strength. His eyes had gone to narrow slits, and we stood, face to face.

"So, Young Will, maybe you believe you have succeeded, but look behind you. My crew comes."

The hair tickled the back of my neck, but I resisted the urge to look. We stood, eye to eye, as I slowly forced his hands together. I slammed his right hand onto his cheek and pushed his left hand closer. About an inch from his cheek, a terrific blue spark jumped. The Supreme Navarch went down

When he fell, his coat opened in the front, revealing three cylinders the size of dynamite sticks with wires attached.

I scrambled for his gun. "José, wake up! José!"

211

I studied the wires. *Not dynamite.* "José!" I kicked his leg. "José!" *Explosives?*

José groaned, but his eyes did not open.

One set of wires went to a switch of some sort. *Which is on or off? Three tubes. Three shocks?* I needed to pull the wires from the switch. *Don't let it touch anything*

In one quick snatch, I jerked the wire loose.

"José!" I shook him, and his eyes flickered.

"Hey, Will. Did we do it?"

"Yes. Can you help me tie him up?"

José shook his head to clear it. "My heart is racing!" With trembling hands we lashed the Supreme Navarch's feet together and tied his hands behind his back.

"Will!" Finn's voice echoed in the array of speaking tubes. "Will! José! We are going down."

I went to a speaking tube. "What's wrong with the engines?"

Finn was panting. "Injector pump failing. I'm holding it together with a crowbar but can't make it pump any faster. Five minutes. Shut down the propellers, or we go down sooner."

I pulled the code key out of the bucket. "José, you better start down. I'm right behind you. Leave your pack."

BB CC GOING DOWN STOP RESCUE HOSTAGES AT LEVEL FIVE FROM BOTTOM STOP NO TIME STOP

I ran up the stairs to the observation dome.

The wheelhouse was beautiful. The glass dome sparkled, giving a beautiful vista. The glass curved under at the edges, giving an eerie view down the sides of the craft. Two banks of brass-handled periscopes lined one section. A large wheel was at the center, and lever after lever was mounted on the floor.

Phillips sat against a bulkhead, head against his chest. *Tie him.* I lifted his chin and slapped his cheek. His eyes fluttered. *Keep us in the air.*

I went to the levers, searching on the floor and along each device for any hint as to what the levers controlled.

There was a wagon brake-like lever that was larger than the others. It was pulled back as far as it could travel. There were eight levers next to it, four on each side. I reasoned that the eight

212

controlled the propeller motors. They were set at Half, and I began to close them, alternating sides.

At first, I could hear no change, but as I moved toward the center, I could hear the propellers slowing. *We need to rise.* When all were closed, I pulled one more time on the levitation lever, making sure it was open all the way.

I looked around the wheelhouse. A gauge said we were at eight thousand feet. *We've been climbing.* I watched the needle move to seven thousand nine hundred fifty feet. I hurried back down the stairs.

I pulled a length of rope from José's pack. *José always has rope.*

I flew up the stairs three at a time. *Seven thousand nine hundred.* I rolled Phillips onto his stomach and hog-tied him, pulling his ankles and wrists close. I double-knotted the final tie. *Still falling.*

I decided to leave José's pack. I slung both rifles over my shoulder and shoved loose shells in my pocket.

José was making steady progress, but I caught him at the fifth level. At the fourth level, we found the hostages beginning to revive. The priest was sitting up and tried to rise when we came in the room. José helped him to his feet.

I opened a side door and went out on the platform. I looked up and waved to the *Cloud Queen.* Laura was in the wheelhouse and blew me a kiss. She turned the wheel, hand over hand, and the ship moved closer.

Inside, another prisoner was awake enough to stand and seemed ready to follow orders. He helped us carry a woman to the outer platform.

Addy ran the gangplank out, and José began to carry the hostages who were still asleep. The man's resilience was amazing.

We were coming closer to the trees; time was running out. The ground under us was steep and rugged.

I carried a woman outside.

José dragged a man to the gangplank and lifted him onto the end.

"How many more?" Addy asked.

José leaned heavily on the gangplank. "Three."

BB FINN COME WE HAVE THE HOSTAGES
WHEN I LEAVE NO MORE THAN A MINUTE

213

COME

Sid joined us. "All knots secure."

No way to save them. The ship lurched, girders groaning.

FINN NOW

We ran back and José, face drenched in sweat, threw a woman over his shoulder in a feat of superhuman strength. Sid lugged a young man. I tried to pick up the last man, but he was hugely overweight. There was a shudder, metal grinding, and the deck tilted.

Where's Finn? No time to find him.

"Finn!" My voice echoed.

I dragged the man by his vest. The bulkheads screamed and the deck buckled under my feet, and the man slid away from the door. Scrabbling for traction, I hunched him toward the bulkhead a few feet at a time. At the door, Sid grabbed the man's feet, and we managed to pull him outside. It took the three of us to lift the man onto the gangplank. Sid pulled himself up, followed by José.

I ran back inside. "Finn! Finn!"

I could hear rapid footsteps below.

Outside, I cupped my hands. "Finn is coming!"

"The whole ship is going over! Jump, Jump!" Laura screamed. José and Sid pulled the huge man further onto the plank.

The *Celestial City* twisted, the gangplank slamming into the landing, sending me to my knees. I scrambled toward the gangplank on all fours.

With my left hand, I managed to grab the walkway chain, and José pulled me up.

The bow of the *Cloud Queen* tipped down. The gangplank was caught on the parapet. I looked over and the safety chain was twisted around a bollard. *I couldn't get that hooked if I tried!* "Hammer! Sledge! Tangled!"

Finn appeared in the doorway. José slid an ax down the tilting gangway. I reached out with one hand, but I missed my grip. The gangway was tilted further, metal grinding. I slammed into the gangway rail posts, knocking the breath out of me. The *Cloud Queen* was being pulled down.

Finn had the handle and swung at the chain. With the third mighty blow, the gangplank swung up suddenly. It clipped Finn's

214

chin, and he lost his footing and fell back. His head slammed against the bulkhead as the *Cloud Queen* rose. A crooked grin appeared on Finn's face, and he gave me a thumbs-up as the *Celestial City* rolled to the side.

Horror rose in my chest, choking me. "Down! Down!"

The stern of the *Cloud Queen* crunched into the side of the mountain, and the ship listed.

José made a long throw with a rope. It swung in the air and fell at Finn's feet. Finn stared at nothing as the *Celestial City* gave way.

I sat on the loading ramp, breathing hard.

The observation dome arced out with increasing speed, the whole ship twisting to starboard. I watched as it teetered for a moment and then fell. A cloud of dust rolled into the air, and rocks tumbled as it slid dome first down the side of the mountain. It came to rest at the bottom of a ravine.

"We have to get Finn! Laura, take us down!"

The airscrews started, and we moved over the wreckage. Steam and smoke billowed out of several levels as the *Cloud Queen* inched lower.

José came and stood by me. "You know Finn is finished."

Tears bit the corners of my eyes, and I nodded. "I need to check."

The *Celestial City* had rolled a quarter turn. We spotted Finn lying on his side, head up, body twisted. Addy brought a hand scope, but it was evident the life had gone from his eyes. A fire burned near the base of the *Celestial City*, and rounds could be heard exploding inside.

José sat with me, feet over the edge of the gangplank. "From the heat, I suppose." Three more rounds echoed. There was a round burn on the right of his chin.

After a long moment, we crawled onto the front deck, and Addy worked the lever to retract the gangplank. I sat on my knees, looking at bodies lying about. Several hostages were seated with their backs to the front cabin.

The priest came forward and placed a hand on my head. "Bless you, son. I am Father Xavier."

"Thank you, Father." I felt blessed.

215

Chapter 39

After we helped the rescued to the back cabins, we gathered around the table in the forward cabin. Time weighed heavily on me. "I don't think we should try to enter the wreckage until it cools."

Addy held a damp cloth to José's cheek.

I studied Laura's face. "You are feeling well?"

Tears began to run down her cheeks. "Yes. I'm just so, so—sad."

Addy poured tea.

I raised the cup halfway to my lips and returned it to the saucer. "The Supreme Navarch wasn't dead. We didn't have time to decide what to do with him." *Couldn't shoot a bound man in cold blood.* "We have to finish this, or he will rise like a Medusa snake."

"We are getting Finn," José whispered.

The room was quiet except for the distant throb of the engine. Addy went to the pilothouse.

"We have tried hard not to become the enemy," I said. "Any of the Supreme Navarch's men alive down there are innocent. When they sober up, they deserve the chance."

Addy returned to the table. "There is a small town, on a road to Denver. It is only a few miles ahead."

I stood. "Before we go down to the *Celestial City,* I'll talk to the hostages. They may want to get back to their homes. Their lives." It sounded good—to get back to our regular lives.

In the back room, several were sound asleep, but I thought it important that all be awake. Father Xavier began to shake the sleepers.

It didn't take long to realize that everyone wanted to go home. These people were not fighters or resisters. I decided to take the prisoners down first.

I stood between the Mayor and Father Xavier. "I have a favor. If we can rescue some of the Freebooters from their ship, will you alert the sheriff and see that they are held until they are sober? I would ask you to remain in town until all is settled."

There was an uncomfortable silence. The Mayor's wife stood. "I will help." She looked around the room.

216

Father Xavier said, "I will help you, Gloria."

Gloria glared at the large man. "Albert?"

Albert wheezed. "I suppose, Dear."

Gloria shook her head in disgust. "You might have to get your hands a little dirty, Albert. It won't kill you."

"No, Dear."

"Then it is settled. We will let you off in the little town below, return to the Freebooter's ship, and see if any are alive."

I went forward and called for Full. Addy brought the propellers up to speed, and Laura steered us toward the village. José talked quietly with Father Xavier as I started to the pilothouse.

Laura and I stood, watching the trees below. Laura touched my arm. "The sheriff might think we are the enemy."

"Yes. Perhaps we should let them off before town."

Laura steered us to a pasture along the road.

Addy and Sid gave each person rescued a drink of water.

"I want to thank you for this." I handed the mayor's wife folded bills.

She looked at the money. "This is more than we will need for lodging."

"You may need travel money. What is left, Father Xavier can use for the church. You don't know what you might find when you get home."

Laura came down. "The town is only a mile down this wagon track."

The Mayor didn't look pleased.

"The walk will do you good, Albert," Gloria said. "About time you worked off some of that weight. I am going to feed you less, and you are not taking a buggy to your office anymore."

José drew near. "Father Xavier is staying aboard until we deliver the prisoners," he said with finality.

I didn't question him, but Laura winked at me.

I let the gangplank down.

Gloria had her husband's arm and was leading him at a brisk walk.

The wind was with us for the return trip, and we came to a standstill over the wreckage of the *Celestial City*. Almost no smoke was coming from the ship.

217

"Will, we must be careful. They are tied, but it has been several hours," José said.

"Are you up to this?" I asked.

"I do not want to slow you down." José touched the burn on his cheek. "I am feeling stronger all the time, but my insides are still shaking."

"OK. First, we'll get Finn. This all started with the three of us burying Uncle John. Finn deserves the same." *We couldn't have done any of this without Finn.*

José let a breath escape between his lips.

The *Cloud Queen* maneuvered for twenty minutes before we got her level with the deck that held Finn. I found myself listening to a voice inside. *The ship needs a reverse.* The stern crunched into pines and rocks, the bow floating over the wreckage. *Finn won't be there to make that happen.*

When Sid and I climbed out to Finn, we wrapped him in a blanket, and gently laid him on the gangplank. José carried the body away and returned with a rifle. "Be careful in there. I will secure any you bring out. Laura thinks she can dock better higher up."

I refused the rifle. "I think I will stick to my pistol. It may be pretty cramped in there."

Sid and I squirmed into the ship. The engine room was still warm, but the piping was broken and bent. We began the awkward task of climbing down the walls, level after level.

The first crew members we found had been killed by the slide down the hill. The *Celestial City* was designed to be suspended from the upper structure. Laying on its side, the frame had buckled and folded in places.

On the fourth level we found two Freebooters uninjured but groggy. Sid took them back up at gunpoint,

I moved down the wall, pistol in hand.

Sid returned in minutes. "Enemy secure. I'm not sure how sober they are. They are almost cooperative." Sid paused to breathe. "The *Cloud Queen* was able to dock outside the engine room. There is a working door—José is attaching the anchor to the *Celestial City*."

We came upon a deck that had buckled and pushed up. Climbing over beams and bulkheads was like crawling over a rock pile.

218

When we arrived at the platform below the control room, the Supreme Navarch was not where I had left him. A coil of frayed ropes lay near the steps.

The door Finn and I had used to enter the ship was against the hillside. The opposite door was fifteen feet up. "He didn't go out that way," Sid grunted.

I pointed down to the control room.

The ladder was almost upside down, and we made our way, stepping on the underside of the steps. We crawled around the railing and looked down into the control room. The dome had shattered, a large hole gaping against the hillside. Phillips lay in the rubble, still hogtied.

"Help me, Sid. Help."

"I'll find the little man. Can you get Phillips out?"

Sid freed Phillips' feet and pulled him up. "I've got him."

I drew my pistol and moved toward the gaping hole in the dome.

Outside, the Supreme Navarch sat with his back against a bent sapling. He was digging feebly at the knots tying his feet.

"Ah, Will, perhaps you have come to your senses. You see that my plan is perfect—that when I rule the world, the world will be in better hands. You could be part of that. Join me, and we will teach the whole planet to behave."

"Why are you out here? Why didn't you untie Phillips?"

The Supreme Navarch smirked. "Phillips was still half asleep, the lazy sot. The air was bad. I came here to collect my thoughts."

He struggled weakly with the ropes that still bound his ankles. "Your knots have proven difficult."

"If you cooperate, I will untie you and help you get out of here."

"Apparently, I have no choice." The Supreme Navarch's eyes narrowed in the sun.

I tied his hands behind his back and checked his pockets. I found a pistol and stuck it in my belt behind my back. I dragged him to his feet and took my knife to the rope binding his legs. As soon as his foot was free, he kicked back like a donkey.

219

I snatched his ankle as his foot grazed my shoulder, lifting until he fell face down in the shale. "Be careful, or I might have to shoot you right here."

I readied my pistol and slipped the knot, freeing his hands.

Back inside the dome, the little man waved at the bent controls. "Genius." He touched a peg of the brass wheel. "There is still time for you, Young Will. I will reveal the instructions you will be given. The Chosen don't follow the same rules as the—little people." He flicked his fingers as if shooing a small child.

"Climb."

As he clawed his way toward the twisted ladder, he continued to plead his case. "With your ships, we will be masters of the earth! I must admit, your man Finn is a gifted inventor. With our combined talents, all things would be possible."

Anger boiled, and I jabbed the gun in his ribs. *You don't get the satisfaction of knowing about Finn.*

We worked our way along the wall of the seventh level. A pine tree trunk was sticking through a broken window.

The little man struggled along, wheezing and whining. I prodded him with the barrel of my pistol.

At the fifth level, the Supreme Navarch tripped and fell. He lay coughing. At last he sat up, leaning against a beam. "You will live well. Dine sumptuously." His face twisted into a sly smile. "You can have your pick of women."

"You have no idea what decent people want!" I growled.

"Have you read Darwin? Survival of the fittest—oh, not huge hulking men, but intellect!" He tapped his temple. "We are destined to—"

"If you're smart, you'll get up and get moving. My patience is waning." I grabbed the shoulder of his coat and dragged him to his feet. "Move." I pushed the Supreme Navarch, and we worked our way to the fourth level.

The higher we went, the more smoke filled the ship. I wasn't sure if it was from the boilers or some electrical device.

I half carried the Supreme Navarch along the wall and then lifted him over the wreckage of the ladder to the engine room. I tugged him to an open door.

220

Outside, the *Cloud Queen* had managed to navigate near. José and Sid stood at the end of the gangway. I put my arms around the little man's waist and lifted him as high as the ramp.

He started kicking my chest, and José slapped his face. "Do not make me hit you again." He pulled the man aboard, where the Supreme Navarch collapsed on the gangplank.

I realized how tired I was when I pulled myself onto the ramp. I put my head on my arm for a moment, relishing the warm sun.

"Are you alright, Will?" José asked.

"Yes, just tired." I stood and jerked the Supreme Navarch onto the front deck. I pulled the cords out of my pocket and reached for the Supreme Navarch's hand. He made a sudden twist and had his arm around my neck. I pulled at his elbow, trying to get my breath.

There was a dull crack as the butt of a rifle hit the side of the Supreme Navarch's head. The arm around my neck went limp, and he fell away. Laura lowered her rifle. The evil man's ear was bleeding.

"This is him? This little weasel?"

"I am afraid so." I was embarrassed I had let him get me in a chokehold.

Sid picked up the ropes and bent down, making quick work of the task.

"Take him back and tie him with double ropes," José ordered. "Tight."

"Do we have everyone?" Laura asked. "Sid brought five of the crew."

I looked back at the *Celestial City*. Smoke still whiffed out of several levels. "That should be everyone." I gestured with my thumb for Addy to take us up.

221

Chapter 40

In the forward cabin, Addy had engine oil on her cheek.

"Where did you put Finn?" It seemed important to know.

José was cooking eggs and bacon. "We wrapped him in another blanket and laid him in the supply cabin." A muscle flicked in his jaw as he flipped the eggs.

Sid stepped to the stove. "Let me finish this." José didn't argue.

"Let's all take some time to clean up, Addy first." I patted her arm. "Good job."

After a hasty meal, I checked the boiler and went to the speaking tube. "Laura, I am taking us to Full. Land as close as possible to the sheriff's office."

When everyone was in fresh clothes, José cleared his throat. "Addy and I have an announcement. Father Xavier is going to marry us." He was wearing a new shirt. Addy joined him in a fresh flowered dress.

A surge of joy washed over me. Laura lashed the wheel, and I shut down the airscrews. Father Xavier assembled us on the front deck. I stood up for José, and Laura stood with Addy.

Laura's eyes met mine, and I couldn't remember when I was last this happy. *If they are half as happy as we are, they will have a wonderful life.*

Everyone was exhausted, but the next few minutes seemed to bring everyone new energy. The father said beautiful things about life, hope, and new beginnings. I believe he was inspired by the new freedom for humanity.

When Father Xavier pronounced them husband and wife, José kissed Addy, and I put my arm around Laura. Addy had never looked prettier, and my friend José's smile reflected his great love.

We started the propellers, and Laura set us on course for the village.

We ate in the forward cabin. For a long time, I almost forgot the work still to be done. For that, I missed Finn's wise counsel.

"What do we do with the Supreme Navarch?" I wondered. "He is a slippery eel and is well able to outsmart his captors and escape."

"He's not going anywhere now," Addy said. She was back in her long coat, tall hat, and goggles. "He's still trussed up like a pig and chained."

"He will devise unusual methods." *Getting me in a headlock wasn't unique—I was only half alert. I felt like a fool.*

"I loathe having him on the *Cloud Queen*, but we must not let him escape," Laura said. "We must turn him over to federal authorities."

"Hard labor on a remote island," José huffed.

"So, it is agreed. We keep him with us until we can deliver him to the proper authorities."

We had a headwind, and it took an hour before we landed in the clearing just outside the town.

Laura gave me a stack of bills. "In case."

Father Xavier, Sid, and I made our way to the sheriff's office with the prisoners. We kept their hands tied with a foot of rope between their feet. They shuffled along but gave us no trouble.

"Can I go home?" one of the twelve asked. "I haven't seen my wife and children for fifteen years."

My heart ached for the man. His children were grown—so much of his life had been wasted. "When you are completely sober from the Blue Vial," the sheriff said.

I shook the sheriff's hand. "Thank you for taking charge of these men. They can't be trusted until a week after their last outburst. Mornings are the worst."

"We will make sure they do no more harm until they are themselves."

I turned to Father Xavier. "Thank you, Father. I'm not Catholic but I feel blessed by your words and the wedding."

He put his hand on my shoulder. "Go in peace, my son."

I turned to go when Sid caught my arm.

"This is the end of the road for me, Will. I'm done. It's time to go home."

How does Laura always know? I pressed the money in his hand. "Cook wonderful food, Sid." A tear pressed the corner of my eye. I

223

put out my hand. "I couldn't have done it without you. Thank you for believing in me."

Sid gave me a nod. "Nor I, without you. Be well, Will." He handed me a paper with his name and town. "Write some time." He turned and walked quickly toward the center of the village.

Watching him go, I felt a mixture of good and bad feelings. I hated goodbyes, and yet was happy Sid could get back to his life—even if Sally would not be there. I jogged toward the ship.

A small crowd of townspeople had gathered at the *Cloud Queen*, with food and pies, and I approached with some humility.

"Hip—hip—hurray" was shouted three times. I moved uneasily through the crowd and stepped aboard. We launched to oohs and aahs, relieved to be in the air.

The code light flashed. DOLPH HERE STOP SS REPAIRS COMPLETE STOP

GOOD MAN DOLPH STOP WE HEAR NOTHING FROM THE FREEBOOTER COMPOUND AT THIS DISTANCE STOP

FREEBOOTERS SOBERING STOP MANY WANT TO GO HOME STOP

Heads were shaking.

HOLD THE FREEBOOTERS STOP WE ARE STARTING IN YOUR DIRECTION STOP WILL BE THERE TOMORROW MORNING STOP CELESTIAL CITY DESTROYED STOP WE HAVE THE SUPREME NAVARCH STOP GET MR SALSBURY AND DYNAMITE STOP

I winced at the thought of Dolph finding out about Finn. "We have to bury Finn. Any ideas?"

"Ira's place where Professor Gruber has been working?" Laura suggested. "They have a family plot on a gentle hill."

"Seems fitting. A lab in the mountains. Finn would like that."

SILVER SEED BRING IRA TO HIS FAMILY FARM STOP

Dolph cried when he heard the news. It was a quiet burial and José carved a marker. Finn's father, Liam, stood quietly.

I cleared my throat. "Finn was one of us. Finn was the brains behind the ships. Finn was brave and worked tirelessly to defeat the Freebooters."

I looked to the sky. "And Friend, we are going to do just that. José has dynamite and fuses. The men and women at the compound are almost sober. We will blow the Air Loom and the entire compound to a pile of rubble. We won."

It seemed silly to be telling Finn what was happening. Perhaps Finn was granted the present view if heaven allowed such fare.

Laura read the verses about fighting the good fight, running the race. "Well done, good and faithful servant."

"I want to stay a minute," Dolph said.

Finn's father stepped back and mouthed, "I'll stay."

We took our shovels back to the laboratory.

"Let's finish this," I said. "Mary, I would like you to take everyone in the compound to jail. There is a village due south of the wreckage of the *Celestial City*. Then, recover the Levitrite from the container at the top of the dome. It is our rock. We need to keep it safe."

"Be careful," she said. "Blow that place to bits."

Inside the compound, we got up a head of steam and started the big generator.

I had never seen the Air Loom. It was a huge polished oak box the size of a small cabin in a large cavern. Tubes running from barrels fed both sides and larger hoses carried the gas to another room.

I couldn't imagine how many thousands of gallons of mind-altering poison had been created there. José had three sticks of dynamite for the Air Loom room alone.

It took the better part of three days to run wires to whole sticks of dynamite. The map Dolph created, showing the layout of explosives, would have made Finn proud.

225

We checked the fuel and water for the generator and moved toward the opening. I stopped in the kitchen and packed the cookbooks Sid had left in his cupboard. I would send them to him.

Dolph turned on the code receiver hooked to the dynamite mechanism, and we took the *Cloud Queen* to two thousand feet. The *Silver Seed,* mission accomplished, hovered high above.

Laura stood in front of the wheelhouse, watching us on the bow. "Go ahead, Dolph. Let her rip."

"OK, but bring the Supreme Navarch. He has to watch."

José and Addy unchained the little man and carried him to the bow. They stood him on his feet, and Addy checked the ropes around his feet and hands.

"Take a good look because your empire is *defeated*," Dolph said through gritted teeth. "This is for my friend Finn, you evil, hateful man!" He touched the key.

For a moment there was silence. Then dust and smoke sent vent covers sailing like pie tins all over the side of the mountain. The mouth of the cavern chuffed out a cloud that blew the roof off the smokehouse. A deep rumble rolled through the sky, and part of the mountain collapsed. The *Cloud Queen* rocked gently.

The Supreme Navarch made a little noise in his throat and spun out of Addy's hands. He made two quick hops and pitched over the side.

Laura shouted, "Oh!" in surprise.

After falling and falling, his broken body lay on the piles of shot rock beyond the tanks.

José took a brief look with a hand lens. "He is dead."

"Well, that took care of that," Laura said.

"Do we bury him?" Addy wondered.

I took off my hat and rubbed my temples. "Laura, please ring for Full. We are going home."

226

Epilogue

Laura and I decided to stay on at Eagle's Crest. With Dolph's help, we built a train of levitating gondolas and began shipping cargo over the San Gabriel mountains. José and Addy joined us in the winter months when the farms needed little tending. Mary piloted the first ship, *The Benjamin,* and she and Nathan seemed quite content. Mr. Salsbury became our agent on the south side of the mountains.

That first fall Laura had a baby boy, and we named him Finn.

Books By George Beckman

Members of the Cast

There is the family you are born into and the family that grows around you.

In 1959, Margo's parents break their promise, leaving her behind for another archaeological dig. She is sent to California to spend her junior year with a great uncle she's only met once. Her parent's interests remain buried in ancient ruins, but Margo begins to discover herself beneath a lifetime of family secrets. For the first time, she has a close circle of friends, a budding romance, and an academic future. But a struggle between herself, the past, and her parents tests all she has learned.

Enter into Margo's world and experience the "California Dream" feel of 1950s Southern California. This is a wholesome book for all ages—a book you can give to your granddaughter or grandmother.

Partway to Wolfskill

Partway to Wolfskill is a collection of poems describing an idyllic childhood in San Dimas Canyon. These lines reflect the beauty of the land and its loss to eminent domain.

Liquid Ambers
They were planted
The year I was born
And we grew there, together...

The Ship from Wolfskill

Young Will and his friends are determined to defend the valley from the Freebooters, a band of ruthless Army renegades pillaging and burning their way north.

Will discovers his uncle's last great invention, an airship styled after a Mississippi riverboat, and he hopes to escape with Laura.

When men from the valley are captured, five young friends sail with the prevailing winds to rescue the hostages. Without conventional weapons, they must rely on their wits to battle the Freebooters.

Airships from the North

Will and his friends are back, fighting off a rogue band of marauders called Freebooters in this second installment of The Wolfskill Trilogy.

As the Freebooter war machine systematically pillages its way north, the young heroes fight back from the decks of the majestic Cloud Queen, a flying steamboat.

This time, the Freebooters are building an airship as well. As the mystery of the Freebooter indoctrination comes to light, Finn designs a sleek, new airship, and the crew lures the enemy to the desert. A dangerous and deadly battle ensues.

Airships from the North is Book Two of this steampunk saga of good and evil. Join this unlikely band of defenders on an unforgettable quest to preserve their world from impending chaos.